THE RETURN JOURNEY

AND

OTHER STORIES

also by Maeve Binchy

Light a Penny Candle
Echoes
London Transports
Dublin 4
The Lilac Bus
Firefly Summer
Silver Wedding
Circle of Friends
The Copper Beech
The Glass Lake
Evening Class
Tara Road
Aches and Pains

Cross Lines (short stories)

THE RETURN JOURNEY

AND

OTHER STORIES

Maeve Binchy

ORION

Copyright © Maeve Binchy 1999
All rights reserved

The right of Maeve Binchy to be identified as the author of
this work has been asserted by her in accordance with the
Copyright, Designs and Patents Act 1988.

This edition first published in Great Britain in 1999 by Orion
An imprint of Orion Books Ltd
Orion House, 5 Upper St Martin's Lane, London WC2H 9EA

Second impression 2000

The stories in this edition originally appeared in two separate volumes,
The Return Journey and *This Year It Will Be Different*, previously
published in USA and Australia

A CIP catalogue record for this book
is available from the British Library

ISBN 0 75282 549 6

Typeset by Deltatype Ltd, Birkenhead, Merseyside

Printed in Great Britain by
Clays Ltd, St Ives plc

To dearest Gordon with all my love and thanks

CONTENTS

CONTENTS

THE RETURN JOURNEY

~⤝ ⤞~

Mother darling,
It's even more green and beautiful than you said. Having a really wonderful time. Will write soon. Keep well and happy.

Gina

Freda,
The card I sent yesterday was for the neighbours. Or rather for you and your paranoia about the neighbours. Anyway its purpose was that it could be left around and looked at, spied on, and inspected by them. The truth is that the place is a shambles, it's raining so hard I can't see whether it's green or yellow. The truth is that I still feel hurt and unhappy and not at all like writing letters. The truth is that I must care about you a great deal, otherwise why am I letting that call from the airport get to me so badly? I believed you when you said you'd watch for the mail. I will write, but just now there's nothing to say.

Try not to worry about what people think and say. Honestly, they aren't thinking and saying much about us at all. They have their own problems.

Gina

Darling Gina,

You called me Freda instead of Mum. I wondered about that for a long while. I suppose it means you're growing up, growing away. I told myself it meant you liked me more, thought of me as an equal, a friend. Then I told myself that it meant you liked me less, that you were distancing yourself.

For someone who claims there is nothing to say, you sure have a lot to say. You say I am paranoid about the neighbours. Well, let me tell you that Mrs Franks came in to say she couldn't help reading your nice postcard and wasn't it wonderful that Gina was having such a good time. So! Do they look or do they not?

You say that you are upset by the call from Kennedy Airport. It was you who called me, Gina. I just said write to me often. You are the one who was crying, I was the one who says what any normal mother says to a daughter travelling abroad ... going to Europe. I said, I'd like it if you wrote to me, is that so emotionally draining? Does it deserve the lecture, the sermon ... the order not to live my life by other people's dictates?

But I only say all this so that you'll know I'm still me, still the same prickly jumpy thin-skinned mother I always was. I like you to call me Freda. Don't stop now because you think I've taken it and run with it, that I've read into it more than there is. And don't stop writing to me, Gina. You know I didn't want you to go to Ireland. But I did say ... I always said it was an unreasonable feeling on my part. There are so many things I want to hear about Ireland, and so many I don't.

I think I want you to tell me that it's beautiful and sad and that I did the only possible thing by leaving it. And leaving it so finally. I think that's what I want you to say in your letters. And when you come home. I love you, Gina, if that's not too draining.

Freda

I'm calling you nothing in this letter in case we get another long analysis. I had an odd day today. I left the B & B, which is fine, small room, small house, nice woman, kept telling me about her son in Boston who's an Illegal. I thought she meant the IRA, but she meant working in a bar without a proper visa or a green card. Anyway I was walking down the street, small houses, hundreds of kids roaming round when school's out, the country is like a big school playground in many ways. *And I saw a bus. It said 'Dunglass.' It was half full. I put out my hand. And it stopped. I asked the driver 'Where is Dunglass?' And he told me . . . But I said is Dunglass not a house, a big house. He said no, it was a town. Mum, why didn't you tell me it was a town? What else did you not tell me? I got off the bus. I told him I had changed my mind.*

Back at the B & B the woman was happy. She had heard from her son the Illegal. It was cold in Boston, lots of ice and snow. I asked her about Dunglass. She said it was a village. She said it was a nice kind of a place, quiet, peaceful but not a place to go in the middle of winter. It would scald your heart, she said. Why didn't you say it was a village that would scald your heart? Why did you let me think for years that it was a big old house with Dunglass on the gate. You even told me what it meant. Dun a fort and Glass meaning green. That much is true, I checked. But what else is?

Gina

Gina my love,
I wish you'd call. I tried to get a number for you, but they don't do street listings like we do. It's five days since you wrote. It will be five days until you get this, ten days could have changed everything. You may have been there by now, for all I know.

I never told you it was a house. Never. Our house didn't have a name that's all, it was a big house, it did have gates, it was the biggest house in Dunglass, which wasn't saying anything great. I just didn't talk about any of it. There are things in your life we don't go over and over. Go see Dunglass, go on a day when there is light and even watery winter sunshine. Go on a day when you might be able to walk down by the lake. Go see the house. Your grandmother is dead and in the churchyard on the hill. There is no one who will know you. But tell people if you want to. Tell them your mother came from Dunglass and left it. I don't think you will tell them. You are always saying that most people are not remotely interested in the lives and doings of others.

I love you and I will tell you anything you want to know.

Your mother Freda, in case you have forgotten my name.

Freda,
Stop playing silly games. And let us stop having an argument by mail. Yes, I will go to Dunglass. When I'm ready.

And don't talk to me about my grandmother. She was never allowed to be a grandmother to me. Her name was not spoken to me, I got no letters, no presents ... there were no pictures of me in a Grannie's Brag Book on this side of the Atlantic. The woman who lies in the churchyard on the hill is your mother. That's the relationship. You might as well face it. Her name was Mrs Hayes. That's all I know. You were Freda Hayes, so my grannie was Mrs Hayes. Don't lecture me, Freda, about forgetting your name, you never even told me hers.

Gina

Dear Gina,
I have begun this letter twelve times, this is the thirteenth attempt, I will send it no matter what. Her name was Annabel. She was tall and straight. She walked as if she owned Dunglass. And in a way she did. It was her family who had the big house. My father married in, as

they say. I never knew why they sent me away to boarding school, why they made me leave such a lovely home. Peggy who looked after me used to whisper about rows, and ornaments being broken, but I couldn't believe that my dad could be like Peggy said he was, two men, one man sober and another man drunk. Everyone admired my mother, because she ran the place. Even after my father went away she never asked for sympathy. She was cold, Gina, she made herself cold and hard. She used to say to me that we didn't need their sympathy, their pity. We needed only their admiration. Perhaps some of that has rubbed off on me, perhaps I care too much about people thinking well of me, rather than being natural.

She had only one daughter, as I have. We could have been more alike than I ever realised. I can't write any more.. I love you. I wish you were here. Or I were there. No, I don't wish I were there, I can never go to Dunglass. But I want you to go and to get some peace and some of your history from it.

Freda

Dear Freda,
Thanks for your letter. I think I'll cool it a bit on all the emotion. Don't forget I have Italian blood as well. The mix is too heady. I could explode. The days are getting brighter, I've been to Wicklow a lot, it's so beautiful ... and I went farther south, Wexford ... the riverbank is like something from a movie ... and Waterford. The Illegal is home from Boston, his name is Shay. He is very funny about Boston, but I think he wasn't happy there, he says his dream is to have a little cottage in Wicklow, and write songs. It's not a bad dream. I have no dreams really.

I'm doing an extramural course in the university about Irish history. It was full of dreams. I'll give you the telephone number in case you're lonely and sad. But don't call just for talking. It's very artificial.

Shay says that when he and his mother used to talk, they both put the phone down feeling like hell. We don't want that, Freda. Now that we're rubbing along OK. Yes, of course I love you.

Gina

Gina,

It was so different then. You can't imagine. I remember the year I met your father. All right. All right. The year I met Gianni . . . the man I married. Does that satisfy you? It seemed as if there was nothing but big funerals that year. Brendan Behan died, Sean O'Casey died. And Roger Casement . . . no, I know he didn't die then, but his body was brought back to Ireland, that's when I met Gianni. I tried to explain it to him. We sat in a café, it was a cold wet day. He was an Italian American. He tried to explain to me about Vietnam. It was 1964. I told Gianni all about the Irish troops leaving on the peacekeeping mission in Cyprus and I showed him where they were building the new American Embassy. And the Beatles went to America that year . . . it seems like a hundred years ago.

And Gianni wanted to know where I was from, so I took him home to Dunglass. And Mother laughed at him because he told her how poor his parents had been when they got the boat from Italy.

And I didn't want to sleep with him, Gina, I was twenty-three like you are now, but in those days we were so different. Not just me . . . everyone, I promise you. But I hated Mother so much for scorning him. And I despised her for saying that she hadn't gone through so much just for me to throw myself away on the son of a chambermaid and a hall porter. Gianni had told with pride how his parents, your grandparents, had got these jobs. And Mother said it in front of Peggy. Just letting Peggy know how little she thought of Peggy's role in life.

I was glad, Gina, I was glad when I was pregnant, even though I was frightened at the thought of living with Gianni forever. I felt it wouldn't last, that we didn't know each other, and that when we did we might be sorry. But we were never sorry, we had you.

And you will admit that, difficult as I have been, and stubborn, I have never said anything bad about your father. He thought he could live in Dunglass and marry in like my father had. But my mother hated him, and she hated me too because I wouldn't stay one minute to listen to her harsh words.

I left my room as it was, my books and letters and papers. I don't know what happened to them. Ever. I closed that door and never opened it.

When Gianni left me I didn't feel as sad as people thought. I knew it would happen. I had my home in America, my daughter, my job in the bookshop, my friends. I may marry again.

I won't, of course, but I say to myself cheerfully like Peggy used to say it may be a sunny day after all, little Freda. My heart is heavy when I think of Peggy. I didn't write to her because I didn't write to the big house, it would have been twisting a knife too harshly into Mother.

Her name was Peggy O'Brien, Gina, they lived in a cottage by the lake. I tried to write after Mother died. But there weren't any words. You were always good with words, Gina.

Love *Freda*

This is a postcard of Dunglass village. I bought it in a Dublin shop. Has it changed much, Mother? I'm going there tomorrow. I'll write and tell you everything. I miss you.

Gina

The time gap is too long. I called you. Shay's mother told me you were still away. You didn't say you were taking Shay with you. It's nearly a quarter of a century since I took Gianni there. Are we going to repeat history all over again? Dunglass hasn't changed very much. I had forgotten it was so small. I wait to hear anything you may write.

Dearest Freda,

Your letter was cold, there were no dears or darlings or loves anywhere. Are you afraid that like my mother and my grandmother, I will marry hastily the wrong man, who will leave me as happened to you and to Annabel? I went to her grave and I laid a big bunch of spring flowers on it. The countryside is glorious. There were little ducklings on the lake, and moorhens and two big swans. You never told me any of that. You never told me that you had a pony and that you fell off and broke your arm. You never told me about Peggy's big soft bosom where I cried like you cried. She bought a lot of your things at the auction. She said she didn't want strangers picking up your books and your treasures. She called them treasures, Freda, and she has them in a room. Waiting for you to come home and collect them. She was left nothing in the will. It all went to charity. She bought them from her wages because she knew one day you'd come back.

I told her it would probably be in June. When the sun shines long hours over the lake and the roses are all out on her cottage. Not far from the one that Shay and I are looking at with our hearts full of hope.

Send me an open postcard to Shay's house so that his mother will know how much you and I love each other. See, I am like you after all. I want them to think well of us. In many ways I'm glad you kept it from me, it came as such a rainbow of happiness. But don't keep it from yourself anymore. There are no ghosts in Dunglass. Only hedges and flowers and your great friends Peggy, Shay, and

Gina

THE WRONG SUITCASE

Annie checked in early. She had come out to the airport in plenty of time. None of this was going to be a hassle. Once she had taken her boarding card and seen the smart new case trundle off with its little tag telling it to go to London Heathrow, she sighed with relief; it was all happening now, nothing could stop it. She was going to have the luxury of really looking at the things in the duty-free shop for once, and maybe trying out a few of the perfumes on her wrist. She might even look at cameras and watches – not buy, but look.

Alan was late; he was always late checking in. But he had such a nice smile and looked so genuinely apologetic, nobody seemed to mind. They told him to go straight to the departure gate, and he did – well, more or less. They couldn't expect him to go through that duty-free without buying a bottle of vodka, could they? He had no sign of fuss or confusion; he slipped onto the plane last, but somebody had to come in last. He settled himself easily into his seat in executive class. With the ease of the frequent traveller, he had stowed his briefcase and vodka neatly above, fastened his safety belt in a way that the air hostess could see it was fastened, and he had opened his copy of *Time*. Another business trip begun.

Annie smiled with relief when she saw her case on the carousel at Heathrow Airport; she always half expected it to be left behind, like she expected the Special Branch men to call her in and ask her business in England and the Customs men to rip the case apart looking for concealed heroin. She was of a fearful nature, but she knew that and said it wasn't a bad way to be because it led to so many nice surprises when these things didn't happen. She took her case and went unscathed through Customs. She followed the signs for the Underground and got onto a train that she thought must be like a lift in the United Nations building: there were people of every nationality under the sun, and all of their suitcases had different little tags. She closed her eyes happily as the train rushed into London.

Alan reached out easily and took his case as it was about to pass by. He helped a family who couldn't cope with all their cases arriving at once. One by one he swung them off the conveyor belt, and when he took one that wasn't theirs he just swung it easily back again with no fuss. The woman gave him a very grateful smile. Alan had a way of looking better than other people's husbands. He bought an *Evening Standard* in the paper shop and settled himself into a taxi. He had already asked the taxi driver if he could have a receipt at the end of the journey; some of them could be grumpy, always better to say what you want at the start and say it pleasantly. Alan's motto. Alan's secret of success. It was sunset; he looked out briefly at the motorways and the houses with their neat gardens away in the distance. It was nice to be back in London where you didn't know everyone and everyone didn't know you.

The train took Annie to Gloucester Road, and she walked with a quick and happy step to the hotel, where she had stayed many times. The new suitcase was light to carry; it had been expensive, but what the hell – it would last forever. It was so nice, she had bought two of those little suitcase initials and stuck them on A.G. At first she wondered if this was a dead giveaway, wouldn't people know that they weren't married if they had different initials? But he had laughed at her and patted her nose, telling her that she was a funny little thing and had a fearful nature. And Annie Grant had agreed and remembered that most people didn't give a damn about that sort of thing nowadays. Most people.

The taxi took Alan to Knightsbridge and the hotel, where they remembered him or pretended to. He always said his name first, just in case. 'Of course, Mr Green,' the porter said with a smile. 'Good to have you with us again.' Alan folded the receipt from the taxi driver into his wallet and followed the porter to the desk; his room reservation was in order. He made an elegant and flattering remark to the receptionist, which left her patting her hair with pleasure and wondering why the nice ones like Mr Green didn't ask you out and the yucky ones slobbered all over you. Alan went up to his room and took a bottle of tonic from the minibar. He noticed it wasn't slimline, so he put it back and took soda. Alan was careful about everything.

Annie opened her case in the small hotel bedroom where she would spend one night. She would hang up her dresses to make sure the creases fell out. She would have a bath and use all those nice lotions and bath oils so that they didn't look brand new tomorrow. The key turned and she lifted the lid. There were no dresses and no shoes. Neither the two new nighties nor the very smart toilet bag with its unfamiliar Guerlain products were in the case. There were files and boxes and men's shirts and men's underpants and socks, and more files. Her heart gave several sharp sideways jumps, each one hurting her breastbone. It had happened as she always knew it would happen one day. She had got the wrong case. She looked in terror and there were her initials; somebody else called A.G. had taken her case. 'Oh my God,' wept Annie Grant, 'Oh God, why did you let this happen to me? Why? I'm not *that* bad, God. I'm not hurting anyone else.' Her tears fell into the suitcase.

Alan opened his case automatically. He would set his papers out on the large table and hang up his suits. Marie always packed perfectly; he had shown her how at an early stage. Poor Marie had once thought you just bundled things in any old how, but, he had explained reasonably, what was the point of her ironing all those shirts so beautifully if they weren't to come out looking as immaculate as they went in? He looked at the top layer of the case in disbelief. Dresses, underwear – female underwear neatly folded. Shoes in plastic bags, a flashy-looking sponge bag with some goo from a chemist in it. God almighty, he had taken the wrong case. But he couldn't have. It had his initials: A.G. He had been thinking that he must get better ones, these were a bit ordinary. God damn and blast it, why hadn't he got them at the time? For a wild moment he wondered if this was some kind of joke of Marie's; she had been very brooding recently and wanting to come on business trips with him. Could she have packed a case for herself? But that was nonsense; these weren't Marie's things, these belonged to a stranger. Shit, Alan Green said aloud to himself over and over again. What timing. What perfectly bloody timing to lose his case on this of all trips.

It took Annie a tearful seventy minutes on the telephone and many efforts on the part of the airline and of the hotel to prevent her from going out to the airport before she realised that she would have to wait until the next morning. Soothing people in the hotel and at the airline said that it would certainly be returned the following day. She had only discovered an office address for Mr Bloody Green, typed neatly and taped inside the lid of the case. An office long closed by now.

Tomorrow, the voices said, as if that was any help. Tomorrow he would have arrived expecting her to be in fine form and to have her things with her. They were going to go for a week's motoring holiday, the first time she was going to have him totally to herself. He was flying in from New York and would hire a car at Heathrow; he had told his boss the negotiations would take longer, he had told his wife . . . Who knew or cared what he had told his wife? But he would not be best pleased to spend the first day of their holiday in endless negotiations at the airport looking for her things. Was there no way she could find out where this idiot lived? If she phoned his home even, maybe his wife could tell her where he was staying. That was if his wife knew. If wives ever knew.

It took Alan five minutes to find the right person, the person who told them that there was no right person at this time of night, but to explain the machinery of the morrow. Yes, fine for those who hadn't arranged a breakfast meeting at seven-thirty a.m., before the shops were open, before he could get a clean shirt. And what was the point of a breakfast meeting without his papers? God rot this stupid woman with her cellophane bags and her tissue paper and her never-worn clothes. Her photograph album, for heaven's sake, and pages and pages of notes, a play of some sort. Hard-to-decipher writing, page after bloody page of it. But there was one page where it revealed the address of Miss Prissy A. Grant, whoever she was, and he was sure she *was* a Miss, not a Mrs. A letter addressed to her had 'Ms' on it, but Alan had always noted that this was what single, not married, women called themselves. Unfortunately it had no address, or he could have sent for an Irish telephone directory and found her mother and father and got the hotel that their daughter was staying at. That's if she had told them. Nutty kind of girls who carry photograph albums, unworn clothes, and plays written in small cramped writing probably told their families nothing.

The man who ran the small hotel near Gloucester Road was upset for nice Miss Grant, who often came to spend a night before she went on her long trips to the Continent; she was a teacher, a very polite person always. He took her a pot of tea and some tomato sandwiches in her room. She cried and thanked him as if he had pulled her onto a life raft.

'Look through his things. You might discover where he is staying,' he advised. Annie was doubtful. Still, as she ate the tomato sandwiches and drained the pot of tea she spread all the papers out on the small bed and read. She read of the plans that Mr A. Green had been building up over the last two years. Plans which meant that by tomorrow he should be able to take over an agency for himself. If things went the way he hoped.

Mr A. Green would return to Dublin at the head of his own company. The arguments were so persuasive that the overseas client would be very foolish not to accept A. Green's offer. There were photocopies of letters marked 'For your eyes only' ... There were files with heavy underlining in thick felt pen, 'Do not take to office.' A great deal of the correspondence was organised so that it showed A. Green's present employers, the people who were paying for this trip to London, in a very poor light. Annie sighed; she supposed that this was the world of business. At school you didn't go plotting against the geography mistress or getting the headmaster to lose confidence in the art teacher. But it seemed a bit sneaky.

Sometimes there were copies of letters his boss *was* shown pinned to those he had *not* been shown. It was masterly filing, and if you read the whole anthology, which up to now had presumably been for Alan Green's eyes only, it made a convincing case. Annie decided that A. Green was a bastard and he deserved to have lost his case and his deal. She hoped he would never find either. But then how would she get back what was hers? And God almighty, suppose he had read her diary.

Alan Green decided to hell with it, he couldn't bear the flat taste of the soda. He opened a calorie-packed tonic water from his minibar and decided that he would do this thing methodically. Look on it as a business problem. Right. He had left his name with the airline, if she called. Of course she would call. Stupid girl, why had she not called already? Stupid A. Grant. She was probably in a wine bar with an equally stupid teacher talking about plays and how to write them in longhand at great length and maximum stupidity. What kind of play was it, anyway? He began to read it. He read of her romance ... It wasn't a play, it was the real thing. This was a diary. It was more than a diary, it was a plan of campaign. It was dozens of different scenarios that could take place on this holiday.

There was the scene where he said he couldn't see her anymore, that his wife had given him an ultimatum. This creepy A. Grant had written out her lines for that one, several times over. Sometimes they were casual and see-if-I-care. Sometimes they were filled with passion, or threats: she would kill herself, let him wait. She had written the whole thing out as if it were a play, even with stage directions.

Alan decided that A. Grant was a raving lunatic and that whoever the poor guy she was going to meet was, he deserved to be warned about her.

He felt glad that she had lost this insane checklist of emotional dramas and how to play them; he was glad that all her finery had gone astray and that she would have to meet the guy as she was. He realised that she had probably done some kind of repair job and washed her tights and whatever just as he had washed the collar and cuffs of his shirt and the soles of his socks. Then he remembered with a lurch that she might have read his dossier on the company.

Annie suddenly remembered she hadn't told the man in the airport where she was staying. She had been too upset. Suppose Mr Conniving Green had rung in with his whereabouts; they wouldn't have been able to contact her. She telephoned them again. Had Mr Green called? He had. This was his number. He answered on the second ring. He would come right around with her case. No, please, gentleman's privilege. Very simple mistake, must be a million A.G.s in the world. He'd come right away.

He held the taxi. She was quite pretty, he saw to his surprise, soft and fluffy. He sort of remembered seeing her at Heathrow Airport and thinking that if she was in the taxi queue he might suggest they share. Remembering the revelations of her diary, he shuddered with relief at his escape. She was surprised to see that he looked so pleasant; she had expected him to look like a fox: sharp-featured, mean pointed little face. He looked normal and nice. She thought she remembered him on the plane up in executive class laughing with the air hostess.

'I have your case here,' she said. 'It's a bit disarrayed, for want of a better word. I was hunting in it to see if I could find out where you were staying.'

'Yours is a little disarrayed too.' He grinned. 'But none of those nice garments you have fitted me, so they're all safe and sound.'

They grinned at each other almost affectionately.

He looked at her for a moment. It was only eleven o'clock at night; in London that meant the evening was only starting. She was quite lovely in a round soft sort of way ...

She wished he didn't have to go. Maybe if she said something about why not go and let's have a bottle of wine to celebrate the found suitcases ...

She remembered how he had described his boss as bordering on senility and how he had given chapter and verse to prove that the boss was a heavy drinker.

He remembered how she had proposed threatened suicide with attendant letters to some guy's wife, his children and his colleagues.

They shook hands, and at exactly the same moment they said to each other that they hadn't read each other's papers or anything, and at that moment they both knew that they had.

MISS VOGEL'S VACATION

Miss Vogel was surprised that she had never married. Not so much upset as surprised. When she was young everyone thought Victoria Vogel would surely be one of the first in the neighbourhood to walk down an aisle.

Fair-haired, soft and pretty, a great homemaker, she even made dresses for herself and her sisters and their friends, as well as baking delicious desserts for any event where good cooking was needed.

The young Miss Vogel had an agreeable manner with everyone; no future mother-in-law would stand in her way, no family would object to the girl who worked pleasantly in her father's bakery. She was much in demand to dance at the weddings of her many friends, and although she caught the bride's bouquet on many occasions, it never led to a wedding of her own.

Miss Vogel didn't look back on her girlhood in New York as a lonely time; she hadn't yearned always for a beau of her own. She always thought there was one around the next corner. She lived happily over the bakery and didn't really notice the years go by.

There were so many other things to think about. Like her mother's illness. The others were all married by the time Miss Vogel's mother took to her bed, so she did the nursing, which made sense because she lived at home.

And when her mother died and her father became gloomy and lost interest in his work, she had to work all that much harder in the bakery to keep it going. There was a manager, of course, Tony Bari.

They spent long hours together trying to see how the bills could be paid, the overheads reduced, and the whole enterprise made sound.

Everyone thought one day they might marry.

Miss Vogel didn't really think they would, even though she would have been happy had their quick embraces led to a proposal.

But she was a practical woman and realised that Tony Bari was very interested in money and had told her several times that any sensible man in business was looking for a rich wife. Miss Vogel knew she wasn't in this category, and even though she did like his company, his big broad smile and the way his moustache tickled her cheek, she didn't weep when he told her he had finally met a lady of property and invited her to his wedding.

Not long after, Miss Vogel's father went to the hospital, and it was known that he would not come out. Tony Bari bought the business. His new wife did not think it appropriate that Miss Vogel continue to work and live there, so, at the age of thirty, she was unemployed.

People said Tony Bari had not paid enough, and indeed, after it had been divided between her sisters and brothers there was very little left.

Miss Vogel had nowhere to live, she had no real qualifications to get a good job anywhere, but with her customary good humour she decided to wait until something turned up. Then she saw a position as a type of janitor or superintendent in a small, new apartment building. A lot of the residents were female, and they had specifically sought a woman super. Miss Vogel, with her calm, pleasant manner, seemed ideal, and she now had a two-room apartment, with an address in a fine part of town.

Her friends were pleased for her.

'You'll meet very classy folk now,' they said.

Miss Vogel didn't mind whether they were classy or not, just as long as they were nice. And mainly they were.

She became involved in all their lives. She walked the little yapping dog, unsuitably called Beauty, for Janet, the discontented widow in Number One.

She baby-sat for the teenage daughter of Heather, who was a workaholic advertising supremo in Number Two. She took in the flowers and arranged them for Number Three, where Francesca the attractive mistress of two businessmen lived. Tactfully, Miss Vogel made sure these two gentlemen never coincided on a visit.

She spent a lot of time in Number Four, where Marion sat and looked out the window, sad because her husband came home so rarely.

There were many others in the building whose lives were familiar to Miss Vogel. Her sisters sometimes said these must be rich, spoiled people who lacked nothing in their lives, but Miss Vogel didn't agree. As she sat in beautifully decorated apartments and drank coffee from a fine china cup or soda from cut-crystal glassware, Miss Vogel knew that unease and unhappiness didn't fly out the window just because you had money. A lot of the people had even more worries than the Vogel family ever had. Sometimes she went past the old bakery where Tony Bari had built a big business with his wife's money. It was now a delicacies shop, and people faxed in their orders for sandwiches, which were delivered to their offices. Imagine!

There were three children. Miss Vogel watched them grow up. She would have liked to have met them properly and known them, to have been invited into the store where she, too, had lived as a child.

But Tony Bari's wife never seemed to want her around.

Miss Vogel thought this was sad. She had always been welcoming and kind to the woman who had come to live there only because of her father's dollars. But then, you couldn't make people like you if they didn't.

Her days and nights were never empty or lonely, because of all the people in the apartments. Miss Vogel did not have what anyone would call a great life of her own, but she went through all theirs, their hopes and dreams for Thanksgiving and Christmas, who would come home, where they would be invited, what they would cook. Their diets for the new year, how many days a week working out at the gym, low-fat foods to be stocked in the freezer. Then she went through their new wardrobes for spring. None seemed to notice Miss Vogel didn't buy spring clothes, plan to lose ten pounds every January, or discuss where she went for Thanksgiving or Christmas.

She was a listening person, not a talking person.

She was interested in their lives.

Now it was time to talk about vacations.

Janet was going to Arizona with her sister, so naturally there was the matter of Beauty, the bad-tempered little dog, Beauty didn't like kennels, so perhaps Miss Vogel . . .

Heather could take only a week and not one day more away from work, so she would fly to Los Angeles. This way, she could fit in one or two meetings on the West Coast as well as take fourteen-year-old Heidi to Disneyland and Universal Studios, so it would be a fantastic holiday for the child. But there was simply no time to get her any vacation clothes. Could Miss Vogel manage . . . one Saturday morning possibly? Just a quick trip to the department store?

Francesca was going to spend one week with one man and the other with the second man, but she had told each she was going to a health spa for the week she would not be with him. Would Miss Vogel mind very much taking the bus to this town two miles away, where the spa actually was, and mailing two postcards for her? You see, men were so possessive and so suspicious these days, and one didn't want to do anything silly.

Marion in Number Four was uncharacteristically cheerful because she and her husband were going to a quiet inn – he said he would like time to talk properly. That had to be good, Marion said, vacations were a time when people found new relationships if they had none or cemented an existing one that needed to be patched up.

That was the wonderful thing about vacations, wasn't it, Marion had said over and over.

Miss Vogel didn't know. She had never had a vacation. There had never been the opportunity, the money, or the time. And now, at fifty-three, there seemed little point in hoping she would find a new relationship, and there wasn't an old one to cement.

Tony Bari and his wife and children were going to Italy. Her sisters, brothers, and their families were going to a lake where they rented chalets every year. Nice for the cousins to get to know each other and keep in touch, they said.

None of them ever thought it might be nice for Miss Vogel to get to know them all and keep in touch, too. But then, she would be out of place. An elderly aunt on her own.

All the holidays seemed to come together. Miss Vogel would have a very empty building to look after. But she enthused about their trips, as she had enthused for so many years about everything they did.

She did all she was asked to do. She studied the feeding schedules of the small, aggressive Beauty to reassure Janet. She took Heidi on an outing to Bloomingdale's and with Heather's dollars bought her bright-coloured clothes to wear in the California sun. She planned the two bus trips so she could send the deceiving postcards for Francesca. She helped Marion pack romantic negligees for her week in the country inn.

And, of course, she would do all the other things that made them think Miss Vogel was an angel. She would turn out their lights, pull their drapes at different times each evening, sort their mail, so, when they came back, it would be in a neat pile on their hall table. She would see their garments were returned from the dry cleaner and hung in their closets; she would admit a television repairman here and an interior decorator there and listen to their holiday tales and look at their holiday photos with great interest on their return.

Often there was fuss and near hysteria at the actual time of departure; limousines had not been ordered in advance, for example, or taxis could not be hailed on the New York streets.

This year, Miss Vogel decided to cut through all the drama and found a neighbourhood car service. She spoke to Frank, a man with a tired, kind face, who was at the desk, telling him she had four trips over two days, to La Guardia Airport for Heather and Heidi, to Grand Central for Janet, to Penn Station for Marion and her husband, and some secret pickup place in New Jersey for Francesca.

'What commission are you looking for?' Frank asked wearily.

'Oh no,' Miss Vogel said. 'I was only trying to arrange something for the people in my building. They'll all pay you the rate. I don't want anything ... I don't want anything for myself.'

'You must be the only person in the world who doesn't, then,' said Frank.

'It's just their vacations. They get very fussed, you know the way people do?'

'I don't know the way people do,' Frank said. 'I've never had a vacation.'

Miss Vogel gave him a big smile. 'Do you know neither have I? We must be the only people in the world who haven't.'

A bond was established between them, and they worked out the times he would be there to pick up the holidaymakers.

He was courteous and punctual, but more than that he was kind.

He waited while Janet kissed Beauty good-bye; he told Heidi she'd love Disneyland – everyone came back from it a new person; he explained to Francesca that he was a genius at finding out-of-the-way spots in New Jersey; he told Marion and her husband that an inn in the countryside was the very best vacation anyone could choose.

Miss Vogel was sorry when the last had gone. She enjoyed Frank's company. She would miss regular visits when she always found time to make him a coffee and give him some of her own home-baked shortbread.

To her surprise, he turned up again.

'I was wondering, Miss Vogel, if you and I should have a vacation in New York,' he began tentatively. 'We could pretend we were tourists here and see it through their eyes.' He looked at her, hoping that she would not laugh at this or dismiss it as a ridiculous idea.

'A vacation in New York City?' she said thoughtfully.

'Well, a lot of people do, you know.' Frank was defensive. 'I drive them to places. I should know.'

'That will be great,' said Miss Vogel. 'But first I have to do a bit of fussing. That's essential.'

'Yes, I'll come around tomorrow morning. Does that give you time enough to fuss?' he asked.

Miss Vogel worked out that she could take a five-hour vacation each day. Then she ironed her clothes carefully and laid out a different outfit for each outing. She went to a beauty parlour on the corner and got her hair and her nails done.

She prepared several picnic lunches they could have and left them ready in the freezer. She got new heels on her comfortable shoes. She checked the weather forecast. She was ready for her vacation.

They went to Ellis Island and spent the day looking at where their grandparents had come into the United States from Italy and Germany, Ireland and Sweden.

'I bet they were four young people who never had time for a vacation once they got here,' Miss Vogel said.

'But they must have been adventurous young people,' Frank replied, 'not the kind of folk who would like to believe their descendants would be stay-at-homes.'

The next day they went to the World Trade Centre to see the view and then back uptown to the zoo. Afterwards, they walked in Central Park in the sunshine.

They drove together companionably to the town where they had to mail Francesca's postcards and talked about how odd life was with so many people living a lie – Francesca herself and the two married men who were each taking her off for a week. They went to Chinatown and on a tour of the stock exchange on Wall Street.

They went back to where Miss Vogel grew up and looked at the big delicacies shop, so much changed in appearance since her youth. They went to see where Frank was raised, changed so very much from when he was a boy. He pointed out where he had lived with his wife for three years a long time ago, and also the hospital where she had died.

Neither had ever been to Carnegie Hall, so they booked a concert.

And as she had seen a ball game only on television, never in reality, they went to Yankee Stadium.

And the week flew by.

Frank helped Miss Vogel to sort the mail, arrange the curtains, and arrange deliveries for the tenants. Miss Vogel went to the car-service office and brightened it up by washing the curtains and putting some colourful ornaments around.

The next week, they could no longer afford five hours a day for vacation. Like everyone else in New York, they would now know that feeling which said the holiday was over.

But for Frank and Miss Vogel, there was something new and wonderful. No longer did they keep their thoughts to themselves, there was someone with whom to talk over the events of the day. Not only holiday memories, but what was happening in the real world as well.

So when Frank drove Heather and Heidi back from the airport, he could report that mother and daughter were hardly speaking and that the girl had been left alone in her hotel room looking at television, since Heather was tied up in meetings all day.

Miss Vogel could tell him that something very odd had happened in Francesca's life – perhaps both men had proposed marriage to her, both would leave their wives, but she wanted neither. Francesca was lying down with a cold compress on her eyes, trying to get the courage to tell them.

Janet told Frank in the car her holiday with her sister had been a huge mistake – there would be no more family get-togethers. What did people want family for, anyway? A good dog was worth twenty sisters.

Marion told Miss Vogel that her rat of a husband had taken her to the inn only to tell her he was leaving her. And amazingly, Marion didn't really mind all that much. Once it was out in the open, she enjoyed the walking and peace of the countryside, and her husband had been startled and annoyed at how well she adapted to the new situation.

But nobody asked Miss Vogel if she had enjoyed her time when they were away. And if they saw Frank around the place a lot, it was because they assumed he was driving people. Sometimes Miss Vogel wasn't quite as available to baby-sit, walk dogs, listen to problems, arrange flowers. Nothing you could put your finger on. And if she looked happier and walked with a spring in her step and smiled with brighter eyes ... they thought she might have lost a few pounds or something.

Tony Bari's wife noticed, however. She had returned from a tedious vacation in Italy with a lot of possessive in-laws and was glad to be back in New York. Her eyes narrowed when Miss Vogel came into the shop. She always suspected Tony Bari harboured feelings for the daughter of the house, and if she had had any money, he would very probably have asked Miss Vogel to marry him.

'Did you have a good vacation, Miss Vogel?' she asked politely, her sharp glance taking in Miss Vogel's improved posture, hairstyle, and general manner.

'Very pleasant, Mrs Bari. I stayed in New York, got to know my own city. It was delightful.'

Tony Bari's wife, who would love to have done the same, was envious.

'Well, at our age, Miss Vogel, we don't expect very much from vacations, do we?' She was trying to remove the pleased smile from Miss Vogel's face. But she was not succeeding.

Miss Vogel paused in her choosing of expensive mushrooms, speciality cheese, and exotic olive oils and smiled confidently at the woman who had taken away her only hope of marriage and a home, merely because that woman's father had money.

'Oh, Mrs Bari, how sad, how very sad to hear you say that,' she said, as deeply sympathetic as if she were offering condolences at a funeral.

Tony Bari was at the other side of the shop. He was fat now and balding, his face set in lines of disappointment and greed. Life had not turned out as he might have wished. How could she ever have thought he would have made her a good husband? Had it all worked out at the time, then she would have just returned from a weary journey to Italy with this bad-tempered man. She would have known no other world but this one; she would never have gone in and out of the lives of the existing people who lived in her building.

She might have looked wistfully at the kind face of Frank, a limousine driver, if she had ever met him, and wondered what it would be like to live in easy companionship with someone who saw beauty everywhere and gain and opportunity nowhere. Tonight, for his birthday, she would cook him a great feast. They had plans for the future, plans young people were making all over the world, but were no less loving and hopeful just because Miss Vogel and Frank were no longer young.

'Oh, Mrs Bari,' she repeated, her voice full of genuine sorrow. She had been about to ask, 'What *is* the point of living at all if we don't expect something from every vacation and every day?' but it sounded a bit preachy, and Miss Vogel had learned firsthand from her apartment complex that happiness does not always go hand in hand with having a lot of possessions, so instead she said that to have unrealistic dreams should not be part of the ageing process.

And head high, her shopping basket full of exotic ingredients, Miss Vogel left the delicacies shop that had once been her father's bakery and, without a backward glance, walked into the sun-filled streets of New York.

THE HOME SITTER

✧

It would be a new start. Not everyone got such a chance, Maura told herself. Three months in a warm climate, and the people were supposed to be very friendly over there. Already she had got letters from faculty wives welcoming her. James would be visiting lecturer in this small university in the Midwest of America. Both fares were paid and they would have a house on campus.

The only problem was their house. James and Maura lived in a part of Dublin where people suspected burglars of lurking in the well-kept shrubbery, waiting till the owners had left each day. If they were gone for three months, the place would be ransacked.

But it was quite impossible to let the place. First there was the fear that you might never get the people out. You heard such terrible stories. Then it would mean locking everything away – no, it would be intolerable. How could they enjoy three months in a faraway place terrified that everything they had was being smashed and they might have to go to the High Court to evict the tenants.

There were no possibilities, either, in their families. Ruefully they agreed that James's mother would be an unlikely starter. She was forgetful to the point where nobody could leave her in charge. The burglar alarm would be ringing night and day, making the neighbours crazy. She did love their dog Jessie, but she would forget to feed her, or else give her all the wrong things. She would allow Jessie out and there would be litters of highly unsatisfactory puppies on the way when they got back.

They couldn't ask Maura's sister Geraldine, either, because she hated dogs. She would leap in terror when Jessie gave a perfectly normal greeting. And Maura feared that Geraldine would poke around, look in drawers and things. There would be so much hiding involved, and having to send Jessie to a kennel, that it literally wouldn't be worth it.

Their neighbours weren't the kind of people you could give a key to. These were big houses with sizeable gardens. Not estates, or back-to-back terraces like Coronation Street, where everyone knew everyone's business. On one side there were the Greens, elderly, mad about gardening, hardly ever out of their greenhouse. Very pleasant to greet, of course. But that was all. And then, on the other side, there were that high-flying couple, the Hurleys, who were always being written about in the papers. They had started their own company. They had three children of their own and had adopted others. They had his mother and her father living in a kind of mews. They always seemed to have at least three students of different nationalities living with them and minding the children. You couldn't ask the Hurleys to take on any more. They'd sicken you with how much they were doing already.

'I don't know *what* we're going to do,' Maura heard herself say for the tenth time to James, and saw with alarm that familiar look of irritation cross his face.

'Everything is a problem these days,' he said. 'Most people would jump at this opportunity. All it does for us is create more and more difficulties.'

She knew that this was true. Other people would see it as an excitement, a challenge, an adventure. She was being middle-aged beyond her years to see the summer as another Bad Thing. She must pull herself together. This trip to America was probably the last chance she would have to make her marriage work. They would be together in a new place, sharing everything as they had ten years before. There would be freedom, there would be time. James wouldn't work late at the college there, as he did at home. He wouldn't stop for drinks at the club rather than coming back to her. He wouldn't invent things to do on weekends to escape the house and the prospect of yet more time mending, fixing, and titivating their home.

Maura reminded herself that she was resourceful, that that was how she had found James in the beginning, her lecturer in college whom everyone had fancied and yet Maura had won. That was how she had found the house. It was good to be hardworking and practical. That was what had saved them both when little Jamie had died, a cot death at three months. Maura had planted the garden and bought a young collie dog. James had always said that she was a tower of strength in those months.

But that had been six years ago, and things had changed a lot since then. It wasn't just the lack of a child. They both knew that. There seemed to be a gulf between them that no amount of shared interest would bridge. There were so many things that they did share already – the house, the garden, the walks with Jessie – and yet there were so many silences. Another child, even if it had come along, would not have cemented them together. James lived more and more in the college, Maura more and more in her office, which she didn't really enjoy, but since the work was routine and simple it gave her plenty of time to think about her home and its constant improvement.

There was something about the frown of impatience on James's face that made Maura realise the urgency of sorting out the house matter without any more fuss.

'Leave it to me,' she said reassuringly. 'I'll think of something. You have enough to do to prepare your lectures.'

The frown went, and there was something of the old James. 'That's more like it,' he said. He was very handsome when he smiled. Maura realised with a sudden lurch of feeling that at least three marriages had ended in the college. It had been shock and horror and scandal at the time, but now all those men had settled down happily with their second choice. The furore had died down except in the hearts of the three women who had been left alone. It could happen with James very, very easily. If someone wanted him desperately enough. If Maura was foolish enough to drive him out of the home with her fussing and creating problems where none existed.

She spent the next day on the phone. Did anyone know anyone? And eventually someone did. An old school friend Maura hadn't seen for years knew someone called Allie.

'Is she an Arab?' Maura asked. The Hurleys had a boy called Ali staying one year.

'No, it's short for Alice, I think. She's a kind of a home sitter.'

'Is she in an organization? Does she get paid?'

The friend, a colourless woman called Patsy, said no, Allie was a law unto herself. 'She's our age, but you'd think she was years younger. She hasn't anywhere to live, no real job, she just moves on from place to place minding people's houses.'

'Sounds a bit unreliable,' Maura said disapprovingly.

'No, she was very good here, actually.' Patsy sounded grudging.

'And what did she do all day?'

'I wish I knew, but she had the place in fine shape when we came back from Brussels. Everyone around spoke highly of her.' There was still something ungiving about Patsy. Maura wondered if she was being told the full story about this Allie.

'You didn't like her, did you?' she asked.

Patsy sounded aggrieved. 'Lord almighty, Maura, you asked for someone to mind your house, I found you someone. Did I like her? I hardly met her. I only saw her twice before we left, and once when we came back. She did everything she said she would, and what more can anyone ask?'

Maura thanked her hastily and took Allie's present phone number. She was minding an art gallery for someone. It would be lovely to go to a home with a dog and a garden, she said.

'And two budgies?' Maura added.

'Super,' said Allie.

She sounded eighteen, not thirty-five-ish. When they met her, she looked much nearer to eighteen also.

Allie had long, dark, curly hair, the kind you knew she shampooed every morning and just shook it dry. She had a great smile that lit up her whole face, she had long golden legs and arms, and she wore what Maura thought was an overshort denim dress.

Allie sat on the grass as she talked to them in the garden. She smiled up at James, and Maura felt a resentment that she had not known possible. Not just at the fact that Allie *could* sit on the ground without falling over. But at the way she looked at James. It wasn't flirtatious or coy, it was just a look that was full of interest. Everything he said seemed worthy of consideration; Allie would nod eagerly or shake her head. She was reacting on a very high level. Not for Allie the nods and grunts and half-attention that James must have been used to from Maura.

To be fair, and Maura struggled to be fair, Allie seemed very interested in her too. She asked Maura about her job, and even James seemed surprised at some of the things he heard about Maura's daily routine.

'I didn't know that,' he said, interested, and Maura realised with a pang that she hardly ever told James anything about work nowadays except to complain about the manager or the difficulty in parking a car or getting any shopping done at lunch hour.

Allie had a big red notebook, and she wrote their names down neatly, and all contact addresses that she would need. She was practical, too, asking about plumbers and electricians, and the number to phone if she smelled gas. She asked them to be sure to put any silver in the bank and to spend a couple of hours assembling all their private papers and documents and to lock them up somewhere.

'We don't need to do that.' James was smiling that slightly besotted smile men in their late thirties smile, Maura noticed.

'Oh, but you do, James.' Allie was firm. 'You see, I come from having minded dozens of homes; you haven't. When you are over in America you'll suddenly remember that you left something out you'd prefer that nobody else saw. This way you'll know you didn't. Also, you can't ask me to pay your dentist's bill or find your income tax for you if it's all locked away, so I'm protecting myself, too.'

Allie had a marvellous laugh; she threw her head back and laughed like a child. She had perfect teeth, and her neck was long and sun-tanned.

Maura felt herself patting her hair. She was middle-aged, frumpish and settled, in her tights and shoes beside this lovely, leggy thing, all canvas shoes and golden limbs. And if Maura noticed it, then you could be sure that James did.

Allie asked about relations and friends, noted their names and numbers. She wrote down that Maura's sister didn't like dogs, and that James's mother didn't lock doors behind her. She seemed to understand everything in an instant.

Allie told them that she would write every week and give them an update on everything. She took instructions about phone messages and redirection of mail.

'Well, wasn't that the direct intervention of God,' James said when Allie had finally left.

Maura felt that this was both going too far and also ignoring her own part in finding the home sitter.

'Yes, well, and my friend Patsy!' she said mulishly.

'Of course.' He didn't care about niceties like this. 'Isn't she a treasure? She's exactly what we want,' he said happily. 'I didn't dream that anyone like that existed.'

A cold, hard knot formed in Maura's stomach. She felt a physical shock, like the feeling you get if you think you've swallowed a piece of glass. She realised she must not show her anxiety.

'Yes, she seems terrific, all right.'

'Aren't you clever?' James said.

Maura could feel the back of her neck get cold and clammy. As she sat in her garden, she knew in a disembodied way that she would remember this moment forever. She knew the time and the date, and the way she sat on the garden seat with her hand stroking the head of Jessie the collie dog. Maura knew, with a certainty that she had never felt before about anything, that Allie was going to bring danger into her life. Real danger, threatening everything she had hoped for.

She had often wondered how women behaved once they knew for certain. But then she supposed few women were possessed of the foresight that she had. Other women had to wait for evidence and proof, or a friend whispering that perhaps she ought to know. Or worse still, the husband saying there was something he had to tell her.

Maura wondered if it was better to know so far in advance. Did it give her any advantage over the others? Were there any points to be gained in the game of trying to keep James for herself, and resist the siren call of Allie, who had already captured his heart?

It wasn't a question of competing. Maura had fine, fair hair; she couldn't grow a mop of dark curls to shake around. Her mouth was small, almost pursed; this had once been thought an advantage, but she couldn't laugh showing all those pearly teeth as Allie did. Maura's legs and arms were white, not long and golden. If it were a straight fight, Allie would have the sceptre and the crown. It couldn't be a straight fight.

They saw her once more before they left – the very morning of the departure. She had brought her own sheets, she told them, and they saw them peeping from a huge straw basket.

'Is that the only luggage you have?' Maura tried hard to stop her voice from sounding like Allie's mother or her schoolteacher.

Allie dimpled back at her. 'I'm a gypsy, you see. I don't need possessions. I use everybody else's. I'll watch your television, look at your clocks, listen to your radio, boil your kettle . . . I don't need to clutter myself up with a lot of things.'

James was listening to this as if it were words from the Book of Revelations. He was also looking at the corner of Allie's sheets. Pretty blue and pink flowers with frilly edges on them. Maura knew that her own dull fitted sheets in white and pink were uninviting by comparison.

It had never been difficult to work out James's thought processes. They were very simple and direct; they went relentlessly from point A to point B.

'We never asked you, Allie, if there is anyone . . . any friend . . . boy . . . man . . .' He broke off in confusion.

'Allie knows she can invite any friend here.' Maura was crisp.

'No, I meant . . . you know.' James looked pathetic; he was dying to know if there was anyone. Maura held her breath, but not with any hope. What she had felt as she sat on that garden seat had not been a suspicion, it had been a foresight. It wasn't a matter of fearing that this golden girl would destroy Maura's life. She didn't just fear it, she knew it.

Allie laughed lightly. 'Oh, don't worry about that, James,' she said. 'I'm between lovers at the moment.'

'I'm sure that state won't last very long.' He was being gallant, arch. Idiotic.

'You'd be surprised.' The smile was easy. 'I have to wait for the right man.'

Maura knew that Allie would wait three months. The right man, James, was being taken out of the country temporarily, but she would wait and plot and plan for his return.

She wrote every week, addressing the letters to Maura, but this was only a ploy. She talked of long walks on the beach in Killiney throwing the sticks for Jessie, chatting with James's mother. A remarkable woman for her age, and so interesting about the year she had spent in Africa.

'Poor Mum, delighted with a new audience,' James said.

Allie had contacted Maura's sister Geraldine; they had, it seemed, been visiting each other a lot. Maura hoped this didn't mean that Geraldine would be dropping in at all hours when they got back.

Geraldine had been frightened by a dog when she was young; this was where her fear stemmed from.

'I didn't know that,' James said.

'Neither did I.' Maura was grim.

The visit to the midwestern campus was a sort of success. Only a 'sort of,' Maura thought.

There was indeed a chance to get closer. Evenings on their own. Walks together. None of the pressures of home, no traffic to cope with or talk about, since they lived in the centre of everything. No duty calls to people, no telephone ringing except from kind neighbours asking them to drop by for a barbecue or a drink.

But the week seemed to be spent waiting for Allie's next letter and analysing the last one.

'Imagine, the Hurleys asked her to dinner,' James said.

Maura had noted that too. 'Very kind of them. They're wonderful at looking after strays,' she said. It had been a mistake. James frowned.

'I don't think you'll find that they classified our Allie as a stray,' he said.

Maura hated her being called 'our Allie.' She also hated hearing in a letter that old Mrs Green was much better now and would be coming home from the hospital soon with a new hip.

'I didn't know ...' James began.

'I didn't know she had a hip replacement either,' Maura said. 'They keep themselves very much to themselves.'

'Not anymore they don't,' James said tersely.

'Will we send them a card?' Maura sounded tentative.

'You were always the one afraid of drawing them on ourselves.'

'Well, since they've *been* drawn ...' She knew her voice sounded sharp.

'Up to you.' He sounded a million miles away. Or a few thousand miles away. Back in that house and garden, in those flowery sheets, on warm terms with the neighbours. Maura felt that cold knot return. Like a flashback in a film, she saw herself sitting with a hand on Jessie's soft velvet fur.

There was a chill in the warm American evening, and she gave a little shiver.

'Are you all right?' he asked, concerned. He would always be kind to her, see that she managed as well as possible in the circumstances. She could see into the future, when he would call around once a year to discuss investments, and whether the roof needed to be redone.

But where would he call? She would *not* give him the house, she would not walk out and let Allie take over that place she had loved and lavished her heart on for ten years.

She would live there alone if need be. Her eyes filled with tears.

'You seem very tense here,' he said kindly. 'If you like, we can get away a little earlier. I mean, I can cram the lectures together a bit towards the end. Be back sooner.'

'What about Allie? She thinks she is staying three months.'

'Oh, she can stay on with us surely? Until she goes to her next place. She's not a fusser, our Allie.'

Maura said she didn't feel a bit tense, she simply loved it here, there was no question of going home early. She knew her smile was small and pinched. Without surgery she would never have a broad, open smile like Allie's.

It was a perfect September day when they got home. Maura rang Allie from the airport.

'How did she sound?' James was eager.

Maura wanted to say that she sounded like an overgrown schoolgirl, laughing and welcoming them back and words tumbling over each other. Instead she said that Allie sounded fine, and that she had arranged a few people to come in. 'That was lovely of her.' James smiled happily. 'Friends of hers, is it?'

'No, friends of ours, I think,' Maura said.

'We don't have that many friends,' James said absently.

'Of course we do,' Maura snapped.

Around them in Dublin Airport passengers were being met, embraced, and ferried out to cars. Maura and James pushed their trolley of luggage to a taxi ungreeted.

'We *could* have been met if we had wanted it,' Maura said in answer to no question.

On their lawn, Allie had set up a table. She had vases of flowers, and jugs of sangria. James's mother was there, helping and feeling as if she were in charge. Geraldine was there with her mute husband Maurice, chatting animatedly to the elderly Mr and Mrs Green, and discussing the success of the operation. The Hurleys were there with their extended family. The children all seemed to know Allie well. Maura had to struggle to remember their names, there were so many of them. A couple from across the road whom Maura and James had never met were among the crowd milling around.

'I do hope we aren't intruding,' the woman said. 'But Allie was so insistent, she said you'd love everyone here.'

'She was utterly right.' Maura strove to put the warmth and enthusiasm into her voice that she knew were called for.

'Have a shower, you must be exhausted.' Allie had thought of everything.

Maura stood under the water while James shaved at the washbasin nearby.

'What a girl,' he said at least three times. He was anxious to be back down there joining in the fun. 'Wasn't this a smashing idea of hers?'

Maura's voice was shaky. 'Great,' she said, hoping the running water covered the sound of a sob. 'Simply great. You go on down. I'll be out in a minute.'

She stood in her bedroom and tried to find something that might look festive and happy to wear. She seemed to see only blouses and skirts or matronly dresses that would make her fit into the generation of James's mother or the Greens.

Allie was leaving that afternoon; she would not stay and destroy Maura's life by taking her husband. Her next job was abroad. Minding a farmhouse in the Dordogne.

But Maura had been right that day on the garden seat. Allie had ruined her life; she had opened up golden doors and shown everyone else how wonderful things could be, but would never be again. James's mother would never again be asked to tell long stories about Africa, Geraldine wouldn't be invited to tell rambling tales of self-pity about barking dogs in her youth. The old Greens would go back into their greenhouse, and the high-flying Hurleys behind their hedge.

The people who lived across the road would never intrude again. James would frown without knowing why, and only Maura would know that nothing would ever be the same.

PACKAGE TOUR

❧

They met at a Christmas party, and suddenly everything looked bright and full of glitter instead of commercial and tawdry, as it had looked some minutes before.

They got on like a house on fire and afterwards when they talked about it they wondered about the silly expression. 'A house on fire.' It really didn't mean anything, like two people getting to know each other and discovering more and more things in common. They were the same age, each of them one quarter of a century old. Shane worked in a bank, Moya worked in an insurance office. Shane was from Galway and went home every month. Moya was from Clare and went home every three weeks. Shane's mother was difficult and wanted him to be a priest. Moya's father was difficult and had to be told that she was staying in a hostel in Dublin rather than a bed-sitter.

Shane played a lot of squash because he was afraid of getting a heart attack or, worse, of getting fat and being passed over when aggressive, lean fellows were promoted. Moya went to a gym twice a week because she wanted to look like Jane Fonda when she grew old and because she wanted to have great stamina for her holidays.

They both loved foreign holidays, and on their first evening out together Shane told her all about his trips to Tunisia and Yugoslavia and Sicily. In turn, Moya told her tales of Tangiers, Turkey, and of Cyprus. Alone among their friends they seemed to think that a good foreign holiday was the high spot of the year.

Moya said that most people she knew spent the money on clothes, and Shane complained that in his group it went on cars or drink. They were soul mates who had met over warm, sparkling wine at a Christmas party where neither of them knew anyone else. It had been written for them in the stars.

When the January brochures came out, Moya and Shane were the first to collect them; they had plastic bags full of them before anyone else had got around to thinking of a holiday. They noted which were the bargains, where were early-season or late-season three-for-the-price-of-two-week holidays. They worked out the jargon.

Attractive flowers cascading down from galleries could mean the place was alive with mosquitoes. Panoramic views of the harbour might mean the hotel was up an unmerciful hill. *Simple* might mean no plumbing, and *sophisticated* could suggest all-night discos.

The thing they felt most bitter about was the single-room supplement. It was outrageous to penalise people for being individuals. Why should travel companies expect that people go off on their holidays two by two like the animals into the Ark? And how was it that the general public obeyed them so slavishly? Moya could tell you of people who went on trips with others simply on the basis that they all got their holidays in the first fortnight in June.

Shane said that he knew fellows who went to Spain as friends and came home as enemies because their outing had been on the very same basis. Timing.

But as the months went on and the meetings became more frequent and the choice of holiday that each of them would settle for was gradually narrowed down, they began to realise that this summer they would probably travel together. That it was silly to put off this realisation. They had better admit it.

They admitted it easily one evening over a plate of spaghetti.

It had been down to two choices now. The Italian lakes or the island of Crete. And somehow it came to both of them at the same time: this would be the year they would go to Crete. The only knotty problem was the matter of the single room.

They were not as yet lovers. They didn't want to be rushed into it by the expediency of a double booking. They didn't want it to be put off-limits by the fact of having booked two separate rooms. Shane said that perhaps the most sensible thing would be to book a room with two beds. This had to be stipulated on the booking form. A twin-bedded room. Not a double bed.

Shane and Moya assured each other they were grown-ups.

They could sleep easily in two separate beds, and suppose, just suppose in the fullness of time after mature consideration and based on an equal decision with no one party forcing the other ... they wanted to sleep in the same bed ... then the facility, however narrow, would be there for them.

They congratulated each other on their maturity and paid the booking deposit. They had agreed on a middle-of-the-road kind of hotel, in one of the resorts that had not yet been totally discovered and destroyed. They had picked June, which they thought would avoid the worst crowds. They each had a savings plan. They knew that this year was going to be the best year in their lives and the holiday would be the first of many taken together all over the world.

The cloud didn't come over the horizon until March when they were sitting companionably reading a glossy magazine. Shane pointed out a huge suitcase on wheels with a matching smaller suitcase. Weren't they smashing, he said; a bit pricey, but maybe it would be worth it.

Moya thought she must be looking at the wrong page. Those were the kind of suitcases that Americans bought for going around the world.

Shane thought that Moya couldn't be looking at the right page; they were just two normal suitcases, but smart and easy to identify on the carousel. Just right for a two-week holiday. But for how many people? Moya wondered wildly; surely the two of them wouldn't have enough to fill even the smaller suitcase. Well for one person, me, Shane said with a puzzled look.

Between the two happy young people there was a sudden grey area. Up to now their relationship had been so open and free, but suddenly there were unspoken things hovering in the air. They had told each other that their friends' romances had failed and even their marriages had rocked because they had never been able to clear the air. Shane and Moya would not be like that. But still, neither one of them seemed able to bring up the subject of the suitcases. The gulf between them was huge.

Yet in other ways they seemed just as happy as before. They went for walks along the pier, they played their squash and went to the gym, they enjoyed each other's friends, and both of them managed to put the disturbing black cloud about the luggage into the background of their minds. Until April, when another storm came and settled on them.

It was Moya's birthday, and she unwrapped her gift from Shane, which was a travelling iron. She turned it around and around and examined it in case it was something else disguised as a travelling iron. In the *hope* that it was something disguised as a travelling iron. But no, that's what it was.

It was lovely, she said faintly.

Shane said he knew ladies loved to have something to take the creases out on holidays, and perhaps Moya shouldn't throw away the tissue paper; it was terrific for folding into clothes when you were packing, it took out all that crumpled look, didn't she find?

Moya sat down very suddenly. Absolutely on a different subject, she said she wondered how many shirts Shane took on holiday. Well, fifteen obviously, and the one he was wearing and sports shirts and a couple of beach shirts.

'Twenty shirts?' Moya said faintly.

That was about it.

And would there be twenty socks and knickers, too? Well, give or take. Give or take how many? A pair or two. There seemed to be a selection of shoes and belts, and the odd sun hat.

Moya felt all the time that Shane would smile his lovely familiar, heart-turning smile and say, 'I had you fooled, hadn't I?' and they would fall happily into each other's arms. But Shane said nothing.

Shane was hoping that Moya would tell him soon where all this list of faintly haranguing questions was leading. Why she was asking him in such a robotic voice about perfectly normal things. It was as if she asked him did he brush his teeth or did he put on his clothes before leaving the house. He stared at her anxiously. Perhaps he wasn't showing enough interest in her wardrobe? Maybe he should ask about her gear.

That did not seem to be a happy solution. Moya, it turned out, was a person who had never checked in a suitcase in her life; she had a soft squelchy bag of the exact proportions that would fit under an airline seat and would pass as carry-on baggage. She brought three knickers, three bras, three shirts, three skirts, and three bathing suits. She brought a sponge bag, a pair of flip-flop sandals, and a small tube of travel detergent.

She thought that a holiday should never involve waiting for your bags at any airport, and never take in dressing for dinner, and the idea of carrying home laundry bags of dirty clothes was as foreign to her as it was to Shane – that anyone would spend holiday time washing things and drying them.

'But it only takes a minute,' pleaded Moya.

'But it takes no time at all if you bring spares,' pleaded Shane. 'The arms would come out of your sockets carrying that lot,' said Moya. 'We wouldn't get into the bathroom with all your clothes draped around it,' said Shane.

They talked about it very reasonably, as they had always promised each other they would do. But the rainbows had gone, and the glitter had dimmed.

It would have been better if they had actually met on holidays, they said, with Moya carrying the shabby holdall and Shane the handsome and excessive luggage. Then they would have known from the start that they weren't people who had the same views about a package tour and how you packed for it. It was a hurdle they might have crossed before they fell in love. Not a horrible shock at the height of romance.

They were practical, Moya and Shane; they wondered if it would iron itself out if they paid the single-room supplement. That way Moya wouldn't see the offending Sultan's Wardrobe, as she kept calling it, and Shane wouldn't be blinded by wet underwear, as he kept fearing. But no, it went deeper than that. It seemed to show the kind of people they were: too vastly different ever to spend two weeks, let alone a lifetime, together.

As the good practical friends they were, they went back to the travel agency and transferred their bookings to separate holidays with separate hopes and dreams.

THE APPRENTICESHIP

It was to be one of the most stylish weddings of the year. Florrie thought that if anyone had been giving odds a quarter of a century ago when she was born whether this child would ever be a guest at something like this, those odds would have been enormous. A child born in a small house in a small street in Wigan didn't seem likely to end up as the bride's best friend at what the newspapers were calling the wedding of the decade. If only her mother had lived, Florrie thought, if only her father had cared. They might have been able to get some mileage out of it, some reward for the long hours of work, the high hopes.

There would be pictures of Florrie in tomorrow's papers, probably a glimpse of her on tonight's television news. She would figure certainly in the glossy magazines, her hat alone would ensure she was well snapped. She would be seen laughing and sharing a joke, probably with some youngish and handsome member of the aristocracy. This would not be hard, because unusually for a society wedding there might not be many young women friends of the bride around. And the groom's friends, being horsey, would not be as photogenic. No, Florrie knew that she would figure in the *Tatler* and *Harper's*. And she knew how to smile without showing a mouthful of teeth and how to raise her chin in a way that made her neck look long and upper class.

She knew that it looked much more classy not to be seen with a glass in her hand, but to appear fascinated by the particular braying chap that she was meant to be talking to.

Florrie knew all of this because she had worked at it, and learned it. Like she had never worked at anything when she was at school. Long ago in a different place and at a different time, with Camilla, except of course that Camilla had not been Camilla then, she had been Ruby. And Ruby and Florrie had been best friends. As in many ways they were still best friends today. The society columns might well describe Florrie tomorrow as a very close friend of the bride. But it would not say that they had grown up together, that they had shared great doorstep sandwiches in their lunch hour, that they had collected old newspapers just so that they could read the society pages and see how people lived in a different and better world.

They had read their subject carefully, young Ruby and young Florrie. No hint of social climbing or being a hanger-on. Not even the most suspicious could fault Camilla or catch her out in a lie today. Camilla had always said she was from way up north, that her parents were dead, that she had hardly any family. Better to stick as close to the truth as possible, she had advised Florrie, less for them to unearth, and you can never be caught out in a lie. Even if they found out she had once been Ruby, Camilla was prepared to say it had been a pet name. She thought it was terribly brave and funny of Florrie to hold on to her name. But then, Florrie was such a character! Florrie had held on to her name because she remembered her mother holding her as a little girl.

'I had a doll once called Florrie,' her mother had said. 'I never thought I'd have a little baby of my own, a beautiful baby to look after.' Florrie was three when she heard this first, hardly a baby, and still further from babyhood when her mother dressed her for school and held her face gently between red rough hands. 'Florrie,' she had breathed in a voice full of admiration and love. 'Such a beautiful name for a beautiful little girl. They wanted me to call you Caroline . . . but I wanted a beautiful name for you, one you'd love . . . Florence. It means a flower, little Florrie, beautiful little flower.'

Ruby's mother might have thought she was a little jewel. She might even have said so, but Camilla never said it. Camilla said nothing about her parents. Except that they were dead. Which was true.

They had died together in a coach crash, on the very first holiday of their married life. Florrie's father had said that's what you got for grand ideas, coach tours to the Continent, no less. Florrie's mother had said maybe they should take in the child. Ruby was eleven, and she had nobody else. Everyone had said it was a great idea. After all, it was unusual to be an only child in their street. Now Ruby and Florrie were like twins. And apart from reading all those 'silly books,' as people called the magazines they read, they were sensible girls, too. Not silly like some, not getting into trouble with boys. Hardworking. On Saturdays they worked in the beauty salon, and they learned how it was all done. The proprietor never had two such willing assistants. As well as sweeping floors and folding towels, they stood entranced watching the facials and manicures.

The customers liked them, two bright youngsters full of unquali-fied admiration. The customers didn't know they had come to learn – as they went to the fashion stores to learn, and as they worked in the good hotel to watch. And they did secretarial courses at night. By the time they had their O levels they were ready for anything. Ruby was ready to leave, to go south to start Stage Two. Florrie could go nowhere, her mother was failing fast.

She sat by her mother's bed and listened to the homespun wisdom, with a heart that was filled with impatience as well as love. She heard her mother beg her to believe that Dad was a good man really. It was just that he was a bit mulish, and drank a little too much. Dad had said no kind word in the seventeen years that Florrie had lived in his house. She nodded and pretended that she agreed with the mother, who would not be leaving hospital and coming home. Her mother said that Ruby was right to have gone to London, she was impatient, she would have been silly to stay around. The woman found nothing odd that the child she had taken in had abandoned her. Ruby has great unhappiness in her soul, she said. Florrie sat by the bed and gritted her teeth. Patience and forgiveness like this were unrealistic. Surely they couldn't be considered virtues. The nurses liked her, the handsome tall girl, a blonde with well-cut hair and long pink fingernails, unlike her stooped and work-weary mother. The daugh-ter had character, the nurses told each other. She wouldn't stay long with the bad-tempered father once the poor woman passed away.

Florrie stayed a week. Her father's farewell was grudging, as every other gesture had been. He had always known she would go, he said, too high and mighty by far for them. No, she needn't keep coming back up, there wasn't all that much more to say.

Florrie was astonished at the change in her friend in ten short months. Vowel sounds had altered, and that wasn't all. Ruby was no longer Ruby. It's only a name, she had explained, it could have been anything.

'I know,' Florrie had said. 'I should have been Caroline.'

'Then *be* Caroline,' Camilla had begged.

'Never.' Florrie's eyes had flashed at the thought.

They looked at each other then, a long look.

'It's only the name,' Florrie had said eventually. 'I'm on for everything else.'

And it was like the old days. They laughed as they heard each other's phrases; you never said you had been to the WC or the toilet, it was the lavatory. You didn't say serviette, you said napkin, and it wasn't posh to have paper ones that you could throw away when they got crumpled. They had plenty of time: it was an apprenticeship, they told each other. They had until they were twenty, then they would be ready. To move among the smart and the beautiful, to be at ease among them, to marry them and live in comfort for the rest of their lives.

It would only be hard if they were unprepared. They had heard too many tales of people being trapped by their humble origins. Camilla and Florrie would be different. They would invent no pedigree that could be checked and found faulty. They would shrug and ask did such things matter anymore. They would look so much the part and seem to care so little about proving themselves that soon they would be accepted. They would try hard but would never be seen to try at all; that was the secret.

And soon they were indeed ready. And it wasn't nearly as difficult as they thought. There was a career structure. Chalet girls in ski resorts, a few weeks working in smart jewellers and in art houses so that they met the right type of girl. They were slow to take up with the right type of men at the beginning. They wanted other girls to be their allies at the start. And anyway they wanted to be ready when they found the really right men. They had noticed that it wasn't only the Royals who liked their girlfriends not to have played the field; a lot of the Uppers thought that girls who had been around a lot might not be good wife material, and after all, one wouldn't like to think that lots of chaps had been with one's wife. What?

And in the meantime, because they *were* so bright and met so many people, they actually got good jobs. Camilla was high up in an estate agency and Florrie was now a partner in a firm of interior decorators. Years of watching for quality and trying to define it had paid off for both of them.

And then Camilla showed a couple of town houses to a chap who thought she was quite super and asked her to his place in the country for the weekend. She went, but she was slower than he thought to begin with a teeny affair, as he called it. In fact, she was adamant about not beginning it. He complained about her bitterly over a bottle of Bollinger to his friend Albert. Albert said that it was very rum, the girl must be mad. He'd like to meet her; he always liked meeting mad people.

Albert was of blood so blue that it almost frightened Camilla off. But she decided to take him on. This was the challenge she had spent years rehearsing for. This was the prize she had hardly dared to hope for.

Albert was intrigued by her. The girl who hadn't been to bed with his friend, who wouldn't go to bed with him either. Who wasn't frightened of his mother, who was casual to the point of indifference about her own background. She was not a gold digger, she had a position of importance in her firm. Nobody could see the potential like Camilla, they said. She dressed well, she seemed to have lots of girlfriends who all spoke glowingly of her. She had no past.

Camilla played it beautifully. She waited until Albert was truly besotted and at that precise moment she told him she was thinking of moving to Washington, D.C. There had been interest and offers; she was vague lest he ask her what interest and which offers. But she had timed it right. Albert couldn't let her leave. Albert's father predictably said she was a fine-looking filly but had she any breeding? His mother unpredictably said she was about the only kind of woman who might make a success of Albert and the rolling acres, and the complicated property investments and the tied cottages. The wedding of the decade was on.

It was decided between them that Florrie should not be the bridesmaid; the press would be too inquisitive, would ask about their origins. Papers nowadays did horrible things. They might send a photographer up to that small street and, perish the thought, find Florrie's father, surly in his suspenders. And he might tell that Camilla was Ruby and that her parents had been killed on their first coach tour abroad.

Better to have six flower girls and Albert's horsey-looking sister. Wiser to have the lovely Florrie stand out among the guests. A young woman of elegance, successful in her field. Further proof, if any were needed, that the bride was the right stuff or as right as you can get in these days of social change and upheaval.

Florrie stood in the old church and looked up at the flags of the regiment that Albert's family had fought in. The stained-glass windows remembered various ancestors, and the pews had brass plates recalling the family. The bishop was old and genial. He spoke of duty and of hope. Florrie listened as she looked at Camilla's beautiful face; she knew that her friend was listening, too.

Then the bishop spoke of love. He told how it conquered everything and that it cast out envy and ambition and greed. His eyes became misty when he talked of love.

The night before, Florrie and Camilla had talked for a long time. They had talked as they had never been able to talk since that day when Florrie had come to London and said she would change everything, everything but her name. They laughed as they hadn't laughed for years, they drank champagne instead of the lemon tea they had learned to like when they were fourteen because they had read it was lower class to take milk.

They had said that the battle had been half won, and now that Camilla was in, she could have the right kind of dinner parties and house parties to launch her friend. Her talented friend with the wonderfully funny name. They had embraced and congratulated each other on their magical apprenticeship.

But they hadn't talked about love. And in the church where Albert's bones would lie one day, very probably beside the bones of her friend Ruby, Florrie shivered. She knew that as far as she was concerned the apprenticeship was over. She had got far enough. Perhaps she had got much farther than her friend who would appear in tomorrow's papers as the bride of the decade, who would be called Lady Camilla, who would live a life without love. They said that young girls' heads were meant to be filled with stories of love, but that had never happened to Ruby or Florrie. There had been no room in their heads, the space was too filled with rule books on how to behave and how to say 'glad to know you' rather than 'pleased to meet you.' It had been too busy an apprenticeship to allow for thoughts of love.

Florrie would make time for it, she thought. She would not list the likely dinner guests that she might trap at her friend's long table, smiling at them confidently through Albert's family silver. When a bishop or vicar or a registrar came to say the word for Florrie, the word *love* wouldn't have an alien ring to it.

She felt somehow that the mother who had thought of her as a flower would have been pleased with her, and she was aware of tears beginning to well up in her eyes. But she willed them back, because the upper classes do not cry at christenings, weddings, or funerals. It is, after all, what sets them apart. Her apprenticeship had not been wasted.

THE BUSINESS TRIP

Lena had loved him for four long years. Not that he knew, of course. Men like Shay wouldn't even consider that they could be loved silently and unselfishly like that. It didn't make sense.

He probably assumed that Lena was fond of him, admired him, and might under the right circumstances be attracted to him. But if he thought of her at all, he might have assumed that she had a private life of her own. He would never have thought that this quiet, efficient assistant of his spent her entire life, both in and out of the office, thinking about him, trying to make his life easier and better, and in her dreams trying to share that life with him.

According to Maggie, Lena was not in love. She was suffering from an obsession, an infatuation. It wasn't healthy for someone who was twenty-six to develop this kind of crush on a man who didn't return it and wasn't even aware of it. And however unwise it might have been to have allowed a temporary fascination to take over, it was positively dangerous to let it continue the way Lena had. She stopped being twenty-six and became twenty-seven, and twenty-eight and twenty-nine. Soon she would be thirty years of age, and what had she to show for it?

Lena said spiritedly that she had as much to show for it as anyone had to show for anything. She had been happy, she had made his life better. She hadn't made a public fool of herself, as so many women had. She hadn't settled for second best, as so many others had done. She loved every second of her working day, which was more than you could say for a lot of people. She was appreciated if not loved in her office, and only Maggie knew her secret. She was not an object of pity. Maggie wouldn't tut-tut and shake her head over coffee with the girls about Lena's foolishness. Maggie was an ally, even if she didn't understand.

Maggie was Lena's aunt. But they had always been much more like cousins or sisters. Only ten years divided them in age, and the teenage Maggie had loved the toddler, Lena, and treated her as a friend. Now Maggie, almost forty, with huge dark eyes and a great mane of black curly hair, looked and acted younger than her niece. Her life was fuller by far. Maggie's problem had never been making men love her. It had been trying to stop them from loving her unwisely. And sometimes trying to stop herself from loving them in return – equally unwisely.

She had been married twice, widowed the first time, separated the second time, but these were only small milestones in the list of Maggie's love: sensible married men, fathers of large and settled families, wanted to throw up everything and move in with Maggie. She often had great trouble persuading them to do nothing of the sort. It wasn't that she gave them unmentionable sexual favours, she told Lena with her big dark eyes full of honesty, it was just that they saw, however foolishly, a kind of life with her where they wouldn't be hassled and troubled. They saw a strange and unrealistic freedom in living with Maggie, something they didn't have at home. Maggie would never ask them to come to the supermarket and push the trolley; Maggie wasn't a one for wanting the grass cut or the house painted, the car cleaned or the patio built up to impress the neighbours. Maggie would be happy to eat a meal of wild mushrooms and brown bread followed by strawberries. Very far from real life. Maggie would agree with them fervently that she was indeed far from real life and they must see her only now and then. The more she protested, the more they wanted her. Lena said she was outraged at the way Maggie got every man she wanted, and yet she, Lena, who kept all the rules, couldn't get just the one.

Lena did keep the rules as written in the women's magazines. She had shiny, well-cut hair, she was tall and slim, she had been to make-up lessons to make the most of her good complexion, her fair skin, and blue eyes. She dressed well and kept her clothes immaculately.

Well, why wouldn't she, Maggie grumbled, if she stayed at home every evening dreaming of lover boy Shay. There was all the time in the world to iron her blouses and sponge her skirts and polish her shoes, handbags, and belts till they shone. But had it done one bit of good in the department where she wanted it to succeed? No. None at all.

Lena's friends and colleagues all said she looked very smart, but their praise and admiration was of no interest to her. Sometimes they wondered why she didn't have a man in her life. She put them off with a laugh. And apart from Maggie, nobody had an inkling.

Maggie's grumbling had always been good-natured. But now it was different. Two things were coming up: Lena's thirtieth birthday, and a business trip with the famous Shay. Yes, he had asked the loyal Lena to London with him. Driving in his car, for a whole week.

Maggie felt it was time to play the heavy aunt for the first time in her life. She sat Lena down and told her to get ready for a serious lecture.

'Oh, not now,' Lena had cried. 'Not now. There's so much to be done, so many preparations. I have to decide what to wear, what to say, what social plans to set up, as well as all his business meetings. Can't the lecture wait till I get home?'

'No, it can't.' Maggie was adamant. 'It's about the trip; this has to be the make-or-break time. When you come back on the ferry and drive off the ramp, Shay must either be involved with you properly or else you will have given up all notion of him.'

Lena's blue eyes filled with tears. 'I don't want anything as definite, as black-and-white, as that. Why does it all have to hinge on this trip?' She looked appalled at having to abandon what was after all the central part of her life.

'Because you are leaving your twenties and for the first time you are leaving the country with this beauty, and you have the rest of your life ahead of you.'

'It's too frightening. I don't want to try and seduce him or something like that.' Lena was trembling at the thought.

'Well, what's all the fuss about what you're going to wear and how you're going to look? If you don't want him to fancy you, why don't you just go in an old sweater and a pair of jeans?' Maggie was ruthless.

'It's different for you, you can make anyone fancy you.'

'So could you if you bothered. It's got nothing to do with well-cut jackets and applying your blusher properly,' Maggie said.

'How, then?' Lena was eager.

'I'll tell you, but only if you promise me that you will decide one way or another at the end of the week. When you come back off that car ferry, you'll either be involved with him properly as two normal people who love each other, or you will leave that job, and put him out of your mind and heart.'

'It's like doing a deal with the Devil,' Lena complained.

'Much more like a guardian angel,' Maggie said.

They sat for three hours, Maggie with her notebook. At no stage were outfits or perfumes mentioned. There was no strategy about booking one room by mistake instead of two. There was to be no research into romantic restaurants in London where the lights would be low and there might even be violins in the background. No, if Lena was to get her man these kinds of cheap tricks were only Mickey Mouse efforts, according to Maggie. And since almost every man who moved in Dublin seemed to fancy Maggie in some way or other, she was worth listening to.

Maggie seemed shocked that Lena had worked for this man for four years, not to mention thinking that she had loved him for this length of time, and still knew so little about him. Maggie asked a string of questions. Lena knew nothing about his schooldays, whether he had liked it there or not, and how he had got into the business world in the first place. She didn't know who his first employers had been, whether he had found it easy or frightening. She didn't know what television programmes he watched, and when he went to a match if it was because he knew all about the game or because he liked the sociability of it. Lena didn't know how he got on with his two brothers and sister, how often he went to see his mother. She didn't know if he liked being with his nephews and nieces. If he felt lonely on weekends, as so many people did in Dublin. How he decided what to eat and whether he had a washing machine or went to the launderette.

'What *do* you know about him, for heaven's sake?' Maggie asked with some impatience.

Lena knew all about his current and past girlfriends, and she knew the restaurants he went to, and the nightclubs, and the bills for bouquets of flowers. She knew that and she knew about him at work, where he was tough and not afraid to go into a meeting and fight.

'Well-briefed by you, of course, with reports you have been working on all weekend when you weren't putting more henna in your hair, hoping he'd notice.'

'I love him,' protested Lena.

'No, you don't love him at all. You don't know the first thing about him apart from these empty social things. You might love him when you get to know him, and he might love you. But you might find him empty.'

Lena refused to accept this but agreed meekly to follow Maggie's advice. In the ship's dining room over a meal she would begin, and in the long drive across Britain she would not veer between business talk and gossip-column chat about nightclubs she didn't even know. She would talk to him about himself.

'Suppose he asks me about myself?' Lena asked fearfully.

Maggie didn't much think he would, but if he did, then she was to tell him the truth. Say she was perfectly happy, she had no wish to change from her life the way it was, assure him it was satisfactory. There was nothing that drove men as mad as that – the thought that women were actually contented the way they were, not scheming and conniving.

'But that's not strictly true. I'm not totally contented the way I am,' Lena complained.

Maggie shrugged. 'You always tell me you are when I try to change you.'

It was unanswerable.

The day before the trip Maggie rang her to wish her luck. 'One thing, Lena, and remember this: he will notice you, he will fancy you. Truthfully, but you may not fancy him.'

'I probably gave you much too shallow a view of him,' Lena whispered in case anyone in the office would hear.

'If that was your view of him after four years of loving him, then I'm sure what you told me was very accurate,' Maggie said.

Lena learned a lot that night at dinner on board ship. She learned that his mother was demanding and never satisfied, that his brothers were discontented and jealous of his success. She heard that Shay's sisters didn't know how to bring up their children properly and gave in to them in everything. She heard that his school was full of sadistic teachers and moronic pupils, that they had ripped him off in his first job and cheated him in his second, and he had seen them coming in his third. He liked to cook but not to wash up; he thought these service apartments he lived in were a bit cramped, but he didn't want to take on the whole palaver of gardens and roofs and drains in a house. He was probably looking for something like a town house.

In the old days, like every day up to this, Lena would have immediately said she would make inquiries about town houses, and go to endless trouble ringing up auctioneers and estate agents. This time she made no offers.

'What about your house or flat, is it what you want?' he asked, almost cursorily, as if he had felt that he might have been talking just a little too much about himself.

'Oh, it's fine. I'm very happy there,' she said. She told him it was a garden flat and had plenty of light as well as nice shrubs and bushes outside big windows. He nodded briskly but seemed to look at her with slightly more interest.

On the long drive to London, they talked about friends. Shay said that he ran with a very lively crowd. No, they weren't around on weekends much, but then, he often came into the office on Saturday afternoons to do a little catching up. Lena knew this only too well. She had to cope with the results of it on Mondays: confused notes, complicated questions. She had begun every week for as long as she could remember by sorting out his thoughts for a secretary to type up. He had got all the credit. Somehow it was disappointing to know he came in only because he was bored on Saturday afternoons. She had thought it was ambition.

He took his washing to his mother, it turned out. She could not believe it, but it was true. He had to go and see the woman once a week anyway, and she had a machine, so it made sense to leave her one load and collect another. And she liked it; what else had she to do?

By the time the signposts saying Central London came up, Lena had opened more doors than she might have wished to in Shay's life.

He suggested they grab something to eat, and she said thank you but no. She had friends to see in London, so unless there was anything they wanted to discuss about work for the conference tomorrow, she would leave him to his own devices.

He seemed quite put out by this. Lena looked at his handsome face scowling with almost childlike disappointment.

'Don't tell me you're going to do the clubland circuit in London?' he asked, not very kindly.

'Lord no, that's not my world at all. Just dinner with friends.'

It was true. Dinner with two old school friends – one a nun, one a nurse. They laughed and talked over old times. Something was lighter in Lena's laugh; she felt it wasn't an effort.

Next day they worked companionably at the conference, but she excused herself at lunchtime to sneak in a little shopping and said that she had a theatre date in the evening. He was thoroughly bad-tempered on the second day of the conference.

'Are you going to keep running away all the time, or will we see each other at all?' he grumbled.

Big blue eyes wide, she said that honestly she was sorry . . . but since they never went out socially at home, she assumed it would be the same here. But, of course, she would be delighted to have dinner with him if he had anywhere in mind.

'I thought you might arrange somewhere,' he said.

'Oh no, I wouldn't dream of it. If you are asking me to dinner, then you must, of course, choose where.'

It would once have been her wildest dream. Not only was the place expensive and romantic, but as he told her tale after tale of being misunderstood, betrayed, cheated, having got even, he took her hand.

'You're very easy to talk to, Lena, and you look very lovely. I hadn't realised.' She had smiled. It was a smile of someone who had known that this was predictable, not of someone who thought it was perfect.

When the evening ended and he suggested a brandy in his room, she said no. Perhaps she would prefer to have the nightcap in her room, he suggested, probably thinking that this was the height of sensitivity. No nightcap at all, Lena said. She who had planned this night for so long, and all it would lead to.

At one stage she began to wonder if Maggie had set her up. Every single harmless question she had asked had brought such a negative response that she had managed to strip Shay, the man she had loved for years of any lovable quality. It was as if Maggie had known the answers in advance.

Maggie hadn't suggested that Lena talk to Shay of love.

But that night she did. They were in a restaurant looking out on the river, and he told her that he thought he loved her – yes, strange as it might seem, and having worked together for so long – but he did think he loved her.

She looked at him for a long time.

'Well, say something,' he said petulantly.

'I don't have any words,' she said truthfully.

He reached for her hands, but she pulled them away.

'What are you thinking about?' she asked him.

'How nice it is to love you, how there you were under my nose all the time.'

At least, she thought, at least he is honest in a childish sort of way. It must be nice for him to think he's found a ready-made love under his nose, as he put it.

For years she had seen how suitable she would be for him, how right as a companion a friend, a wife. How much she would help his career and cope with his weaknesses.

Until tonight she had never seen what it would be like for her. A lifetime of putting up with his moods, building him up when he was low, lying for him, pretending for him. And turning a blind eye when he wanted to run with a lively crowd and do the clubs and walk the blondes.

She smiled at him affectionately. It was the way she had seen her aunt Maggie smile at a multitude of men.

'What are *you* thinking about?' he asked. He was sulking now; his declaration of love had not only not been returned, it had been smiled at, patted down, soothed away.

'I was thinking about going home, about driving out of the ferry and going home,' she said.

This was a very puzzling response. 'Why, what will you do then?' he was anxious to know.

Lena wondered what would she do. She wouldn't leave her job just because he had said he loved her and she wouldn't love him back. She liked her work, she would stay there and overtake him if necessary. She would not fight with him or explain or apologise – Maggie never did that. She was happy in her garden flat, and now she was free as well. If some man came along – as men came along for Maggie – that she really did like, then she was free to love him.

'What will I do?' she answered him almost dreamily. The world was so full of possibilities now that the question was hard to answer. 'What will I do when I get home? I think I'll telephone my aunt.'

THE CROSSING

'It's like a real cruise, isn't it?' Mary said, then wished she hadn't said it. What did she know about a real cruise except reading the brochures?

'I was just thinking that too,' said Lavender, the older woman. 'Not that I was ever on a cruise, mind, but it feels like we should have two weeks, and visit exotic places every day instead of just getting out at Liverpool.' They laughed, united in never having been on a luxury cruise liner, united in admiring the seagulls, and valuing a few minutes away from the family.

'Are you going or coming back?' Lavender asked. She had a kind face and bright, interested eyes. Mary felt you could talk and she really might care what you said.

'Going over. The children have never seen their grandparents. It's a bit of an ordeal really.'

Why had she told that to a stranger? She hadn't told any of her neighbours, nor her best friend Kath, nor her sister Betty. Why did she blurt it out to a woman with a North of England accent on the B & I boat?

'Oh, I know,' Lavender consoled her. 'It's always an ordeal, isn't it? Maybe we should have to live with our in-laws all the time in the same tribe and never move, or else we should never see them at all. It's the in-between bit that causes all the guilt.'

This was so exactly true that Mary almost jumped to hear her own feelings echoed . . .

'Did you have that kind of ... well, that kind of thing, you know, with your husband's parents? Wanting to make it all closer and then getting it a bit wrong?'

'Tell me,' Lavender said.

And Mary did. Every bit of it. Slowly, hesitating sometimes, going back over bits in case they hadn't been fair. How she met John when he was on a cycling holiday in Ireland. John was unhappy at college, he found it was hurting him inside his head, the stress and the worry. It wasn't only exams and study. He didn't think he would ever be happy as a teacher. He was too anxious in the classroom practice, he wouldn't be able to keep control, and he could not look forward to a life that would be a constant battle and a series of confrontations in the classroom every day.

'Why don't you do something else with your life, then?' Mary had asked him. 'We only get to come onto the earth once. Wouldn't it be a pity to spend it all doing something that makes you unsettled?'

It was like a revelation to John. There and then he decided to abandon the idea of being a teacher. He wrote to the college, he wrote to his parents and to his girlfriend in London. He said he had been feeling a bit lost; now he was going to find himself in Ireland. He was going to work on a farm while he was finding out what to do with the rest of his life.

Nobody was pleased – not the college, which worried about his grant, not his girlfriend in London, who worried for four weeks and then sent a card telling him it couldn't matter less whether he found himself or didn't, since she had found somebody more normal. And his parents worried most of all. He was an only child; they had their hopes set on his being a teacher, and now he was a farmhand in Ireland, for heaven's sake. They were very disapproving. They were not people who wrote letters much or made cross-Channel phone calls. But they disapproved nonetheless. Heavily.

And when John and Mary got engaged, they assumed that it was a shotgun marriage, which it wasn't, and that it would be in a Roman Catholic Church full of images of saints and the Virgin, which it was. And they said they couldn't come to the wedding.

Mary sent pictures of the children, Jacinta, now eight, and John Paul, who was born the day the Pope came to Ireland and was seven.

Looking back on it, Mary wondered if she should have chosen different names for the children. But surely that wasn't important. John's parents could hardly disapprove of a child's name as being from a different tribe. And Mary had been careful to send pictures of the children at Christmas rather than the First Communion snapshot that she felt the instinct to send each time.

Lavender was full of praise. Mary had done more than her share. And where was the problem?

It wasn't exactly a problem; there was no out-and-out war, just a distance in every sense of the word. And a dread of meeting these people, who wouldn't come to Ireland, who had never shown any greater interest than a dutiful card at Christmas. Mary was not looking forward to hearing what a brilliant career had been cut short when John had met her in Ireland ten long years ago.

She didn't want to make excuses for the life they led in a small country town where John worked happily on a farm and Mary was a dressmaker.

And they were going now because John's father was unemployed, had been for a year, and the word had trickled back from a woman neighbour that John's dad was taking it hard. Mary had suggested they visit Ireland and as usual it had been turned down, so, gritting her teeth, she had then suggested that they take the children to visit their grandparents, and this had been agreed to. Ungraciously, of course. 'You'll have to take us as you find us.' But still agreed.

It was a two-week visit. Too long, Mary thought, but it was a huge undertaking, four of them to go to London; it would be a great waste to go for less time.

Lavender said that Mary was a positive gem among women. She said she was sure that the parents-in-law would be so pleased that in a few days they would all wonder whether the distance could possibly have been in their imaginations.

'Would you like a little advice?' she asked, almost shyly.

'Oh, I'd love anything you could tell me, you being English and a bit older, not that you'd be as old as them or anything, but you know ...'

Lavender leaned her back against the rail, squinted into the sun, and talked not directly to Mary but as if she was speaking to herself. She looked very much like a woman who should be on a luxury cruise liner waiting for an executive husband to come back from a game of deck tennis with the captain.

'I wouldn't apologise or explain too much. Maybe let them think they were part of your lives, even though they weren't. The children should know a bit about them, like their birthdays and their names, and where they grew up themselves. And perhaps you might ask, all of you, about your husband as a little boy, you know, when he was seven or eight, what he read and what toys he played with. They probably have them still. And it could be assumed rather than said that one day, soon, but not a fixed day, the grandparents would come to Ireland.'

Lavender seemed apologetic. She felt she had talked too much.

'I wish you wouldn't say you were laying down the law. I'm just overjoyed to get some ideas. That's a very good thought, you know. I don't know their birthdays and the children don't know anything at all about them.'

'There'll be plenty of time on the train to London.'

'You have children yourself?' Mary was diffident.

'One, a daughter.' There seemed to be a full stop.

'That's nice,' Mary said. 'Or isn't it?'

'Not much at the moment, it isn't.'

They had started to walk around the deck. People sat in chairs lathering themselves with Nivea. Duty-free bags were being tucked under the sunbathers, children ran round excited, passengers had all started to talk to each other in the relaxed way of holidaymakers. There might be long drives, or train journeys, or even family ordeals ahead, but on the ship they were suspended. It was time out of time. People spoke, as they often had no time to speak when on land.

'I'm sorry,' Mary said to Lavender. 'You're so easy, you should have a good time with a daughter.'

'I did until she was fourteen. Then she met this lad. Oh, I think a hundred times a day how different life would have been if she hadn't met him.

'She never opened a schoolbook from that day to this. We were before the courts for her every month of the year. If it wasn't truancy it was shoplifting, then it was glue sniffing, then it was a stolen car.'

It had certainly not been the life they had hoped for their Emma.

'And did she get over the lad?' Mary sighed, thinking that all this might easily lie ahead for her with Jacinta in a troubled world.

'No, she'll never get over him. She's eighteen now and she misses him so much that she just sits and cries. She's sitting down in the restaurant now with her dad, crying. I couldn't take it anymore; she cried all through this holiday in Ireland we took specially to give her a treat. I couldn't see it for one second more. That's why I came up on deck.'

'I'm glad you did,' Mary said.

'So am I,' said Lavender. 'But you can see I'm not one to be handing out advice. You see how poor my own situation is. I can't even sit and talk to my own daughter.'

'Wasn't it nice of you to bring her to Ireland on a holiday, though?' Mary said admiringly. 'A lot of mothers would not have done, with a girl who got into all that sort of trouble. She's lucky.'

'She doesn't think so, she thinks she's cursed with middle-aged, old-fashioned parents. She'd like to be left alone with that yobbo.'

'Still, she came with you. She's eighteen, grown up, she needn't have come unless she wanted to.'

'True.' Lavender's face was sad.

'What would be the best that could happen? The very best?'

Lavender was thoughtful. 'I used to think if he disappeared off the face of the earth that would be the best. But in their mad white-faced Mohican-hair way with chains dangling and safety pins all over their ears . . . they love each other. So I suppose the best that could happen is for them to love each other without breaking the law and for him to be a bit civil to us. We are part of Emma's life too; for years we held her by the hand and dreamed of what she would do. If he took that into consideration a bit . . .'

'That's why you told me to ask John's parents about the toys, wasn't it?' Mary said.

'Love, it's a different world to yours. You're a lovely warm woman trying to build bridges; he's just a yobbo with a face like the devil trying to break up everything he comes across.'

'They must have thought that about me too,' Mary said. 'I only realise it now. I was so alien and so determined. All the time I was annoyed they couldn't be a bit warmer. But I never thought what it was like to *be* them, having held John's hand for years and listened to his baby talk and watched him starting out to school.'

They walked companionably on their tour. They would never meet again, nor write to each other. Mary would never know if the yobbo reformed, or if Emma dried her tears over him. She wouldn't even know what Emma looked like, or her father, who was sitting patiently handing her more and more paper table napkins to wipe the sad, pale, punky face.

And Lavender would never know if the visit went well, and if John's parents took out his old train for John Paul to play with and if Mary became friendly with his mum and helped in the kitchen. She would never hear if the invitation to Ireland, which would be just assumed rather than stated, would in fact be taken up.

Their lives would never cross again.

But while they did cross on a sunny day on a blue sea they talked as all shipboard passengers do in a way that would sound to the seagulls above that these people were friends for life.

And Lavender told Mary that all her sisters had been called after flowers and Mary told Lavender that in her class at school there were eleven girls called Mary and it had been very confusing.

They never knew that their husbands were having a drink at the bar.

Emma's tears had dried, John Paul and Jacinta had found a new friend, and it happened that Lavender's John and Mary's John were standing having a pint. They talked about golf, they talked about the shambles the World Cup had been, and they talked about prices and Ronald Reagan and trade unions.

And Lavender's John and Mary's John had a second pint and that was it. They were getting near Liverpool now, and so they found their families and their luggage, and one family went north and one went south.

THE WOMEN IN HATS

It was very exciting watching people come on board, said the purser. After a few journeys you could size them up pretty well. That woman would fight with her husband two days out, he would spend all his time with the bar people, she would find a younger man and a little shipboard romance. That woman over there, she would keep her husband by her side with a rod of iron; she was one of these so-called 'invalids' who had nothing wrong with them, except a very serious case of self-importance.

The purser was a beautiful dark-eyed gay Canadian who missed his boyfriend terribly, and rang him from every port and regarded his job as so much torture necessary in order to save enough money for a house on the Great Lakes.

He liked talking to Helen; she was forty and friendly and didn't show any dangerous tendencies of jumping at him some night and assuring him of her powers of being able to make the earth move for him. She played gin rummy with him, told him funny tales about the people at her table, and seemed very interested in his tales of Garry. Helen used to advise him not to call Garry so much. 'Telephone calls are very unsatisfactory and expensive,' she had said. Paul the nice agreeable purser was beginning to think she was right. He would miss her when she got off at Singapore. He'd have to find a new friend.

Leaning over the side at Piraeus, Paul saw a good-looking man squinting up into the sunshine. A pang of infidelity to Garry swept over Paul, but it was gone as soon as it arrived. Anyway the handsome man didn't look very available. A very beautiful woman with sunglasses in her hair rather than on her face with a golden suntan, and a blue flowing dress exactly the same colour as her eyes, seemed to have her hand possessively on his arm.

'What do you make of that pair?' he asked Helen.

'Honeymooners?' wondered Helen.

'No, they don't have that absorbed look,' Paul said. 'They seem to be talking about something, not just "Imagine, this is us getting on a ship." That's the way honeymooners go on.'

The tanned girl had a huge blue and white hat tied by a ribbon around her neck. For no reason she annoyed Paul. People should put sunglasses on eyes, and hats on heads. What was she looking at anyway? He followed her gaze.

At the top of the gangway was the fattest woman Paul had ever seen. She wore a huge pink and white hat, on her head, he was relieved to notice. She had a flowing pink and white dress that could easily have been a tent for several people. She carried an enormous beach bag, white but with a name embroidered on it in pink. 'Bonnie,' it said.

Paul couldn't see her face, but he got the feeling she was young. Immediately Paul felt protective towards her. Even if it wasn't his job, he would look after her. In fact, she might become his friend when Helen left.

'Let's ask the pink elephant lady to have a drink with us?' he said to Helen. 'I think she's on her own and she'd appreciate it.'

'No,' said Helen. 'She's not on her own, she's with the non-honeymoon couple – I saw them all get out of the same taxi. But I'm all for a drink with anyone anytime.'

Paul looked at Helen with affection. She had talked him out of phoning Garry because of the time difference, the known unreliability of Greek phones, and all the unnecessary angst he would cause himself if there was no reply. Helen must have been through all this love business too, but unlike most women, she didn't seem to want to discuss it or recall it way into the night. Paul called her a purser's joy, someone who didn't complain and who helped other people to enjoy themselves; he said she should really be getting a fee, not paying a fare.

Paul thought Helen must be wrong about big Bonnie. She couldn't be with the golden couple; she wasn't old enough to be the mother, she wasn't young enough to be their child. But when he went to see how they were all settling in, he found the threesome was as Helen had said.

The good-looking boy sat in the middle and on either side of him huge hats bobbed, one blue over the slim tanned girl, one pink over the enormous smiling Bonnie.

'I'm Paul Preston, the purser ... you are very welcome on board.' Bonnie looked up with a big welcoming smile and offered him a huge hand to shake.

'How nice and alliterative,' she said. 'I'm Bonnie and this is Charlie and this is Charlotte ...' She waved delightedly at the golden couple. Paul still couldn't figure out what relation they were to her.

'That's pretty nice and alliterative too,' he said about their names.

'I'm always saying that about them,' said Bonnie. 'It's the most amazing coincidence, my two best friends in the world both called after some no-good Stuart king.'

Paul thought it was more of a coincidence that two people called Charlie and Charlotte should have met and married each other than to have turned out to be friends of Bonnie's, but he decided not to follow that line of chat.

They discovered he was from Ottawa originally, would like to live on the Lakes, had been a ship's purser for four years and was aged twenty-nine. He discovered they were from Australia originally, but had lived so long in Europe now they had almost forgotten the Outback. Bonnie was twenty-nine and Charlie and Charlotte were twenty-seven each. Another coincidence. They had been living in Greece for the summer, all three of them, and now they were going to Hong Kong on this ship to see if they could set up a little import-export company, and then they were all going to take a cheap flight back to Australia where they would stay until Christmas. None of them were very enthusiastic about going back home. Bonnie said her parents were dead and she had no ties. Charlie said his father thought people who left Australia were traitors. Charlotte said that her mother wanted her to marry a man who had a big share in a sheep station. They all seemed so easy and relaxed in each other's company that it looked as if they had been friends for years.

Had they been in business long together, he wondered? No, they had only met that spring. All of them had been working in London. Bonnie had advertised for fellow Australians to set up a venture, and that was how they had met.

'And that's how you got together?' said Paul, smiling at the two golden heads of Charlie and Charlotte as they sat together near Bonnie's knees on the deck. They looked like an advertisement for something, so healthy and happy did they seem.

'Yeah, that's how we all met,' said Charlie, sounding puzzled.

As the days went on Paul saw no way of making Bonnie into a special friend, since she was never alone. If Charlie and Charlotte, or one of them, weren't with her, she was surrounded by others. She had offered to embroider people's names on their towels or bags, and was doing a roaring trade. Paul was sure that some bylaw said she couldn't charge fees, but he never looked it up.

In Ceylon he bought a beautiful shirt for Garry. Helen had said it was much wiser than spending money on a telephone call, everyone knew how unreliable the Sinhalese telephone service was.

He was admiring the shirt lovingly when a big shadow and a soft footfall came upon him. It was Bonnie.

'Shall I do your name on it?' she asked. 'In off white on the pocket, so that you'd have to strain to see it, that would be nice.' In fact, that would be very nice. Paul admired her taste.

'Could you put "Garry" on it?' he asked shyly.

'Is that your boyfriend?' asked Bonnie.

'Well, yes,' Paul said. He didn't feel at all at ease with her like he did with nice comfortable, undemanding Helen. In a funny way this enormous woman seemed to consider herself quite socially acceptable. Was there even a hint of a flirtation with him and a sense of regret that there was a Garry in the background?

Paul began to wonder was he losing his reason. He must be imagining it. He must.

They sat in the sunset for a bit, then he told her about the flying fish that sometimes came up on deck, and she told him how much she loved embroidery and sewing and she was going to make herself a huge patchwork cape someday with a hundred colours in it. It would shine out everywhere and nobody could ignore her.

This made Paul strangely uneasy again. With someone like Helen he could have said what came into his mind, which was that he didn't think it a good idea for a gigantic woman to call further attention to herself. He had told Helen several times that she would look nicer if she wore lipstick, and eventually she bought some and wore it just to please him and everyone admired her. He would love to say this to Bonnie, that she should be more restrained, there was no need to go around like a lighthouse. But he didn't dare. Nor did he dare to suggest that she should have white wine and soda instead of the great pint of beer she was drinking as the sun went down.

So Paul didn't become a friend of Bonnie, but he became, to his great amazement, a great observer of her. He noticed the way she settled herself by the swimming pool early with her embroidery, how Charlie and Charlotte would appear and consult her about how the day was to be spent. Bonnie had four sundresses, each one louder and more attention-getting than the one before. Some had sunflowers, some had huge roses, one even had multicoloured designs. And there was always a huge hat as well, usually matching the dress. The hat upset Paul most of all. It was like a flag saying 'Look at me.' It was especially tasteless, he thought, since Charlotte also wore huge hats. Hers looked lovely, they made her seem like a slim Mexican boy, while Bonnie looked like a giant toadstool.

And it wasn't a question of disliking her. She was one of the most easygoing pleasant people he had met. He couldn't work out why he felt uneasy with her. He even discussed it with Helen.

'You've been obsessed with her since they came aboard,' said Helen grumpily. 'In a way I'm a bit jealous. I don't know why you are doing all this analysing. It's very simple to understand.'

'Well, I wish I understood it,' said Paul.

'You want to patronise her, pity her, bring her out of herself, get her to join in things . . . and it isn't necessary. She doesn't need pity, she's already out of herself, she does things without your having to organise it, in fact she's on a nice little number with all that sewing people's names on things. She's taken in a couple of hundred dollars.'

Paul thought about this. Well, there was a little truth in what Helen had said . . . just a little. He wasn't upset because Bonnie rejected his friendship . . . it was just that she seemed quite complete without it. That's what was the little pique, the slight wound.

But he was drawn to them all, like someone charmed. He watched them every day, Charlie with his lithe athletic body playing deck games, Charlotte looking like an advertisement for the glamour of cruising, and Bonnie more ridiculous looking, more calm and sure of herself every day. Paul's mother had been fat. Back in Canada she had hardly moved outside her house. But then his mother had been a lady, she had dignity. In a million years she would never have understood this Bonnie who behaved ... well, like a normal woman.

The words pulled him up short when he felt himself thinking them. Of course, in many ways his mother and Bonnie were normal women, they actually were ordinary people, just fatter than the accepted shape. But Mother had known that it was dignified not to go out and about if you looked different to other people, and when Mother had to go out she wore dark concealing clothes, the most restrained garments she could find. Bonnie with her big mad hats, wide smile, and her red lipstick would have been like a creature from Mars.

He wondered, were Charlie and Charlotte attracted by her in the same mesmerised way as he was? Did they have this mongoose/snake thing with her that he did? One day he decided to discuss it with Charlotte. She was sitting alone for once, feet up on the ship's rail, hat hanging from its ribbon around her neck. She looked very gentle and beautiful.

He wondered, how did Charlie feel able to share her so much? Not that Paul was any authority on women, but he did feel that if you were married to such a dazzling woman as Charlotte you might want her for yourself rather than spend all your time in an odd trio.

'What are you thinking about?' he asked the still girl.

'Oh, I was thinking about how undemanding life is on board a ship. Somebody else decides where you're going, how long you'll stay. I love not having to make any decisions.'

'Do you have to make all that many in real life?' he asked.

'Constantly. How to earn money, who to live with, who to trust, where to be, when to leave ... all the time.'

'But that's all over now, I mean can't you do it as a team?' asked Paul. He assumed that Charlie must make at least fifty percent of the decisions for the couple.

'Yes, that's the great safety of being with Bonnie,' said Charlotte.

'Well, I meant Charlie really,' he said.

'Oh, Charlie feels the same, he's often said it to me. He said he felt such a wave of relief when he proposed to her and she said yes. He knew he'd be safe for the rest of his life . . .'

'When he proposed to Bonnie?' Paul stuttered, confused.

'Well, not proposed, asked her to marry him, whatever people do,' said Charlotte. Then suddenly, 'What's wrong?'

'I thought you and Charlie were married,' he said, 'to each other, I mean.'

'No, I'm not married to anyone. Charlie and Bonnie were married in spring. You must have known they were married, or together anyway. I mean, they have a cabin and everything . . .'

Paul was digesting this very slowly indeed.

'I didn't know,' he said. Even as he said it he didn't know why he was so shocked. He couldn't sit here and think about it anymore. He got up quickly and made some mumbled excuse – so inadequate that the lovely Charlotte actually sat up in her deck chair to watch him disappearing off down the deck. She shrugged and went back to her book.

Paul found Helen.

'Did you know that he's married to Bonnie, not to Charlotte?' he said.

'Oh yes, I discovered that a couple of days ago. I heard someone call them Mr and Mrs.'

Paul was annoyed that she took it so calmly.

'It's ridiculous. They're so unsuited.'

'I think they get on particularly well,' said Helen, spiritedly. 'I mean, look at the other couples on the ship who are fighting or yawning or sulking. I think Bonnie and Charlie are a tonic.'

Paul felt affronted. He was astonished at the violence of his own reactions. He liked them all, he loved none of them. Why should it matter who was hitched to whom? But it did. It really did. He felt very adrift.

Helen looked at him sharply.

'You really have been building up some kind of fantasy about these three, haven't you?' she asked, not unkindly.

'I don't know what you mean,' he said defensively.

'You're obsessed by them, and Bonnie in particular. Now, you're the last person on board to realise that it's she who's married to the young blond Adonis. It may have caused a momentary flicker in the rest of us, it's nearly knocked you down.'

'I think she's gross,' he said suddenly. Helen looked shocked.

'No, of course you don't. She's not nearly as gross as that retiring German missionary who got on at Bombay, and she's not nearly as fat as the Greek woman who has to lift her stomach up in front of her. What can you mean, Paul? She's just a fat girl with a lovely face. You can't ever have looked at her properly if you don't realise that she's absolutely dazzling looking. Just too much fat.'

'My mother was very attractive until she let go,' said Paul in a mulish small-boy voice. 'But she never went around in such garish colours calling the full attention of the world to herself.'

'Did she go around much at all?' asked Helen with interest.

'No, she had respect for herself. She knew she didn't look well, so she hid herself away. She was very dignified.'

'And probably very depressed, too,' said Helen very sharply. 'How have you the slightest idea whether your mother was dignified or was going nutty as a fruitcake having to stay in the great Canadian indoors just because her pretty little son and her handsome husband might be a teeny bit embarrassed if she ventured out. You don't know anything about anyone.'

'You said I was getting upset. You're the one who's shouting now,' said Paul, startled by this change in easygoing Helen.

'You make me shout, intolerant insensitive little pansy,' said Helen. 'Yes, pansy, pouf, queer, I can't remember the other words, but I'm sure they're there. Ten years ago, that's what people would have called you. Ten years ago your particular minority didn't go out very much, it was dignified and depressed and hid itself.

'Stop looking wounded and betrayed. I only say this because you annoy me so much with all your unliberated attitudes. You think it's modern to be able to tell me about Garry . . . I think it's just so much rubbish. You can't see that your own mother was a victim to your narrow-mindedness about physical appearance. You want a world of beautiful identical robots. You want a Nazi world, only the fittest and the finest shall be tolerated . . . You want to grow up, Paul.'

Paul was still for a while.

Then he said, 'Helen, I don't want to upset you, perhaps you're right, but why do you take it so badly? You're not fat, you can't have an axe to grind for Fat Rights. Tell me what it is that makes you feel so strongly.'

'I might have told you once. I might have given in to this seductive shipboard thing of confiding. I thought you were a gentle kind boy with a new open soul. But not now, I'll never tell you. You'll have to guess, and you can spend months guessing, and you'll never know.'

Helen laughed at him, not unaffectionately.

'No, little Paul, you'll never know whether I had a fat lover who died from slimming, or whether I was once fat, or whether someone I cared for was hurt by cruel insensitive attitudes such as yours. But that doesn't matter very much. It's just one shipboard story fewer to hear. What does matter is that you realise you are the one out of step, not big Bonnie. She's modern and liberated, she's no prisoner because of her flesh. I don't have an ounce of sympathy for that girl, she's a happy soul, she's got an adoring husband, she's got a good business sense. She's not gross, Paul – you could be. You and Garry could end up in some community where people don't like gays . . . and I'd hate to think where your courage and inner resources might be then.'

She gave him an awkward kind of matey hug as she left the room. She didn't want to close every door to him.

With a numbness a bit like the way you feel after having a tooth filled, Paul walked to the upper deck and looked down below. It was sunset, and at sunset every evening, the glorious Charlie sat sipping a drink, flanked by the women in hats, and they were all laughing contentedly in the pinky red light.

EXCITEMENT

❧

Everyone said that Rose was immensely practical. She was attractive-looking, of course, and always very well groomed. A marvellous wife for Denis, and wonderful mother for Andrew and Celia. And a gifted teacher. People said that Rose was a shining example. Or if they were feeling less generous, they said that they had never known anyone to fall on her feet like Rose. Married at twenty-five to a successful young man, two children, a boy and a girl, a job to stop her going mad in the house all day, her own car, her own salary every month, no husband grousing about the cost of highlights. Why wouldn't she be a shining example?

It had been Rose who suggested the idea of Sunday brunches. They had all come from the tyranny of family lunches with great roasts and heavy midday meals. So they moved from house to house every Sunday, everyone bringing a bottle of wine and some kind of salad thing. They all dressed up. The children played together. If any couple wanted to bring along a friend, they could.

They congratulated themselves, it kept them young and exciting, they thought. Not dead and lumpen like their parents had been. And it had been Rose's idea in the first place.

Of course, another example of Rose's luck was that her mother lived way down in Cork. She wasn't constantly on the doorstep, criticising the way the grand-children were being brought up. Twice a year Rose's mother came up to Dublin; twice a year Rose took the

79

children to Cork. It was yet another example of how well she organised her life.

So they would have been very surprised if they had known how discontented Rose felt as half-term was approaching. She seemed to have been teaching forever. The same things every year, and in the same words. Only the faces in front of her were different, the younger sisters of the children she had already taught.

Then, on the home front, there would be the same arguments with Andrew, six, and Celia, five, about which place to visit when they went to the zoo: Andrew wanted snakes and lions, Celia wanted birds and bunnies. And there would be the same discussions with the au pair. A different name every year, but always the same discussion – the time she came home at night, the long-distance phone calls. And Denis? Well, he was pretty much the same too. There would be the usual jokes about life being a holiday for teachers, about the workers of the world like himself having to toil on. In a million years he would never suggest the two of them went away together. It wouldn't matter what kind of a place. Even a simple guest house. But it wouldn't cross his mind. And if Rose were to suggest it, Denis would say he really shouldn't go away. Business was different from teaching – you had to stay in touch. And then what about Sunday? Surely Rose wouldn't want to miss their Sunday with all the gang? Rose began to wish she had never invented these Sundays. They were a lash for her back.

Always being bright and cheerful, always thinking up a different little dish to make them ooh and aah, blow-drying her hair, putting on make-up, reading the Sunday papers so as not to be out of the conversation, bribing Andrew and Celia to behave. It was always the same.

Rose was quiet as the time came up towards the half-term holiday. Nancy, her friend in the staff room, noticed.

'Where's all the zip and the get-up-and-go?' she asked. Nancy was single and always saying in mock despair that she would never find a man.

'A bit of the magic seems to be going from it all,' Rose said more truthfully and seriously than she had intended to.

'Maybe he has the seven-year itch,' Nancy said. 'A lot of men get it just because they think it's expected of them. We poor spinsters keep reading about such things just so that we'll be ready for marriage, if it ever comes. It'll pass, though, it usually does.'

Rose looked at her in disbelief. Really, Nancy was as thick as the wall. It wasn't Denis who had a seven-year itch. It was Rose. She was thirty-two years of age and, for the foreseeable future, her life was going to be exactly the same as it was now. A lifetime of smiling and covering her emotions had made Rose very circumspect. She was, above all, practical. There was no point in having a silly row with her friend and colleague Nancy.

'Maybe you're right, let's hope that's all it is,' she said with her mind a million miles away from the mild expression on her face. Because Rose now realised the truth. She was restless and unsettled. She was looking for something, a little spark, a little dalliance. Possibly even a little affair. She felt a shiver of excitement and disbelief. She wasn't that kind of person. She had always thought wives who strayed were extraordinarily foolish. They deserved all they got, which was usually a very hard time.

Rose found that, in the days that followed, everything had become even more samey than it used to be. Denis said, 'Sorry, what was that?' to almost every single sentence she spoke to him, sometimes not waiting until she had finished. Every day Maria Pilar said, 'I mess the buzz, the buzz was late.' It was useless to tell the stupid girl that either she was late or the bus was early. Rose gave up trying. Andrew said every day that he hated cornflakes and Celia, to copy him, said the same thing. Rose's mother phoned from Cork regularly to say how good the life was down there, how dignified, gracious, and stylish compared to the brashness, vulgarity, and violence of Dublin. Rose listened and murmured, as she felt she had been doing for years. A meaningless murmur.

And then it was Sunday again. She prepared a rice salad with black olives and pine nuts for the gathering at Ted and Susie's. She knew before they even rang at the door what Susie would say. Susie, a colourless woman who would have looked very well if she had dyed her eyelashes and worn bright colours, in fact did say, exactly as Rose had known: 'How clever you are, Rose. You always think of marvellous things. I don't know how you do it.'

Rose had the urge to scream at her that occasionally she opened a bloody cookbook, but stifled it. It would not be practical to shout at a friend, a hostess. She smiled and said it was nothing. She went into the room – there they all were, each playing the role that could have been written for them.

Bill was talking about the match, Gerry about the cost of airfares, her Denis was nodding sagely about business expansion schemes, Nick was telling them about a horse he knew. And the women had roles, too. Annie talked about the litter in the streets, Nessa about the rudeness of the people in the supermarket . . . Susie, as she always did, apologising and hoping everything was all right.

Rose's mind was a million miles away when Ted, standing beside her and spooning some of the rice salad onto his plate, said into her ear: 'Very exotic.'

'Oh, it's quite simple, really,' she began mechanically.

'I didn't mean the rice, I meant you,' he said, looking straight at her.

Ted. Ted with the new car every year and the fairly vague job description, married to mousy Susie, who had the money.

'Me?' Rose said, looking at him with interest.

'Well, your perfume, it's very exotic indeed. I always fancy that if we were all in the dark I'd find you immediately.'

'Well, it's hard to prove seeing that it's broad daylight.' She laughed at him, her eyes dancing like his.

'But it won't be daylight on Tuesday,' he said. 'Not in the night-time, that is.'

'Now, *what* made you make a deduction like that?' She was still playful but didn't sound puzzled or outraged. It was as if she were giving him permission and encouragement to go on.

'I'm going to Cork on business . . . overnight . . . and I thought that perhaps we could test out this theory of the perfume, you know. See whether I knew what part of the room you were in. What do you think?'

It was the moment to ask did he mean to include anyone else. It didn't need to be asked. 'And have you thought out how this could be managed?' she asked. She spoke in her ordinary voice, as if they were talking about any of the same things they talked about in each other's houses for the last seven years.

'I gave it a load of thought,' said Ted, 'like it's your half-term and you could be staying with your mother, as it were.' He was leaning on a shelf and looking at her. Interested. That's what he looked. It was a lovely, almost forgotten feeling to have someone looking at her like that. Rose felt a tightening of her throat, and a small lurch in her stomach.

'You've thought of everything,' she said.

'I don't see any obstacles, do you?' Ted might have been talking about garden furniture.

'Only the messy one of upsetting people,' she said.

'Ah, but you and I wouldn't do anything like that. It's not as if we're falling in love or leaving anyone or breaking up any happy homes. It's just a bit of . . . well, how would I describe it . . .?'

'A bit of excitement?' Rose suggested.

'Precisely,' he said.

She thought it was very sophisticated of them indeed not to make any plans and think up any cover stories. If it was going to happen, which she thought deep down it would, then these would all come later. They rejoined the group.

Rose let her glance fall over the others, Nessa and Susie and Annie, Grace. Did none of them ever ache for a little excitement in their lives? And if they did, whom would they have found it with? Hardly her own Denis. He had barely time and energy for that kind of activity in his own house without thinking of arranging it with someone else's wife. The Sunday ended, as every Sunday did, with a visit to the pub. They had their traditions in this too. No big rounds, meaning that people stayed all night. Each family bought their own drink. It was very civilised, like everything they did. And very, very dull, Rose realised.

As they left the pub for the car, Andrew said he hated fizzy orange, and Celia, who had drunk very little other than fizzy orange in her life, said she hated it too.

Denis opened the door of the car for Rose. 'Don't we have marvellous friends?' he said unexpectedly. 'We're very, very lucky.'

She felt a hard knot of guilt form in her chest. But she swallowed it and agreed.

'But we work at it, of course,' Denis said. 'Having friends means a commitment of time and effort.'

Rose looked out the window. If working to achieve a Sunday exactly like this every single week was the result of time and commitment, then she was absolutely within her rights to want a day off, a night out.

The knot of guilt had quite disappeared.

Ted rang casually and told her there was a great place to leave her car in for an overhaul, only a few miles beyond Newlands Cross. Rose took down the details and thanked him. If the call had been bugged by every private detective and secret service in the world, it would have seemed totally innocent. Rose went into town and bought herself a black lace night-dress, a bottle of full-strength perfume with matching talcum powder, and body lotion. If she was going to have a bit of excitement with Susie's handsome husband, he was going to remember it for a long time.

'I want to go to the zoo tomorrow,' Celia said at supper.

'That sounds nice,' said Denis, not looking up, 'Mummy's on half-term.'

Rose looked at her son, hoping he would speak on cue. He did. 'I hate the zoo,' Andrew said.

'I hate the zoo too,' said Celia.

'That's settled, then. Maria Pilar will take you out for a lovely walk and an ice cream.'

'I get tired when I go on a lovely walk,' said Andrew.

'So you can go on the buzz. Maria Pilar loves the buzz.'

'Eet is not the buzz, eet's the bussss,' said Maria Pilar, hissing across the table.

'So it is, I keep forgetting.' Rose got up briskly from the supper table. 'Now, I've got lots to do, I'm off to see Grannie tomorrow.'

'I want to see Grannie,' Celia said.

'I hate Grannie,' Andrew said. Before Celia remembered that she hated Grannie also, Rose said no, this was a flying visit.

'Are you taking the plane?' Andrew asked with interest. His hatred of his grandmother might be tempered by a new experience like going in an airplane.

'Sorry, what was that, you're going to see the old bat?' Denis asked.

'Has Grannie got a bat?' Andrew was very interested now.

'I want to see the bat,' Celia said.

Rose glared at her husband. Now she would have to pretend that Grannie did have a bat. 'It's out a lot,' she said. 'Especially at night.'

'It's too much down and back in one day,' Denis said.

'I know, I'll stay the night.' Rose was surprised how easy it came when it had to, the lie, the cover-up. She always thought that women who weren't used to this would bluster or redden and give themselves away.

'You're doing your purgatory on earth, that's all I can say.' Denis left the supper table and went into what they called Denis's Den. He would be there until midnight. There were a lot of figures to be sorted out – coming up to sales conference time, he would tell her if she protested. Or Annual Report time or the AGM or the Visiting Firemen. There was always something.

Rose slept a guilt-free sleep. No woman was meant to sign on for such a dull life. That had been part of no bargain. Somewhere in the air there was a little clause allowing for a few excitements along the way.

Ted was waiting exactly where he had said at ten o'clock. He was relaxed and easy. They transferred Rose's little overnight bag into his trunk.

'This is great fun,' he said.

'Isn't it just?' said Rose.

On the journey, they flirted with each other mildly. Rose said he drove the car in such a masterful way. Ted said she curled up like a kitten in a very seductive way. They played Chris de Burgh tapes. Ted had to do a few calls, but he had booked a table for lunch somewhere he thought Rose would like. Perhaps she'd like to settle into the hotel first and meet him at the restaurant. They didn't mention Denis or Susie. They told each other none of the cute little things said by Andrew and Celia or by Ted and Susie's children. This was an Excitement, time out and away from all that.

Rose examined the bedroom with approval ... She hung up her good dress, hid all the perfumed unguents in her case. She didn't want it to look as if everything had come out of a bottle. She looked at her own face in the mirror. She was exactly the same as she had been last Sunday morning, only two days ago before Ted had come up with the offer of the Excitement. The same, but a little more carefully groomed. She had waxed her legs. Always a dead giveaway about affairs, people said, but Denis wouldn't have noticed. She strolled happily along to the restaurant, where she was greeted by a cry that froze her blood. 'Rose, Rose, over here.' It was her mother.

Sitting with Nora Ryan, the most horrible person in the South of Ireland or maybe in the whole of Ireland. A woman with beady eyes and a tongue that shot in and out like a snake's tongue. Delivering harsh, critical words every time. They were sitting at a table for three, and they pulled out the third chair for her. Rose felt a pounding in her head. It was as if they had expected her.

'How did you know I was . . . um . . . coming to see you . . .?' she stammered.

'Well, I rang. I rang and that not very bright girl said you were in zee Cork.'

'Europeans,' said Nora Ryan, casting her eyes up to heaven.

'We're all Europeans,' snapped Rose before she could stop herself.

'How observant of you, Rose dear,' said Nora Ryan with three flashes of her thin, serpentine tongue.

'And what did you say?' Rose spoke to her mother.

'I said that's great, and that Nora and I were having lunch here, but that stupid girl couldn't understand a word I said.'

'Spaniards!' said Nora, her eyes nearly reaching the brim of her hideous hat.

'So what did you do then?' Rose felt a sense of blind panic that she had never known before.

Now the unthinkable had happened. Her mother must have told her husband there had never been any question of a visit. Was there a hope in hell Rose could pretend it had been meant as a surprise?

'I had a very odd conversation with my grandson, who seemed to think the house was infested with bats and that you were coming down to deal with them.' Rose put her head in her hands. 'So then obviously I rang Denis at the office to find out what was happening.'

'And what did he say?'

'Questions, questions, really, Rose, you're like one of these interrogators on television,' said Nora Ryan.

Rose flashed her a look of pure loathing. 'Mother, what did Denis say?'

'He said he was well, he said he was busy coming up to the sales conference . . .'

'Before I have to take you by the throat and beat it out of you,

Mother, what did he say about my coming to Cork? What did he say?'

'Really, Rose,' Nora Ryan began.

'Shut up, Mrs Ryan,' said Rose.

They stared at her. Rose tried to recover the lost ground. She spoke very slowly, as if talking to someone of a very low IQ. 'Can-I-ask-you-Mother-to-tell-me-what-did-Denis say?'

Rose's mother was fingering her throat, the one that Rose had threatened to shake her by. She seemed almost afraid to speak. 'I don't see *why* you're talking like this, Rose, I really don't. I told Denis that if you called before you went out to the house this is where we'd be having lunch. To save you . . . to *save* you the journey out to the house . . . that's what I was doing and inviting you to lunch in a nice smart place like this . . .' Rose's mother had taken out a handkerchief and dabbed the corner of her eye. 'I most certainly didn't expect dogs' abuse and interrogation about it.' She was hurt and she didn't mind them knowing it.

Mrs Ryan was now in the totally unaccustomed role of being a consoler. 'Now now, now now now,' she said, patting the shaking shoulder awkwardly and flashing glances of hate at Rose.

'Did he know I was coming to stay with you?' Rose's voice was dangerously calm; the words came out with long spaces between them.

'Of course he knew,' her mother sniffled.

'How did he know?'

'I told him.'

'How did *you* know, Mother?'

Rose's mother and Nora Ryan looked at each other in alarm. Perhaps Rose was going mad . . . seriously mad.

'Because Maria Pilar had told me, my grandchildren had told me . . .'

The breath seemed to come out of Rose more easily now. 'Yes. Well, that's fine, that's all cleared up,' she said.

And at that moment Ted came into the room, carrying a single red rose wrapped in cellophane. The blood drained from her head yet again.

He saw her and came over. 'What a surprise. What a huge surprise,' he shouted like a very bad actor in an amateur play.

The two older women looked at each other; again their alarm increased.

'Good God ... it's Ted,' cried Rose. 'Of *all* the people in the world!' She looked around the room as if she expected to see a few other equally unexpected people, like Napoleon.

'I'll tell you the most extraordinary thing,' Ted shouted, unaware that the entire dining room was now looking at them and could not avoid listening to them.

'This is my mother,' screamed Rose. 'My mother that I was coming down to Cork to visit.'

'How do you do?' Rose's mother began, but she might as well have been talking to the wall.

'The *most* extraordinary thing,' Ted repeated. 'I was back at the hotel before ... um ... before coming alone here, and who did I meet but Susie's brother and his wife. Susie is my wife,' he said to the sixty or so people who were now part of his listenership. 'They are in Cork and staying in the same hotel.' He paused to let the words sink in with all the diners. 'The very same hotel.' He didn't get the reaction he wanted, whatever it might have been, so he said it in a different form. 'The *selfsame* hotel, I think you might say,' he said triumphantly.

Rose began to babble. 'That's lovely for you, Ted, you can all be together. I'd love to stay in a hotel myself sometime, but I'm staying with my *mother*.'

Mrs Ryan looked at her with narrowed eyes. 'I'm sure your mother wouldn't mind at all if you were to stay in a hotel,' she said pleasantly.

'No, no, no, I can't. And anyway, Mother has a lot of bats in the house,' she floundered wildly to Ted, 'so that's where I'll be staying.'

Ted might not even have heard her.

'So the odd thing was that when they thought they saw me, they asked at Reception was that me and Reception, of course, goddamn interfering nosy parkers that they are, said that Mr and Mrs Ted O'Connor were there.'

Rose said, 'What did you do?'

'I told them that suddenly at the last moment Susie couldn't come and then Reception said did I want to move to a single room because it would be cheaper, and I said yes, but that I'd rush up and pack my things and so I did and they're in the back of the car, if you know what I mean.'

Rose looked at him. His face was scarlet; he looked like a madman talking to other very mad people.

'If you get my drift,' he roared.

Rose felt a sudden maturity sweep over her. She knew now that she had enough excitement to last her a long time. On the grounds that she was helping Ted to park his car, she left with him, retrieved her suitcase. They were both too shocked to speak.

She returned to the restaurant, where the diners looked up with interest, hoping for Round Two.

Ted had given the red rose to Mrs Ryan. 'I bought it for you,' he had said without explanation. Nora Ryan saw nothing odd in this. In her youth it had happened a lot, she said.

Rose spoke courteously to her mother, planned the night in the house that she had forgotten was bat free and worked out what train to get back to Dublin and how to retrieve her car from beyond Newlands Cross. To begin what she hoped would be a fairly even-tempered and unexciting period of her life.

HOLIDAY WEATHER

❧ ❦

Robert said that after dinner they would curl up with the map of the South of France and plan the journey. Frankie was looking forward to it. This was always a great part of the holiday, when he would sit on the sofa with his arm around her, the fire crackling in the grate, glass of wine at hand, and together they would point out magical names to each other. It had been like this last year, when his conference had been in Spain and they had hunted for little Spanish idylls for their rambles afterward. And the year before, when it had been in Italy, and their fingers had traced the names by the lakes.

Of course, Frankie knew that the evening would not organise itself. She would have to escape down to the shops at lunchtime to buy something she knew he would like, and this was getting more difficult since he had begun to worry about his waistline. Gone were the evenings of fillet steak, mushrooms, and garlic bread. Perhaps she might get some monkfish – very expensive, but it did seem special – and a small selection of vegetables. She could even top and tail them at work; there would be so little time when she got back to her flat. She would have to rush around it tidying, of course, getting rid of all the work things that littered the place. Well, Robert hadn't been around for over a week, so she had been doing her Open University course every evening.

Frankie thought happily about the evening ahead. She would wear her green dress, the one that he had once said matched her eyes. A long while ago. But of course he still loved her, and people didn't have to go on about eye colour forever. It would have been unnatural, and possibly a bit repetitive.

The only good thing about working for a man like Dale was that it took up such a small amount of time and so little brain. All that the awful Dale wanted was someone to sit in his front office and look pleasant, ask them to wait a moment while they could thumb through some of the fairly horrible cuttings about Dale's success in the world of public relations, and then ask them to go straight on in. Frankie was far too intelligent for this job, and that knowledge alone gave her great satisfaction. But by being with Dale and his outfit, she had an excuse to see Robert almost every day. And as far as Frankie was concerned, she would work in a coal mine or as a steeplejack if it meant being close to Robert.

Robert needed excuses to meet Frankie. Robert was married to his boss's daughter – marriage of convenience that he had entered into at a time before he knew what true love, real love, was like.

Robert and his wife had two children, who were eight and seven. They were at the age when they could not be upset by things that had nothing to do with them; it wasn't their fault that Robert had found true love too late. Robert was the rising star in the organisation; he must work harder than ever now that he intended to leave home and set up two establishments. He must make himself totally indispensable to his boss, his father-in-law, so that there would be no question of letting him go once the divorce was brought up. Frankie didn't ask when that was going to be but thought that it would be unreasonable to expect it before the children went to boarding school. Three years, perhaps?

She would wait. Naturally.

But in the meanwhile there were wonderful things like the great summer honeymoon. They always called it that: Our Italian, Our Spanish, and now Our Riviera Honeymoon.

Frankie made her shopping list and took out the map of France. Whenever Dale passed by she looked as if she were making notes or looking up a reference. Dale would not stop to question her.

Frankie looked fine for the job, with her long dark curly hair and her bright green eyes. And even more important, she was the friend of Robert the whiz kid in Benson's. Dale would have employed any kind of person in that front desk if it kept him well in with Benson's. He regarded it as a bonus that Frankie was both bright and beautiful.

The only thing that bored Frankie was that she had to put in the actual hours in her horseshoe-shaped desk. If only she could have slipped away for the afternoon. She could have gone to the hairdresser and even had a manicure as a luxury; her hands would be greatly in view tonight as they traced the route south through the Côte d'Azur down from Cannes past St Raphael to Saint-Tropez. Or should they go the other way from Cannes, over past Antibes to Nice and Monte Carlo? It was heady stuff even saying the names. Perhaps Frankie would even buy a little guide-book at lunchtime so that she would appear knowledgeable tonight.

It was all a rush, as she knew it would be. But the dinner had gone well. Robert was relaxed; he had loosened his tie and kicked off his shoes. Frankie had been able to wash her hair, and she had bought green earrings at lunchtime.

'They're lovely,' he said. 'The colour of your eyes.'

She felt that the fuss and the bustle had all been worthwhile. She even felt glad that she had spent that money on a dishwasher. It had been very extravagant, but Robert adored it. His wife was playing Earth Mother, according to his reports, refusing modern gadgets, but for them it was all right – there was the help and the au pair. In Frankie's flat, however, he loved to see technology. Cuts out all the fuss, he had said. They arranged the china and glass and cutlery carefully and listened to it humming away in the kitchen as Frankie got out the map.

'Darling,' he said. 'Wrong map, I'm afraid.'

'It says Provence on top, but it's all Cannes and Nice and everywhere down on the coast,' Frankie said, surprised. Normally Robert knew where everywhere was; that was why she had studied it so much in advance all afternoon.

'We're not going, my love,' he said.

Her heart lurched with the kind of jump that almost reached her throat.

'I don't understand.'

'Neither do I, but it's true. Listen, don't think I'm pleased . . . Stop looking at me like that, hey?'

'Why can't I come? We've always been able to swing it before. I tell

Dale I'm taking my vacation, you tell Mr Benson you need someone from Dale's to run over the implications of the conference with you. Why can't I come this time? Why?' Frankie knew she was sounding like a seven-year-old, but her disappointment was so huge she couldn't hide it.

She had bought her clothes, her terribly expensive shoes, the knockout beach gear. The operation was foolproof – why was he pulling out now? Was it possible that he had found someone new? If he had cheated on his wife once, then obviously he could do it again. But don't go down that road. And don't *cry*. Frankie forced her face to stop puckering.

Robert sounded weary and resigned.

'It's not you, sweetheart, it's me. It's a nonstarter.'

'But you always go to the conference. You *are* Benson's.' She was aghast. And yet there was a seed of hope. Suppose he had been discovered, and maybe even demoted. Did that not mean that the day they could be together might be nearer than they had thought?

'This year being Benson's means going somewhere else and shoring up someone else's cock-up,' he said. 'A whole project is going down the Swanee, and apparently I'm the only one who can sweet-talk us back where we were. What a bloody crowd of fools he employs. I'd have got rid of three quarters of them. I will – I tell you I will one day.'

This was an old refrain. Frankie didn't want to hear it all over again – Robert's plans for the day when he ran the place himself. This was an old set of lines they had said to each other; she wanted to know what was new.

What was new was Ireland. A new plant, a lot of bother, nobody had been there to straighten it out, to tell the people on the ground what was happening, what was expected of them, what they could expect.

'They're bound to be suspicious of us, think we're in it for what we can get out of it.'

Frankie said nothing; for once she didn't murmur her usual words of encouragement. In fact, she knew that Benson's was in it for what they could get out of it, that's what business was about.

'So you see what's happened. In the very week of the conference in Cannes, I have to be over in the middle of the boglands talking to the mutinous forces over there and promising them wealth beyond their wildest dreams.'

'Can't you go now? Before the conference?'

'Don't you think I asked that? But old man Benson is adamant. It has to be that bloody time, something to do with some European thing or other that's being held there. They're much more interested in Europe over there, for some reason that escapes me. God, I could kill them for not setting it up right at the start, allowing all these discontents to grow up. If we don't go in and fly the flag or show our face or whatever the expression is ... then the whole thing could collapse like a house of cards.' He looked so handsome when he was annoyed. She could understand why so many people were impressed with him.

'Will we have any honeymoon together this year, you and I?' she asked in a small voice, looking down at the ground lest he see all the pain in her green eyes.

'You could come to Ireland,' he said doubtfully. 'I can't be tied up with them all the time. We'd have some time together.'

'To do what?' She had no maps of Ireland, she had no magical names like Juan les Pins, like Saint-Tropez.

'I don't know, darling, I don't know, give me space. I only heard about this today, this afternoon. We'll do something. It could be a rest for you, getting away from it all, and then I'd escape when I could.'

A more courageous woman would have told him to forget it. A tougher woman would have told him in no uncertain terms what he could do with this half-hearted offer.

Frankie was neither brave nor tough. Which was why she found herself in the small hotel on the west coast of Ireland. A hotel called the Greener Grass standing on a low cliff over a long, empty beach. When you looked across that sea the next stop was America, they told you. Frankie could believe it – it looked endless. And on the first days it looked grey and lonely. The seagulls calling to each other and other seabirds coming in to perch on rocks. She saw a school of porpoises go by one day, and she became familiar with the habits of a cormorant and a kittiwake and a tern and a gannet.

'I could do another Open University course in the habits of

seabirds,' she said ruefully to the proprietor as he set her lobster before her at a table, which, for the third time had been set for one.

'There are worse ways to spend your time, you know.' His voice was soft, but it was distant. He was Shane, he said, a returned Irish American. He had called his place the Greener Grass because of the grass always seeming greener when it was far away. He had saved up for seven years to buy his own small hotel.

He was different from the other local people, who wanted to know all about Frankie and Robert, and what was their business in the place, did they have any children, where had they been for holidays before. Did they love the Irish way of life? Shane asked none of these questions. He had the air of someone contented with his own way of life. She saw him choosing his own vegetables from the fields where he had tilled the land to grow them. She watched him sometimes writing the menus in slow, careful, calligraphic script.

Robert set out in the early mornings and was rarely back to the Greener Grass before dark.

'Not much of a honeymoon, is it, darling?' he said more than once. Frankie saw his face, white and tired.

'The honeymoon bit is at night, remember?' she said, laughing.

But at night the weary Robert slept suddenly and soundly as soon as he got into bed. Some nights Frankie sat at the bay window, where there was a lovely three-part window seat, and looked out at the night sky over the water. Sometimes she saw Shane and his dog Tracey walking.

So he couldn't sleep either, Frankie thought, even though he had saved seven years to build his dream and had it now in his hands.

She saw Shane bend to pick shells by the moonlight. He looked peaceful, she thought, and somehow at ease. Even though he didn't really belong here, not like locals – he had been away too long, and he had a slight New York tinge to his voice.

Next morning at breakfast, she asked him about the shells.

'You sat at the window and looked out over the moonlit sea,' Shane said. Robert seemed annoyed somehow. 'You didn't tell me you couldn't sleep.' She felt she had been disloyal.

Later Shane came and gave her some cowrie shells. 'You could do another Open University course on these and still know nothing about them,' he said with a smile.

Robert liked to think that it was somehow a rest for her, that sharing some fraction of his life was reward enough for the broken promise, the conference that never was ... the ribbon of the French coast not visited.

'I bet this is doing you no end of good,' he said each morning as they ate brown soda bread and fish just in from the sea.

For the first few days she had smiled bravely, and taken a book disconsolately to walk along the hilly cliff or down to the rock pool, and try to stop thinking that her life was as grey as the skies all around her.

But then one morning the sun came out, and everything was different. Even Robert seemed loath to go.

'It's very beautiful, this place, you know,' he said as he stood beside his hired car about to head off for the day with the mutinous men he was finding it harder to placate than he had thought possible.

Frankie looked down at the beach she had walked so often in the dull days. Today it sparkled, as if there were little particles of precious metal hidden behind the rocks instead of soft sand. She thought she could see the cowrie shells that Shane had been collecting. The sea was twenty different colours of green and blue, with little white flecks.

'I might have a swim,' she said.

'Yes, well, be sensible. It's the Atlantic Ocean, don't forget.'

'Next stop, America.' Frankie laughed.

Robert looked at her, puzzled.

'I hope I won't be too late,' he said, but doubtfully. 'This lot seem to need conversation and explanation way into the night, as well as all day.'

He drove away along the road, and as Frankie looked after him up at the purple mountains and over beyond the small green fields with their stone walls to a dark, velvety forest, she began to feel as if a film had just turned from black-and-white into Technicolor.

She ran lightly upstairs to fetch the red bathing suit that had cost her so much in the days she thought it would be seen on the Côte d'Azur. As she came down, carrying the pricy beach bag and her red and white fluffy towel, Shane's dog Tracey came up and looked at her hopefully.

'I'd be very grateful if you would,' Shane said. 'He needs a walk, and with today's weather I'll have the world and its wife for lunch, so I can't take him.'

'I don't know a lot about dogs,' Frankie began.

'Well, Tracey is half sheepdog and half setter, we think. A lovely nature, and he'll bark if you start to drown or if anyone comes and bothers you.'

'Who'd come and bother me?' Frankie laughed, looking at the empty beach.

'I haven't seen you in that swimsuit, but it might attract a bit of local attention.' He laughed too; the good weather made him seem less remote.

'Would he run away or get into a fight or anything?' It had never been part of her life, walking with a big, bounding dog.

'Not a chance. And as a reward, I'll come and find you and take you a little late lunch and take Tracey off your hands.'

'Oh no.'

'Oh yes. It's the minimum fee for dog minding. There's a nice flat rock in the next bay. It makes a good table.'

She had never spent a day on a beach like it. Tracey ran for sticks with never-ending energy. She really thought she could see his foolish face smile at her as she threw them again and again.

Tracey barked at the waves, but swam in and paddled near her as if to look after her when she swam. She collected shells and laid them out on the flat table rock.

Soon, far sooner than she had expected, Shane arrived with a picnic basket.

'You abandoned your lunchers. How can you expect to earn a living!' she said sternly.

'You're not wearing a watch. It's after three o'clock – they've all been and gone. You must be starved.'

Imagine. She had been playing with this idiotic dog for hours on a shell-covered beach, no cloud had come across the sky, and no thought of Robert and their situation had come across her mind.

Companionably they shared the picnic, local prawns, homemade bread, cheese made by some nuns in a convent across the valley, red shiny apples from the small orchard behind the Greener Grass.

'It's like heaven.' She sighed as they drained the bottle of wine to the dregs.

'Thank God we don't get weather like this all the time,' said Shane.

'Why do you say that? Because you'd have to work too hard?' Frankie had been about to say the very opposite; she had been on the point of wishing that every day could be so sunny.

'Because we would be parched and dry, it would not be a green island, and we'd be so used to it we wouldn't be calling out our thanksgiving to the very heavens as we are today,' he said.

'Yes, I know, and that's a point, but what about your business? If it was much sunnier, there would be many more people here. This beach would be full.'

'And could you and I and Tracey have had such a picnic if the beach were full?' he asked.

'We had meant to go to the South of France,' she said suddenly.

'Yes, so your husband told me, when he called to book.' Shane had his distant face on again. 'He seemed very disappointed and told me in several different ways that this was not his first choice.'

Frankie was going to explain that Robert was not her husband, but she let it go. Instead she apologised for him.

'He's normally very charming and would never have given you that impression. He has work problems to see to here. We had thought we could have made a holiday out of a conference in Cannes.'

'But why did he take you here, and leave you all alone?'

'I'm glad he did,' Frankie said positively. 'Now, do you think it's an old wives' tale about not swimming after lunch, or should we risk it?'

'Just as long as we don't go out too far, any of us,' he said, and they raced to the edge where the foam was breaking and drawing out the sand with it as it gathered for another wave.

'Have you ever been to the South of France?' he asked.

'No.' Her voice sounded small.

'Neither have I, so let's pretend this is a hundred thousand times better,' Shane cried, and threw himself into the waves.

'You caught the sun,' Robert said when he got back earlier than usual. He had phoned to ask if dinner could be kept for him, and had been surprised and not altogether pleased to hear Shane say that his wife had had a late lunch.

'Did you tell him we were married?' Robert asked as they sat at a window table and watched the sun set, leaving red and golden paths and crisscross lines across the bay.

'No, darling, I didn't, but in this country they are likely to assume it if we check in to the same room and you have booked us as "Mr and Mrs."'

Robert looked at her sharply but decided not to make it something to argue about.

'Is it better? You know, are you sorting it out up at the plant?' Frankie asked.

'Yes. I think they believe our heart is in the right place,' Robert said.

'And it is?' Frankie's face was innocent, bland.

'What are you trying to say?'

'Well, I mean that a lot of them came back from jobs overseas because they really believed that it was going to be a proper plant, not something that would pack up and fold its tent when things got a bit hairy.'

'Oh, come on, Frankie, what do you think Benson's is, part of Mother Teresa? Of course we have to be practical. If things get hairy, as you put it, we can't stay on here forever, bleeding hearts keeping returned emigrants in beer money.'

'That's all right, as long as they know it.'

'That's all right whether they know it or not,' Robert flashed.

'You remind me more and more of Dale,' Frankie said. 'The same cynical way of looking at everything.'

'You are beginning to remind me more and more of my wife. The same way of picking a row and nagging over everything.'

Frankie had read somewhere that you know when something is over, you know that this is the moment, but you won't accept it. You try to say it was because one person had too many tiring days negotiating, and the other person had too much unexpected sun.

Robert probably knew, too, because when he was called to the phone he went with eagerness and came back to say that some of the men needed him for a further conference.

They parted pleasantly, almost with relief.

Frankie went walking on the beach in the last rays of the sun. She felt Tracey rushing up to her before she knew Shane was on the beach as well.

'I had a friend in New York, a great friend, she was going to come here and run the Greener Grass with me. You know, a joint enterprise. Then she said she'd join me later. Then she said she needed thinking time. Then she said she'd write.'

They walked in silence; there seemed no need to say anything. Frankie thought about all those years, and those two honeymoons where she had felt she needed to entertain Robert all the time, talk to him, be bright, show no hurt, no loneliness.

'He's not my husband,' she said after a long time.

'Oh, I know,' said Shane.

'How?'

'Labels on suitcases, his instructions about not ever calling him to the phone if the office rang but always taking a name and a time he should call at. If you were married, he would have asked you to take the messages.'

After another long time Frankie asked, 'Is it all right? You know, running the place as a single venture, not a joint one as you had thought?'

'Yes, it's all right. It mightn't always be single. You never know your luck.'

The sea was calm now. They skimmed flat stones and made them hop.

'He'll be going back soon, I imagine,' Shane said. 'The lads tell me it's all settled.'

'Yes, well, they wouldn't want to rely on that too much.'

'They're smarter than they sound,' Shane said with a laugh. 'All us fellows who worked over the water learned a bit about business.'

'We had planned to stay on a bit when it was settled, but I don't think so now.'

'No, he'll want to be off. He might even catch the tail end of the Cannes thing.'

'A place where the sun shines all the time and there's no sense of surprise?' Frankie smiled at him.

'The very spot,' Shane said.

'And what's the weather forecast like here?' she wondered.

'Optimistic but unknown,' said Shane.

'I'll stay,' said Frankie. 'I'll certainly stay on awhile until I know how it turns out.'

They walked back to the Greener Grass in a companionable silence, because they knew there was no need to say anything, or plan anything, or spell anything out, or indeed say anything at all.

VICTOR AND ST VALENTINE

Victor was brought up in a home where they made a huge fuss of St Valentine's Day. His sisters spent weeks wondering if anyone would send them a card; his mother cooked a very special meal for her husband that evening and served it by candlelight. His father bought something romantic like a heart-shaped charm for her bracelet, a little pendant, a glass vase for a single rose.

No wonder he thought it was a special day.

In the real world, he discovered, things were different. At school, for example, fellows didn't send girls cards unless they were jokey ones, often with hurtful remarks on them.

Nobody made any mention of St Valentine's Day ceremonies in their homes, so Victor stayed quiet about his own household. No point in *inviting* mockery. It was quite enough that he was already the subject of a lot of ridicule because of gentleness, good manners, and a lack of interest in beating up his classmates in the playground.

Then, later, when he went to train as an electrician, they did make a bit of a fuss and celebration at Technical College for a St Valentine's Day dance but mainly the chat was about which girls would be likely and which would not.

Victor never wanted to talk about people being likely; he thought it was too personal a thing to be speculated over in the bars. So the others more or less gave up on him in this area.

His first boss was not a man with much time for St Valentine. A load of commercial claptrap, he said.

Around that time Victor sent a valentine card to a nice girl called Harriet who had gone to the pictures with him several times. Harriet telephoned him at once.

'Listen, Victor, I'm sorry, there has been some awful misunderstanding. I wasn't being serious or committed or wanting to marry you or anything.' Victor was alarmed.

'No, heavens no, neither was I,' he said, panicking at the very thought.

'Then why did you send me this card with all the roses and violets and sign your name?' she asked.

'Because it's St Valentine's Day,' he said.

'But you signed your own name. Naturally I thought you wanted commitment.' Harriet was outraged at the misunderstanding.

'I'm very sorry,' Victor said humbly. 'I'll never do it again.'

But of course he did do it again, when he met Muriel, and did fancy her greatly.

Muriel said he should have had the courage to come straight out and say it if he loved her rather than relying on a card and somebody else's verses and sentiments. She couldn't see a future for them. She was sorry.

Victor decided he was not good with women. He wasn't without dates, a social life, and indeed the odd little romance, but none of them led to anything.

He was, however, a very good electrician. He had a pleasant manner and a lot of skill, and soon he didn't have to have a boss at all – he had his own business. A mobile phone, a business card, and a lot of word-of-mouth recommendations, and Victor had more customers than he could deal with.

Sometimes they asked him about his private life. 'Never met the right woman for me,' he would say. 'And here I am a hopeless romantic. But the girls don't take me up on it at all.'

He was thirty-eight, tousled hair, a warm smile.

People didn't really believe him. They thought that he might have a very colourful private life but just wasn't telling.

People liked Victor and told him things. And he liked listening to them, because in his own way he was a little lonely.

He would have liked a companion to go out with on weekends. Someone to go on vacation with.

Victor had saved money for a holiday, but it wasn't quite the same going alone. So he enjoyed talking to his clients. Like the couple who were going to adopt a baby, and were so excited when it arrived that they invited Victor to the welcome party.

'Are you a relation?' somebody asked him.

'No, but I rewired the nursery,' he said, and again nobody believed him.

And there was the man who dared not tell his wife that he had been made redundant; Victor had many a cup of tea with him on a day when he was merely meant to be putting in new sockets.

And mainly there was old Mrs Todd.

She was very fond of Victor. She told him all about her family, her son Frank who was so protective of her that he had set up this door-entry system where she could see on a little screen who was there before letting them in. Mrs Todd hadn't wanted it all, but her son Frank had insisted; the world was full of bad, dangerous people, he said.

Frank didn't come much to visit his elderly mother, which Victor thought was a pity, but Frank laid down the law a lot from a distance. Mrs Todd said that Frank had given instructions she was not to invite any new people that she met to coffee. This was hard, but she was sure Frank must be right.

Victor thought Frank sounded like a bully but was too tactful to say so. Frank's daughter, Amy, had gone off to Australia as soon as she was old enough to leave.

Mrs Todd said that Amy wrote regularly; she lived in Sydney, she worked in a flower shop there, and she was very happy. She wished that her gran would come out and see her.

'Why don't you go?' Victor encouraged her.

He was in Mrs Todd's apartment yet again over an allegedly loose connection. He knew and she knew that there was nothing wrong electrically speaking, but that she was very, very lonely. He would arrange to call on her at a time that suited him to when he was in the area, and she paid him a token fee to keep the thing on some kind of professional basis.

'Oh, I couldn't go for lots of reasons,' she said. 'I'm not really able to travel on my own, and anyway it would be a bit awkward. You know Amy doesn't get on with her father, so even if I were strong enough to travel there alone, it would cause a family upset, and we don't want that.'

Victor sent her a Valentine's Day card, but after his earlier frights in such matters, he didn't sign it.

It was on her mantelpiece when he next called to check the mythical mystery of the immersion heater.

'Thank you so much for the valentine, Victor,' she said.

'What makes you think I sent it?'

'Apart from my late husband, you are the only really romantic person I know,' she said.

The months went on. Her son Frank appeared less and less and gave yet more and more directions.

The letters from Amy were more and more yearning. 'Please come out here, Gran, I want to show you my Australia. You are not old, because you have a young heart. I'm saving to send you the fare.'

Around Christmas, when it was cold and wet in London, Victor made a decision.

'Mrs Todd, why don't you and I go there early next year together? I'll deliver you to your granddaughter, then I'll go off and see a bit of the Outback. I might hire a car and drive to Broken Hill. I'd enjoy that. Then I'd come back and take you back home.'

Her eyes filled with tears.

'You are such a kind man, even to *think* of it. Believe me, that's enough to make me very happy.'

'No, Mrs Todd, you must believe me, this is for me as much as you. I've always wanted to go to Australia. I've had the money saved and waiting, I just couldn't find the excuse.'

'But Frank?'

'Frank will have to accept it.'

'No, Victor. That's easy for you to say, you're a young man. I'm an old woman. Frank is all I have. He wouldn't dream of letting me go out all that way with ... with ...'

'With the electrician,' Victor finished for her.

'Well, yes, in a word.'

'Then I'll have to be a friend of Amy's, that's what we'll say.'

They smiled at each other. The adventure had begun.

*

It didn't take long to become a friend of Amy's, much less time than anyone would have thought possible, and all because of e mail.

Every morning he got a message from her. It was night-time in Sydney, and Victor sent one back, before she went to sleep. Bit by bit they put together the subterfuge, they invented a way in which they had met and become friends. They rejoiced at each other's inventiveness.

She said nothing hostile about her father, but made it clear that they were people who, while minimal courtesies would be maintained, would never have a meeting of the minds.

Frank was told, as he had to be, about the upcoming trip. He had a dozen objections, all them rehearsed, and answered by the three conspirators. But he was up against unequal odds.

And then they were on the plane. Mrs Todd and Victor. They laughed when the steward thought they were mother and son.

'No, we are partners in an enterprise,' Mrs Todd explained.

They drank Australian wine to get into the mindset of the New World. They slept and woke.

And slept. They got out for coffee in the Middle East and for Tiger Beer in Singapore. Neither of them thought it the slightest bit odd to travel together to a continent on the other side of the earth.

They watched movies, they read magazines, and they talked about their past. Mrs Todd told Victor about Mr Todd, who had been a wonderful, kind man who brought flowers home every Friday night and had told her she looked like a flower herself.

Victor told Mrs Todd about the various ladies in his life and how he had been a little too romantic for them. Perhaps his luck would change. No he didn't, he didn't really think it would in Australia. They were very modern there, forward looking, they would think he was a silly old Pom.

Mrs Todd said there were romantic people everywhere in the world, and he must not make generalisations.

Then it was dawn, and they saw the Opera House and the Bridge and all the things they had dreamed of, and they landed.

Crowds waited in the sunshine.

Victor wheeled Mrs Todd out in her chair.

A girl with a wonderful smile was waving at them. She had on pink shorts and sunglasses. Long black curly hair, dimples in her cheeks.

He knew immediately it was Amy.

'We're here,' he shouted.

'It's about time,' she called back.

Mrs Todd and her granddaughter embraced each other. They hugged and cried, and looked at each other with amazement. Around them the same scene was being acted over and over again. Australians welcoming the relatives from Britain.

Victor the electrician stood a little apart. Then they remembered him.

'This is Amy,' said Mrs Todd with huge pride.

'Welcome to Australia,' said Amy. She had a warm smile.

Suddenly he wished he hadn't made such firm arrangements about leaving Sydney to drive to the Outback. Sure it would be exciting, and that was one of the reasons he had come all this way. But Sydney looked as if it had a lot to offer as well. And he had only given himself three days to see it.

Amy showed them the city in style. She drove them over the famous Harbour Bridge and got them on a ferry to sail under it. She rightly regarded nothing as being too tiring or adventurous for her elderly grandmother.

She brought them to small restaurants where she knew the Greeks and Italians who ran the place. She liked that, it was all so international, she said.

'London's getting like that, too,' Victor said.

'Oh, London.' Amy shrugged.

'They're not all like your father,' Victor said before he could stop himself.

But she only smiled.

'Just as well,' she said.

They had pretended to be old friends as a ruse to fool her father. Already they felt they *were* old friends.

He longed to give her a valentine's card before he drove off across the bush, down the ribbon road that would take him past scrubland and ostriches. Amy had told him to be very careful of the kangaroos at sunset, they could jump out in front of the car. But Victor reminded himself of the many times his greetings had been misunderstood.

Perhaps there was a chocolate koala bear with hearts on it. But then, there was no point in sending a jokey thing; he couldn't understand a whole industry based on that.

He wanted to say thank you for lighting up our lives. Why should it have to be dressed up as a joke?

He came to say good-bye, and Amy handed him a single red rose. There was a card on it: 'I'll miss you, Victor Valentine.'

When he could speak, he said, 'I was thinking I needn't stay away all that long.'

Amy said, 'And I was thinking maybe we might come with you.'

CROSS LINES

❦

Martin tapped his fingers in irritation on the phone. He was unsure of himself in his new and unfamiliar world of the arts where he was heading. There were already too many stresses involved in this whole business without having to part from Angie in such an unsatisfactory way. Beautiful Angie, why hadn't she got up and pulled on a track suit? Why hadn't she said she'd drive him to the airport, they'd have coffee and a croissant together; it would have been so good. It would have calmed him down, to have sat with Angie, looking into her big dark eyes watching the passersby envy him with this girl with the great mane of streaked hair and the big slow smile. He would have felt a million times more confident about the venture ahead. Instead of edgy and jumpy.

In the next booth he saw one of those kind of career women he disliked on sight. Short practical hairdo, mannish suit, enormous briefcase, immaculate make-up, gold watch pinned to a severe lapel. She was making a heavy statement about being equal and coping in a man's world. She was having a heated discussion with somebody on her telephone. Probably entirely unnecessary, shouting at someone for the sake of it. He would give Angie another three minutes and dial again. She had never been known to talk this long to anyone. And at nine-thirty a.m.

Kay wished the man in the next phone box would stop staring at her; she had enough to cope with with one of Henry's tantrums. She had explained to Henry over and over how important it was for her to be at the trade fair a day in advance; that way she could supervise the setting up of the stand, make sure they had the right position, the one they had booked near the entrance, see that the lighting was adequate, decorate the booth, get to know the neighbours on her right and left so that she could rely on them and call on their support once the doors opened and the day's business began.

Henry had said he understood, but that was yesterday; today he was in one of his moods.

Kay would be gone for five days; she *hated* leaving him like this, it was so uncalled for, he had nothing to fear from her trip to another town. She would be far too weary and exhausted to consider going out partying at the end of a long day; all she would want was a warm little telephone conversation every night, reassuring her that he loved her, that he was managing fine but not so fine as he managed when she was around and how he greatly looked forward to Friday. She had called him at the office to try to dispel his mood before it got a grip of him.

It had been a mistake. Henry's black disapproval came across the phone line loud and clear.

She had made her choice. She had decided for an extra day on this junket, and against going with him to his staff party. It was quite simple; she could take the consequences.

'What consequences?' Kay shouted, turning her back on the arty pseudo-bohemian in the next phone box.

He was handsome, she supposed, in that vain peacock way that a lot of actors or showbiz people adopt, mannered and self-aware, stroking his cravat. The kind of man she most disliked. But it was increasingly hard to talk to Henry, the kind of man she most admired. He was showing none of those qualities that had marked him out when she met him first.

He pointed out that if Kay, his constant companion, was not going to bother to turn up at an important corporate gathering, then he would regard himself as a single and unattached person with no commitments.

'That's blackmail of the worst kind.' Kay was appalled at herself for reacting like a teenager.

'The solution is in your hands,' Henry said coldly. 'Come back from the airport now and we will forget the whole incident.' She hung up immediately, not trusting herself to speak to him.

Martin told himself that Angie's deep sleep was always important to her. She was a model; her face had to be unlined, untired at all times. She must have taken the telephone off the hook. His brow cleared when he remembered this, only to darken again when he remembered that as he kissed her good-bye he had said he would call from the airport and she had said that would be super. Why, then, had she cut off his way of getting through to her?

Lost in their thoughts, neither Martin nor Kay realised that they had in fact been seated beside each other on the plane . . . They looked at each other without pleasure. Martin took out the long, complicated report on arts funding that he was going to have to explain to various theatrical and artistic organisations, all of which were going to brand him as a cultural philistine. Kay read a report on last year's trade fair, and noted all the opportunities missed, contacts lost, and areas of dissatisfaction. Their elbows touched lightly.

But they were unaware of each other. From time to time they lifted their eyes from the small print in their folders and Martin thought of all the times *he* had driven Angie to her modelling assignments and Kay remembered all the corporate functions in *her* firm that Henry had refused to attend without even the flimsiest excuse.

Above the clouds it was a lovely day, bright and clear. Kay felt her shoulders relaxing, and some of the tension leaving her. They were far above the complications and bustle of everything they had left behind: buildings, traffic, rush, corporate functions. She breathed deeply. She wished they could stay up here forever.

At that moment Martin sighed too, and with the first sign of a pleasant expression that he had shown, he said that it was a pity they couldn't stay up here forever.

'I was just thinking that. At exactly this moment,' Kay said, startled.

They talked easily, he of the problems ahead trying to convince earnest idealistic artists that he was not the voice of authority spelling out doom for their projects. He had been trying to dress like arty people, as he knew that otherwise he would be dismissed as a Man in a Suit, which was apparently marginally better than being a child molester.

She told him of the poor results the company had achieved at last year's promotion, and how this was her first year in charge. There were many in the organisation who hoped she would fail, and she feared they would be proved right. She knew that people thought she had got the post through some kind of feminine charm; she was dressing as severely as she could to show them that she wasn't flighty.

They were sympathetic and understanding. Martin told her what Henry never had, that perhaps she was overcompensating, making herself look too stern and forbidding, killing off the good vibes she might otherwise have given.

Kay told Martin something that Angie had never thought of – that possibly the cravat might be over the top. There was the possibility that the disaffected artistic folk might think he was playing a role.

They fell into companionable silence in the clear, empty blue sky. And Martin thought that Angie probably didn't care about him at all, she cared only about her face, the magazine covers she appeared on, and what bookings her agent might have for her next week. He would call her when they landed, a cheerful call, no accusations about taking the phone off the hook, she would wish him well, and he would take the whole thing much more lightly from now on.

Kay wondered if Henry would seriously take up with someone else, as he had threatened. And would she mind very much if he did. She decided she would ring Henry's secretary and say how sorry she was to miss this evening's function, she would wish it well and say that sadly work had taken precedence. She would ask that Henry not be disturbed but insist that her message of goodwill was passed to those in the right places. This was a professional businesslike approach, not a very loving one. But Kay didn't feel very loving anymore.

Then, just at the same moment, she and Martin left their private thoughts and turned to each other to talk again. Angie wasn't mentioned, nor was Henry, but strategy was, and optimism was exchanged.

Kay encouraged Martin to be straight with the groups, to tell them the worst news about funding first and try to work back into a position they felt was marginally more cheerful. Martin advised Kay to let her colleagues in on her hopes for their joint success, let them think they were creating it too. By the time they left the plane they were friends in everything but name. Martin considered asking her name but thought it might sound patronising. Kay wondered about giving him her card but feared it would look stereotype female executive.

There was a bank of telephones facing them in Arrivals. They both headed towards them.

Kay paused with her hand on the receiver. In the next box she saw Martin's fingers, not drumming this time but hesitating. Through the transparent walls they smiled at each other.

He looks less affected, she thought, the velvet jacket's fine really.

She is quite elegant in spite of all that power dressing, he realised. Neither of them made the phone call.

But it was too soon for any sudden decisions. There was work to be done. If they met each other somewhere again, well and good.

They wished each other luck and got into separate taxis.

As they settled back into their separate seats they each gave their taxi driver the name of the same hotel.

A HOLIDAY WITH YOUR FATHER

Rose looked at the woman with the two cardboard cups of coffee. She had one of those good-natured faces that you always associate with good works. Rose had seen smiles like that selling jam at fêtes or bending over beds in hospitals or holding out collection boxes hopefully.

And indeed the woman and the coffee headed for an old man wrapped up well in a thick overcoat even though the weather was warm, and the crowded coffee bar in Victoria Station was even warmer.

'I think we should drink it fairly quickly, Dad,' said the woman in a half-laughing way. 'I read somewhere that if you leave it for any length at all, the cardboard melts into the coffee and that's why it tastes so terrible.'

He drank it up obediently and he said it wasn't at all bad. He had a nice smile. Suddenly and for no reason he reminded Rose of her own father. The good-natured woman gave the old man a paper and his magnifying glass and told him not to worry about the time, she'd keep an eye on the clock and have them on the platform miles ahead of the departure time. Secure and happy, he read the paper and the good-natured woman read her own. Rose thought they looked very nice and contented and smiled, cheered to see a good scene in a café instead of all those depressing gloom scenes you can see like middle-aged couples staring into space and having nothing to say to each other.

She looked at the labels on their suitcases. They were heading for Amsterdam. The name of the hotel had been neatly typed. The suitcases had little wheels under them. Rose felt this woman was one of the world's good and wise organisers. Nothing was left to chance; it would be a very well planned little holiday.

The woman had a plain wedding ring on. She might be a widow. Her husband might have left her for someone outrageous and bad-natured. Her husband and four children might all be at home and this woman was just taking her father to Amsterdam because he had seemed in poor spirits. Rose made up a lot of explanations and finally decided that the woman's husband had been killed in an appalling accident that she had borne very bravely and she now worked for a local charity, and that she and her father went on a holiday to a different European capital every year.

Had the snack bar been more comfortable, she might have talked to them. They were not the kind of people to brush away a pleasant conversational opening. But it would have meant moving all her luggage nearer to them, which seemed a lot of fuss. Leave them alone. Let them read their papers, let the woman glance at the clock occasionally, and eventually let them leave. Quietly, without rushing, without fuss. Everything neatly stowed in the two bags on wheels. Slowly, sedately ... they moved towards a train for the south coast. Rose was sorry to see them go. Four German students took their place. Young, strong, and blond, spreading coins German and English out on the table and working out how much they could buy between them. They didn't seem so real.

There was something *reassuring*, she thought, about being able to go on a holiday with your father. It was like saying thank you, it was like stating that it had all been worthwhile ... all that business of his getting married years ago and begetting you and saving for your future and having hopes for you. It seemed a nice way of rounding things off to be able to take your father to see foreign cities ... because things had changed so much from his day. Nowadays young people could manage these things as a matter of course; in your father's day it was still an adventure and a risk to go abroad.

She wondered what her father would say if she set up a trip for him. She wondered only briefly, because really she knew. He'd say:

'No, Rose my dear, you're very thoughtful, but you can't teach an old dog new tricks.'

And she would say that it wasn't a question of that. He wasn't an old dog. He was only sixty, and they weren't new tricks since he used to go to Paris every year when he was a young man, and he and Mummy had spent their honeymoon there.

Then he would say that he had such a lot of work to catch up on, so it would be impossible to get away, and if she pointed out that he didn't really have to catch up on anything, that he couldn't have to catch up on anything, because he stayed so late at the bank each evening catching up anyway ... Well, then he would say that he had seen Europe at its best ... when it was glorious, and perhaps he shouldn't go back now.

But he'd love to go back, he would love it. Rose knew that. He still had all the scrapbooks and pictures of Paris just before the war. She had grown up with those brown books, and sepia pictures, and memos and advertisements, and maps carefully plotted out ... lines of dots and arrows to show which way they had walked to Montmartre and which way they had walked back. He couldn't speak French well, her father, but he knew a few phrases, and he liked the whole style of things French, and used to say they were a very civilised race.

The good-natured woman and her father were probably pulling out of the station by now. Perhaps they were pointing out things to each other as the train gathered speed. A wave of jealousy came over Rose. Why was this woman – an ordinary woman perhaps ten years older than Rose, maybe not even that – why was she able to talk to her father and tell him things and go places with him and type out labels and order meals and take pictures? Why could she do all that and Rose's father wouldn't move from his deck chair in the sun lounge when his three-week holiday period came up? And in his one week in the winter, he caught up on his reading.

Why had a nice good warm man like her father got nothing to do, and nowhere to go after all he had done for Rose and for everyone? Tears of rage on his behalf pricked Rose's eyes.

Rose remembered the first time she had been to Paris, and how Daddy had been so interested, and fascinated, and dragging out the names of hotels in case she was stuck, and giving her hints on how to get to them. She had been so impatient at twenty, so intolerant, so embarrassed that he thought that things were all like they had been in his day. She had barely listened, she was anxious for his trip down the scrapbooks and up the maps to be over. She had been furious to have had to carry all his carefully transcribed notes. She had never looked at them while there. But that was twenty, and perhaps everyone knows how restless everyone else is at twenty and hopefully forgives them a bit. Now at thirty she had been to Paris several times, and because she was much less restless she had found time to visit some of her father's old haunts ... dull, merging into their own back-grounds ... those that still existed ... she was generous enough these days to have photographed them, and he spent happy hours examining the new prints and comparing them with the old with clucks of amazement and shakings of the head that the old bakery had gone, or the tree-lined street was now an underpass with six lanes of traffic.

And when Mum was alive she too had looked at the cuttings and exclaimed a bit and shown interest that was not a real interest. It was only the interest that came from wanting to make Daddy happy.

And after Mum died people had often brought up the subject to Daddy of his going away. Not too soon after the funeral, of course, but months later when one of his old friends from other branches of the bank might call ...

'You might think of taking a trip abroad again sometime,' they would say. 'Remember all those places you saw in France, no harm to have a look at them again. Nice little trip.' And Daddy would always smile a bit wistfully. He was so goddamn gentle and nonpushing, thought Rose, with another prickle of tears. He didn't push at the bank, which was why he wasn't a manager. He hadn't pushed at the neighbours when they built all around and almost over his nice garden ... his pride and joy, which was why he was overlooked by dozens of bed-sitters now. He hadn't pushed Rose when Rose said she was going to marry Gus. If only Daddy had been more pushing then ... it might have worked. Suppose Daddy had been strong and firm and said that Gus was what they called a bounder in his time and possibly a playboy in present times ... just suppose Daddy had said that. Might she have listened at all or would it have strengthened her resolve to marry the Bad Egg? Maybe those words from Daddy's lips might have brought her up short for a moment ... enough to think.

Enough to spare her the two years of sadness in marriage and the two more years organising the divorce.

But Daddy had said nothing. He had said that whatever she thought must be right. He had wished her well, and given them a wedding present for which he must have had to cash in an insurance policy. Gus had been barely appreciative. Gus had been bored with Daddy. Daddy had been unfailingly polite and gentle with Gus. With Gus long gone, Rose had gone back to live in Daddy's house. It was peaceful despite the blocks of bed-sitters. It was undemanding. Daddy kept his little study where he caught up on things, and he always washed saucepans after himself if he had made his own supper. They didn't often eat together ... Rose had irregular hours as a traveller and Daddy was so used to reading at his supper ... and he ate so early in the evening. If she stayed out at night there were no explanations and no questions. If she told him some of her adventures there was always his pleased interest.

Rose was going to Paris this morning. She had been asked to collect some samples of catalogues. It was a job that might take a week if she were to do it properly or a day if she took a taxi and the first fifty catalogues that caught her eye. She had told Daddy about it this morning. He was interested, and he took out his books to see again what direction the new airport was in ... and what areas Rose's bus would pass as she came in to the city centre. He spent a happy half an hour on this, and Rose had looked with both affection and interest. It was ridiculous that he didn't go again. Why didn't he?

Suddenly she thought she knew. She realised it was all because he had nobody to go with. He was in fact a timid man. He was a man who said sorry when other people stepped on him, which is what the nicer half of the world does ... but it's also sometimes an indication that people might be wary and uneasy about setting up a lonely journey, a strange pilgrimage of return. Rose thought of the good-natured woman and the man who must be ten or fifteen years older than Daddy; tonight they would be eating a meal in a Dutch restaurant. Tonight Daddy would be having his scrambled egg and deadheading a few roses, while his daughter, Rose, would be yawning at a French restaurant trying not to look as if she were returning the smiles of an ageing lecher. *Why* wasn't Daddy going with her? It was her own stupid fault. All those years, seven of them since Mummy had died, seven years, perhaps thirty trips abroad for her, not a mention of inviting Daddy. The woman with the good-natured countenance didn't live in ivory towers of selfishness like that.

Almost knocking over the table, she stumbled out and got a taxi home. He was actually in a cardigan in the garden scratching his head and sucking on his pipe and looking like a stage image of someone's gentle, amiable father. He was alarmed to see her. He had to be reassured. But why had she changed her mind? Why did it not matter whether she went today or tomorrow? He was worried. Rose didn't do sudden things. Rose did measured things, like he did. Was she positive she was telling him the truth and that she hadn't felt sick or faint or worried?

They were not a father and daughter who hugged and kissed. Pats were more the style of their touching. Rose would pat him on the shoulder and say: 'I'm off now, Daddy' or he would welcome her home clasping her hand and patting the other arm enthusiastically. His concern as he stood worried amid his garden things was almost too much to bear.

'Come in and we'll have a cup of tea, Daddy,' she said, wanting a few moments bent over kettle, sink, tea caddy to right her eyes.

He was a shuffle behind her, anxiety and care in every step. Not wishing to be too inquisitive, not wanting, but plans changed meant bad news. He hated it.

'You're not *doing* anything really, Daddy, on your holidays, are you?' she said eventually once she could fuss over tea things no longer. He was even more alarmed.

'Rose, my dear, do you have to go to hospital or anything? Rose, my dear, is something wrong? I'd much prefer if you told me.' Gentle eyes, his lower lip fastened in by his teeth in worry. Oh, what a strange father. Who else had never had a row with a father? Was there any other father in the world so willing to praise the good, rejoice in the cheerful, and to forget the bad and the painful?

'Nothing, Daddy, nothing. But I was thinking it's silly my going to Paris on my own. Staying in a hotel and reading a book and you staying here reading a book or the paper. I was thinking wouldn't it be nice if I left it until tomorrow and we *both* went. The same way . . . the way I go by train to Gatwick . . . or we could get the train to the coast and go by ferry.'

He looked at her, cup halfway to his mouth. He held it there. 'But why, Rose dear? Why do you suggest this?' His face had rarely seemed more troubled. It was as if she had asked him to leave the planet.

'Daddy, you often talk about Paris, you tell *me* about it, I tell *you* about it. Why don't we go together and tell each other about it when we come back.' She looked at him ... he was so bewildered she wanted to shout at him, she wanted to finish her sentences through a loudspeaker.

Why did he look so unwilling to join? He was being asked to play. Now, don't let him hang back slow to accept like a shy schoolboy who can't believe he has been picked for the team.

'Daddy, it would be nice. We could go out and have a meal and we could go up and walk to Montmartre by the same routes as you took in the good old days. We could do the things you did when you were a wild teenager ...'

He looked at her, frightened, trapped. He was so desperately kind, he saw the need in her. He didn't know how he was going to fight her off. She knew that if she were to get him to come, she must stress that she really wanted it for her, more than for him.

'Daddy, I'm often very lonely when I go to Paris. Often at night particularly I remember that you used to tell me how all of you ...'

She stopped. He looked like a hunted animal.

'Wouldn't you like to come?' she said in a much calmer voice.

'My dear Rose. *Sometime*. I'd love to go to Paris, my dear, there's nothing in the world I'd like to do more than to come to Paris ... but I can't go just like that. I can't drop everything and rush off to Paris, my dear. You know that.'

'Why not, Daddy?' she begged. She knew she was doing something dangerous, she was spelling out her own flightiness, her own action of whim of doubling back from the station ... she was defining herself as less than levelheaded.

She was challenging him, too. She was asking him to say why he couldn't come to a few days of shared foreign things. If he had no explanation, then he was telling her that he was just someone who said he wanted something but didn't reach for it. She could be changing the nature of his little dreams. How would he ever take out his pathetically detailed maps and scrapbooks to pore once more with her over routes and happenings if he had thrown away a chance to see them in three dimensions?

'You have nothing planned, Daddy. It's ideal. We can pack for you. I'll ask them next door to keep an eye on the house. We'll stop the milk and the newspaper, and, Daddy, that's it. Tomorrow evening in Paris, tomorrow afternoon we'll be taking that route in together, the one we talked about for me this morning ...'

'But, Rose ... all the things here ... my dear, I can't just drop everything ... you do see that.'

Twice now he had talked about all the things here that he had to drop. There was *nothing* to drop. What he would drop was pottering about scratching his head about leaf curl. Oh, Daddy, don't you see that's all you'll drop. But if you don't see and I tell you ... it means I'm telling you that your life is meaningless and futile and pottering. I will not tell *you*, who walked around the house cradling me when I was a crying baby, you who paid for elocution lessons so that I could speak well, you, Daddy, who paid for that wedding lunch that Gus thought was shabby, you, Daddy, who smiled and raised your champagne glass to me and said: 'Your mother would have loved this day. A daughter's wedding is a milestone.' I won't tell you that your life is nothing.

The good-natured woman and her father were probably at Folkestone or Dover or Newhaven when Rose said to her father that of course he was right, and it had just been a mad idea, but naturally they would plan it for later. Yes, they really must, and when she came back this time they would talk about it seriously ... and possibly next summer.

'Or even when I retire,' said Rose's father, the colour coming back into his cheeks. 'When I retire I'll have lots of time to think about these things and plan them.'

'That's a good idea, Daddy,' said Rose. 'I think that's a very good idea. We should think of it for when you retire.'

He began to smile. Reprieve. Rescue. Hope.

'We won't make any definite plans, but we'll always have it there, as something we must talk about doing. Yes, much more sensible,' she said.

'Do you really mean that, Rose? I certainly think it's a good idea,' he said, anxiously raking her face for approval.

'Oh, honestly, Daddy, I think it makes *much* more sense,' she said, wondering why so many loving things had to be lies.

THE FIRST STEP OF CHRISTMAS

❧ ❦ ☙

Jenny and David gave wonderful Christmas parties. Always on the Sunday before. They asked the whole family, his and hers, they produced Timmy for just enough time for everyone to think he was adorable and never for that one moment too long when people would tire of him. They made the party a huge buffet so that nobody was too trapped with anyone else. The house was festooned with decorations, usually real holly and real ivy gathered from the countryside where it was growing wild. There was nothing vulgar about their tree. Clever ribbons and angels and paper flowers, not expensive-looking packages. But everyone *knew* that somewhere, discreetly, were the gift-wrapped presents that must have poured in to a couple so loving and considerate as David and Jenny.

As the years passed, five Christmases to be precise, Jenny stood sometimes in her immaculate kitchen listening to the murmurs of appreciation. David's first wife had never done anything like this. Oh, no one had been invited across the door in Diana's day. Diana had been far too hoity-toity to bother with family.

That was Jenny's reward. That was the glory for the weeks, no, months, of preparation and planning and shopping and making it all seem so effortless. David had grumbled slightly when Jenny said they should have a second freezer, but then he wasn't there when she made the mountains of mince pies and the stacks of savouries. David didn't know how Jenny worked in that kitchen on the nights he had meetings or had to stay out of town. He would never know. She would be as different from the beautiful, selfish Diana as it was possible to be. And her child Timmy would be an angel, not a devil, as Diana's child had turned out. Not a dangerous, destructive girl like Alison.

Alison had been nine when Jenny met her first. Very beautiful, with untamed curly hair almost covering her face. She had made no pretense at politeness.

'How much did that cost?' she had asked Jenny about the new dress.

'Why do you want to know?' Jenny was spirited from the very start.

'I was asked to find out.' Alison shrugged as if it didn't matter very much.

'By your mother?' Jenny could have bitten out her tongue the moment she said it.

'Heavens no, Mother wouldn't be remotely interested.' The way she said it, Jenny knew she was speaking the truth; the lovely, lazy Diana would not indeed have cared.

'Who then?'

'The girls at school. One of my friends said you must be after Father for his money.'

It hadn't really got any better.

When she was ten, Alison had come to stay for a weekend and had tried on all Jenny's clothes and used all her make-up. It wouldn't have mattered so much if every single lipstick had not been twisted out of shape, and every garment marked with make-up.

'She was only dressing up; all little girls like doing that,' David said, his eyes pleading.

Jenny decided not to have their first row on the losing battlefield of the stepchild. She managed a smile and planned a lengthy session at the dry cleaners. When Alison was eleven, Timmy was born. 'Did you forget to take your pills?' she asked Jenny when her father was out of the room.

'We wanted him, Alison, just as your mother and father wanted you.'

'Oh yeah?' Alison had said, and Jenny's heart was leaden. It was true that she had wanted the child much more than David had. How could this monstrous step-daughter have found her vulnerability?

When Alison was twelve, she was expelled from school. The counsellor said that it was all to do with feeling her father had rejected her. She must be allowed to spend more time as part of his life. David was out at work all day, and so was Jenny; they treasured the time they took together with Timmy. Time when the quiet Swiss au pair went to her room and left them to be a family. Now they had Alison on long visits sulking, yawning, contributing nothing, criticising everything.

When she was thirteen, she didn't want to come near them, which was bliss, except that it made David feel rejected. Jenny worked in a publishing house. She told colleagues ruefully that she could see why there were so many books on step-parenting, she had read them all and she could have written half a dozen more. But none of them had ever had to face anything like Alison.

When Alison was fourteen, her mother died. Suddenly and unexpectedly, after a routine operation. David had gone to Alison's boarding school. 'I expect you'll have to have me now,' she had said to her father. David said it had nearly broken his heart to think that his only daughter considered herself a package to be passed from one place to another. Jenny forced herself to think about Diana, dead before she was forty. Dead without ever having lived properly. She put the thought of Alison to the furthest part of her brain. She knew it would spoil everything. There were going to be no happy endings in this story, no one would walk hand in hand into the sunset swearing undying friendship. She would do it, she would do it for David and, oddly, for the dead Diana, whom she had feared and mistrusted in life. If Jenny were to die young, she would like some other woman to look after Timmy, to try to make a life for him.

She slaved as never before over their Christmas party. Sometimes she got up ludicrously early in the morning. David would come down to breakfast and find a smell of cooking in the kitchen, even though all the mess had been cleared away.

'You are a funny little thing,' he said to her, giving her a squeeze.

Jenny was not funny, nor was she a little thing. She would look at herself thoughtfully. She was tall, not as willowy as Diana, but tall. She was deadly serious about her family and her work. Why was it the action of a funny little thing to get the party right? He used to tell her how much he loved it, that he had always been one for ceremony and for celebration, but Diana had never wanted to bother. But Jenny would pick no fights, manufacture no rows. Not at the festive season.

Alison arrived a day earlier than she was expected. Jenny came back from work and found her halfway through eating a tray of intensely complicated hors d'oeuvres. Each one had taken three minutes to assemble, they would take one second to eat, and Jenny had made sixty of them, shaping the curls of filo pastry with endless patience, and leaving them to cool before freezing them. It represented three hours of her life. She looked at Alison with pure hatred.

Alison looked up from behind the curtain of hair.

'These aren't bad. I didn't know you were a home-maker as well as a career woman.'

Jenny's face was white with rage.

Even Alison noticed.

'These weren't for supper or anything, were they?' she said with mock contrition.

Jenny took the deep breath that all the books on step-parenting seemed to recommend. It was so deep, it reached her toes.

'Welcome home, Alison,' she said. 'No, these weren't for supper . . . not at all. They were just something for the party.'

'Party?'

'Yes, on Sunday. We have the family. It's a tradition.'

'I think things have to be more than just three or four years to be a tradition,' Alison said.

'This is our sixth Christmas together, so I suppose that feels like a tradition.' Jenny's shoes were hurting; she wanted to take one of them off and beat her stepdaughter senseless with its high sharp heel. But she felt it would have been both unseasonal and counterproductive. There was no way Jenny was going to enjoy this Christmas; what she must try to do was to contain it. She tried to remember that phrase people used – what was it, damage limitation? She had never known quite what it meant. Had it something to do with saving what you could? She often found at work that if you thought of something quite irrelevant and allowed your mind to click through the motions, then it prevented you from flying off the handle.

She saw Alison looking at her with interest.

'Yeah, I suppose six years is a tradition,' Alison agreed, as if she were struggling to be fair.

A glow of sympathy towards the girl began to shine through the mists of dislike and resentment. But Jenny was too experienced to mistake it for the swell of violins surging at the end of the movie.

'About the party,' Jenny said. 'Are there any of your mother's relations that we might ask?'

Alison looked at her in disbelief. 'Ask here?'

'Yes, it's your home now, they are your relations, too. We want to make it a family Christmas, we would be very happy to have them.'

'What for?'

'For the same reason that anyone asks anyone under their roof at Christmas, for goodwill, for friendship.' Jenny hoped her voice wasn't getting tinny, she could feel the edge developing.

She willed her eyes away from the tray of canapés that she had worked on so meticulously. The crumby, mangled remains. Even those that had not been eaten were somehow used-looking.

'That's not why people have Christmas parties, it's for showing off,' Alison said.

Jenny took off her shoes and sat down at the table. She reached out for the perfectly formed pastries with their exquisite fillings. They tasted very good.

'Is that what you think?' she asked Alison.

'I don't think it. I know it.'

Jenny did a calculation in her head: fourteen now, Alison might be with them until she was eighteen. With any luck, this school might not expel her, so it was only the school holidays and half terms they had to consider; four Easters, four summers, four Christmases. Timmy would grow up in the shadow of this moody girl. He would be a grown-up seven-year-old by the time Alison left their home. She would lose these lovely years because of the hostile girl who sat at her kitchen table. She wondered what she would do if it were a problem at work. But that was not a useful road to go down. If Alison had been a mulish, mutinous junior, she would have been sacked or transferred with such speed that it would have electrified everyone. She contemplated telling this discontented girl that life, far from being a bowl of cherries, could often be a bed of nettles and that everyone had to make her own happiness. But Jenny was familiar enough with teenagers to know that they wouldn't share that kind of pain as an older woman might. Someone of Alison's age would shrug and ask, Why bother?

She wondered, was there a chance that Alison might be into the bond of the friendship? Should she offer to exchange some of her blood with her and swear eternal solidarity?

But sadly, she remembered the school reports. They had all stressed how much Alison resented any of the school conventions, even those enjoyed by her peers. No, the sisterly loyalty act didn't look as if it would work.

She ate her fifth canapé, thinking that this now represented a quarter of an hour's work early that morning. Soon David would be home, tired and anxious to have a restful evening. She hadn't even seen her beloved Timmy since she came in the door.

All over the country, families were getting ready for Christmas, some of them certainly had tensions ... but not one family, in the entire land, had Alison. The time bomb. Theirs for four long years, ready to explode at any time.

She saw Alison's luggage strewn all around the place. She would *have* to get an agreement with David that Alison keep everything in her room. Her room! Nothing had been done to it.

In fact, it was filled with boxes; worse still, packets of fir cones and a huge canvas bag of holly sprigs. If ever the child was going to feel unwanted and unwelcome, it would be because of Jenny. She had intended to leave many, many clothes hangers and a small understated vase with greenery and a couple of flowers as welcome ... nothing that could be considered showy or vulgar or uncool, or whatever were the favourite hatreds of Alison this festive season.

She had been silent as she had been glumly rejecting every possible method of relating to her stepdaughter. Alison must have noticed the lack of chatter. Her eyes followed Jenny's and landed on the luggage.

'I suppose you want me to take all that out of your way,' Alison said in the voice of a martyr who had met a particularly unpleasant torturer.

'About your room ...' Jenny began.

'I'll keep the door closed,' Alison groaned.

'No, not that ...'

'*And* I'll keep the music down,' she said, rolling her eyes.

'Alison, it's the room I wanted to explain ...'

The girl stopped in her bag-laden trudge to the bedroom.

'Oh God, Jenny, what is it *now*? What else can't I do?'

Jenny felt so tired, she could cry.

'I just wanted to explain what there was in there . . .' she said in a weak voice. Alison had opened the door.

She stood looking around her at all the preparations, the trimmings and the garnish for a festive Christmas. She lifted a fir cone and smelled it. Her eyes went all around the room as if she couldn't take it all in. 'We didn't think you were coming until tomorrow,' Jenny apologised.

'You were going to decorate my room.' Alison's voice was husky.

'Well, yes. Well, with whatever you thought . . . you know.' Jenny sounded confused.

'With all this?' Alison looked around her.

Jenny bit her lip. There was enough greenery in that room to decorate a three-storey house, which was what they lived in. The child couldn't possibly have thought it was all for her bedroom.

Then with one look at Alison's radiant face she realised that that was exactly what the tall, rangy Pre-Raphaelite with the wild hair and the sullen mouth was. She was a child. A motherless child who was going to have a room decorated for the first time.

In publishing they always told you that the best decisions, the best books, came by accident, not by dint of long and clever planning.

'Yes, well, with most of it. I thought we'd make it look really nice, nice and welcoming for you. But now that you're here . . . maybe . . .'

'Maybe I could help?' Alison said with eyes shining.

It wouldn't last forever, Jenny knew that. The road ahead was not lit with soft, flattering lighting like a movie. They wouldn't fall into each other's arms. But it would last a little bit. Maybe through the party and through Christmas Day.

She heard the sound of her son running to find her.

'Where were you, you didn't come and see me?' he called.

She picked him up in her arms. 'I was just welcoming your sister home,' she said, almost afraid to look at Alison's face.

Alison leaned out and tickled Timmy with a frond of ivy.

'Happy Christmas, little brother,' she said.

THE TEN SNAPS OF CHRISTMAS

❧ ❧

Maura loved Christmas. Jimmy endured it. When Maura was a child they used to make a great fuss of it, an Advent calendar opening a window each day, the Christmas cards examined with all the verses read aloud, then each one threaded on coloured string. They would start talking about the tree as early as October, and every present was lovingly wrapped and labelled and laid under the tree for at least a week's squeezing and prodding in the hope and even fear of finding out what it was.

When they got married, first Jimmy thought this was very endearing, he used to kiss her on the nose and say she was sweet. As the years went by, Maura noticed that it had become less sweet, like so many things. So she kept her sense of Christmas excitement a secret that she hugged to herself and the babies as they arrived one by one. This year there was only Rebecca for Santa Claus. Rebecca was four, John and James and Orla were far too old. But you couldn't be too old for trees and lights and candles and a holly wreath for the door. Maura worked alone and happily, and didn't burden Jimmy too much when he came home from work in the evenings. She only consulted him about what Big Present each child was to get.

James was ten: he would get a bicycle. John was eight: he would get the electronic game that had been much hinted at. Rebecca would get a dozen small, noisy things – she wasn't old enough for the Big Present yet, but Orla . . . what would they give the tall fourteen-year-old? Maura said she thought Orla might like a voucher for clothes in that trendy shop where her school friends spent hours just looking in the window. Jimmy thought that Orla might like a typewriter and a quickie typing course. They could come to no meeting of minds over this at all. Maura said to give anyone a typing course for Christmas was like giving a woman a diet book or a membership to Weight Watchers. Jimmy said to give a child a voucher for a shop like that was like a license to buy perverted transsexual clothing with a parental imprimatur. It had better be neither of these. They decided they would give her a Polaroid camera. The kind that would take pictures instantly there and then. Festive for the season and urgent for today's generation. So that was what they bought, and wrapped it in many other boxes and corrugated paper so that Orla prodded it a hundred times and still had no idea what it contained until the day itself.

Maura bought some heated hair rollers for her mother, who came to stay for Christmas. Her mother was glamorous and fashion-conscious in Maura's mind; in Jimmy's mind she was mutton dressed as lamb, a woman who refused to grow old gracefully. He never objected to her Christmas visit, but he didn't look forward to it either. His own parents were kept at a safe distance, presents posted and a call on Christmas morning to wish them the compliments of the season. Jimmy's family was a lot less demonstrative.

Maura bought a nice Tara brooch for Marie France, the French au pair girl. Marie France had this disconcerting habit of wondering were things real silver or pure silk or was the wine vintage or if they had the best seats at the theatre. At least with something so obviously ethnic and Irish she could hardly complain. Marie France was all right, Maura thought, a bit pouty and shruggy and eyes-up-to-heavenish, but maybe that was the way twenty-year-old French girls banished to learn English behaved. She did exactly what she was asked to do with Rebecca and about preparing the vegetables and vacuuming the downstairs, but not one single thing more. Maura had often wished she had set out a slightly more demanding timetable; after all, Marie France had a room of her own, three marvellous meals a day, and endless time to study as well as go to her course. But nothing, not even the minor sense of grudge toward Marie France, could spoil Maura's Christmas, she felt the familiar excitement just as soon as they started to play 'Mary's Boy Child' and 'The Little

Drummer Boy' over the tannoy at the supermarkets . . . and that was fairly early on. By the time the streetlights were up, Maura was in a high state of happy fuss. Her mother arrived with a yet more outrageous outfit than usual, her friend Brigid who had left her husband again wondered was it possible if she could join the family, and Maura said, 'Of course,' for Christmas was a time to be happy and Brigid had been a friend since school. Jimmy groaned a bit about Brigid. He said she was a nutcase and that the husband was well rid of her, but he agreed that since she could only eat a plate of turkey and ham, and since the day was ruined already by the presence of Maura's mother, then honestly he saw no objection to Brigid coming, and sure sure if she brought her sleeping bag why not, why not let her sleep in the sitting room on the sofa. Since the crazy mother-in-law was taking up the guest room why not?

They sang carols on Christmas Eve. Maura closed her eyes in happiness and in gratitude for all she had. Her face was so happy that even Orla who thought it was yucky, and Grannie who thought it was over the top, and Brigid who thought it was barking mad, and Jimmy who thought it was pathetic, all joined in. James and John thought it was funny and sang one louder than the other. Rebecca thought it was a game and banged on her tambourine in what she thought was in time with the music.

Next morning after Mass they sat around in a circle while the presents were given out. Maura's mother loved the hair rollers and took a plug off one of the lamps immediately in order to try them out. Marie France shrugged and pouted over the Tara brooch, Jimmy was genuinely pleased with the anorak because he hated waste and he wanted one anyway, and Maura showed pleasure at the carpet sweeper, which Jimmy said might be useful on those occasions when she didn't think it worthwhile taking out the vacuum cleaner.

Orla was very quiet all morning as the gifts were being opened. Maura felt a pang of regret. Perhaps she should have fought harder for the voucher for the child. It was becoming harder and harder to talk to her, but all mothers said the same about teenage daughters, and really it was only now when she was well and truly married and had a grown family that she could relate properly to her own mother. Maybe that was one relationship that would never work. It would be the same when chubby, adorable Rebecca had a decade behind her.

Orla wasn't rude or surly like other people's daughters. She never defied them or insisted on her own way. It was just that recently she seemed ... well ... a little bored with them. It was as if she didn't rate them very highly as a family. Nothing you could put your finger on and certainly nothing you could say to Jimmy, who thought the sun and the moon and all of the stars shone out of his eldest daughter. It would look like some kind of criticism, which it was not. Maura had decided on this occasion, as on many others, to say nothing. But she chewed her lip as Orla's long blond hair fell over the well-disguised present and finally revealed the camera that would take instant pictures.

'It's beautiful, thank you, Dad, thank you, Mum,' she said in roughly the same voice that Maura had thanked Jimmy for the carpet sweeper.

'You can get people to take pictures of you so that you can chart your progress from ugly duckling to swan,' said Maura's mother.

'Thank you, Grannie,' said Orla.

'Or you could take pictures of fellows and congratulate yourself later that you had nothing to do with them,' said Brigid, who was sitting smoking, angrily rejoicing in her abandoned husband.

'Yes, terrific idea, Auntie Brigid,' said Orla.

Maura could see the annoyance, but yet she too felt disappointed. If only Orla knew what she had been saved from ... a typing course to be taken during the school holidays at Easter and a reconstituted typewriter and a book to practice from. If Orla knew that, maybe she might smile more warmly at her mother. Again Maura wished she had stood out for the gift token. If Orla had that in her hand, maybe the day would have been filled with dreams of gear to be bought, to be discussed, tried on, rejected, taken out on approval. Still it was done now and a camera with a whole film of ten snaps in it was a marvellous gift for a fourteen-year-old girl.

'Will you take one now?' James was anxious to see if it worked.

'We'll all make faces.' John wanted it to be a joke.

'Let me take the rollers out first.' Maura's mother was already testing the strength of her new gift and her head was a forest of spikes.

Orla shrugged. She was developing this very unattractive shrug, Maura thought. Far too like Marie France, far too distant.

'It's Orla's camera, she can take what she likes,' Maura said, and hoped for a grateful smile, a thank-you look. But Orla just shrugged again.

'It doesn't matter,' she said. 'I'll take one if you want to.'

They spent a long time posing. Marie France had to put on her lipstick, Maura noticed she didn't bother to put on the Tara brooch. Soon they were assembled, five adults on the sofa, the three children in front. Orla pressed the button and like magic it came out a piece of grey-green that turned in front of their eyes into a picture of them all.

They looked oddly dead, Maura thought, and some of them had devil-like red eyes.

They all said it was very clever and wondered what would savages who had never heard of such things think if they saw one.

They had little jobs for the Christmas lunch; the boys had to clear up all the paper and put it in a neat pile. Jimmy was to get the wine, Grannie was to arrange the crackers on the table and lay out the chocolates on little glass dishes to be served later. Brigid was given a new linen dishcloth to polish the glasses. Marie France had been given nothing, so nothing was what she would do. Maura went out to do the gravy and the bread sauce. Everything seemed to boil at once, the dishes were heavy, and Rebecca was under her feet at every turn. Sharply she ordered the child out of the kitchen and then felt guilty. It was Christmas Day, why was she being so irritable? She just felt that something was wrong. It was one of those silly fears, like recovering from a bad dream. In her annoyance and confusion she let the turkey slip right off the dish onto the floor. She grabbed it furiously by the legs and rammed it back in the baking tin. Thank God her mother and Jimmy hadn't been in the kitchen, they were both great at wrinkling up the nose and sighing at what were called Maura's slapdash methods. What they don't know won't harm them, she thought as she rescued the sausages from under the cooker and picked off the surface dust. She hadn't noticed Orla in the kitchen, but the child was there still examining the camera thoughtfully.

'Do you really like it, my love?' Maura asked kindly.

'Oh yes, didn't I say I did?' The girl was withdrawn. She would only resist any attempt at a heart-to-heart.

'Did the flash go off just then? I was wondering was I seeing lights in front of my eyes, or was it lightning?'

Orla shrugged. I'm going to get that bloody shrug out of her without having to go as far as physical violence, Maura thought purposefully. The boys came into the kitchen.

'Will you take another? Take one of us outside,' they begged.

'No.'

'Oh go on, Orla, that's what it's for.'

'No, they said I could take what I liked.'

'What *are* you going to take?' They were impatient with her now.

'Just casual pictures here and there; you know, to get a picture of Christmas the way it really is, not all people just posing and smiling.'

They lost interest in her. Maura beamed, however. Perhaps Orla did like the gift and she might even take up an interest in photography. That would be marvellous. Maura didn't praise the idea too much in case Orla might shrug it off.

Orla went to the shed where the wine was kept. Daddy didn't hear her come in and had no idea she was there until the flash and the soft whir announced her.

'*Orla,*' he roared, moving towards her very fast. It was almost like a speeded-up film to see how quickly he had drawn away from Marie France and how his arms had fallen from her. Marie France looked at the door with a half smile. She was straightening her blouse.

'What kind of a silly trick is that?' Her father wasn't quick enough. Orla was back in the house and Maura had come out to see what the commotion was.

'Nothing, I'm just taking my own pictures for myself like you said I could.'

'Oh leave her, Jimmy. It's her camera, let her take what she likes.' Maura went back to the kitchen.

'It's just a game, you know, a sort of Christmas game,' Jimmy said, desperate, but Maura had lost interest and Orla had gone off somewhere to examine the picture in peace.

Brigid was in the dining room thoughtfully polishing the glasses for the festive lunch, but her thoughts were in no way pleasant. Why was she being forced to camp out in someone else's house, share another family's Christmas because of that bastard? She would show him. She would certainly punish him for this. If only she had some money. Life was so unfair. Look at all this cut glass and silver in Maura's house, they hardly bothered with it. That little dish on the sideboard might be worth a few pounds, and there it was with pencils and sticky tape in it.

As she slipped it into her handbag Brigid heard a hiss and saw the flash. Orla stood impassive at the door.

'I was just dusting it Orla, you know, rubbing it against something in my bag.'

'I know, Auntie Brigid.' Orla was gone before she could be asked to show the picture.

In the sitting room where Grannie was meant to be sorting sweets and crackers, Grannie was actually drinking the festive brandy from a bottle that she was holding by the neck. She nearly choked when Orla came into the room and her look was wide-eyed when she heard the camera make its whishing sound.

'Don't be a silly child, that's a very babyish thing to do wasting your ten snaps, throwing them away.'

'I know, Grannie, but I *am* very babyish,' said Orla.

It was almost time for lunch, soon there would be excited calls from Maura and everyone would gather. The boys were suspiciously quiet. Orla went to their room and entered without knocking. John was coughing over his cigarette but James was flourishing his in fine style.

'Captured for the future generations,' Orla said as the camera flashed.

'We'll be killed,' James said simply. 'It'll ruin Christmas.'

'Only if they see it,' Orla said.

In her own bedroom as she waited for her mother to call, she laid out her collection. The group on the couch and the floor, scarlet-eyed and sure of themselves. Then her mother and the turkey on the floor, her father and Marie France, her grannie drinking the brandy from the bottle, her mother's friend stealing the silver, her two brothers smoking in their bedroom. She still had four more to take. Maybe one when the plum pudding came in and one when they were all asleep with their mouths open.

'It's ready.' She could hear her mother's excited voice from below.

She tore the picture of the turkey into tiny pieces. Her mother was kind. Pathetic but kind. Orla's eyes went back to her gallery. And look at the great Christmas that her mother had as a result of being kind. No, there was no need to keep the turkey disaster, but she would keep the rest.

She went down to her Christmas lunch with her head held high. She knew somehow she would be a person of importance this year. A person not to be taken lightly anymore.

MISS MARTIN'S WISH

꧁꧂

Elsa Martin had never been to New York. She had a passport, even a visa to go to the United States, dating from when she had thought that she was going on her honeymoon in Florida.

That was when she had thought she was going to have a honeymoon.

The passport lay there in a box. It was in the same drawer as her grandmother's little silver bag, and all the good-luck cards in an album that the children had made for Miss Martin. She could have thrown them out, but the children had gone to so much trouble, put so many horse-shoes and wedding bells on them, such glitter and decoration. It would have been like breaking up blossoms or standing on seashells.

For a while she had kept Tim's letters there; the letter where he told her he had never really loved her and couldn't go through with it, where he begged her forgiveness. But then after a year Elsa had taken the letter and burned it because often she found herself going to read it over and over again. As if she might find some insight, some reason why he had left; some thread of hope that he might be coming back.

People said that Elsa had been magnificent, they said that Tim must have been a rat or mentally unstable. They said she was well rid of him, and they marvelled that she had taken it so calmly, ten days before her wedding day. She had returned gifts with a courteous and noncommittal note: 'Since by mutual consent our marriage will now not take place we would like to return your generous present with

143

our gratitude for your kind wishes.' And she had continued teaching the following term as if nothing had happened, as if her heart had not broken into two separate pieces.

The children were more honest.

'Are you very sad you didn't get married, Miss Martin?' a child might ask.

'A little sad, not very sad,' she would admit with a smile.

In the staff room they didn't ask about the cancelled wedding, and Elsa didn't want to fill them in, so it remained one of life's mysteries. Probably a mismatch, better they found out before the ceremony, really, than afterwards.

Elsa's sisters had never liked Tim because he had small eyes. They told each other, but did not tell Elsa, that their little sister had had a lucky escape.

Elsa's friends hadn't really got to know Tim very well. They were sympathetic but vaguely relieved. Tim had come out of nowhere very quickly and taken all Elsa's mind and attention. Perhaps it was doomed from the start. And the years went by, five of them. The children grew up and forgot that Miss Martin had ever planned a wedding for which they had all made cards. The other teachers in the school forgot too. If a new teacher came and inquired about Miss Martin's private life, they would have to root around in their memories of the incident some years back. A wedding called off at the last moment? It didn't rate as important in their lives. But it was still the centre of Elsa's life. She tried everything possible to uproot the burning anxiety to know why someone thought she was a fine person to share his life hopes and dreams with one day, and the next day was able to say that it had all been a mistake. If it wasn't anything she had *done*, then it must be something to do with the person she *was*. It was a huge matter to put behind you, but of course you had to pretend to – otherwise people accused you of brooding and tried to take you out of yourself, which was wearying and irritating. Elsa's friends thought she was very absorbed with her school work, her colleagues thought she had a busy life with friends. It was easy to remain within yourself, which was where she wanted to be.

Christmas was always meant to be the poignant time, the season that pointed out what the lonely were lacking; but, oddly, Elsa never found that Christmas was any worse than other times. One year she had gone to one sister's, a tense household in South London where a lot of the discussion centred around alcohol and whether her brother-in-law was possibly partaking of too much of it. Another year to another sister's, a haphazard home where Elsa did most of the cooking and clearing up; and then to a colleague's house where they had rather too much carol singing and rather too little food. Last Christmas she had spent walking in the Scottish Highlands with a recently divorced friend who wanted to talk angrily about the innate badness of men and how they should all be wiped from the face of the earth.

And now it was the fifth Christmas. For some reason this year she refused every offer, always grateful, always assuring them of something else long planned, but never specified. At the Christmas concert in the shabby prefabricated annex that served as a school hall, she adjusted the wings of the angels, the fleece of the shepherds, and the crowns of the three wise men as she had done for so many years in this school. The children were overexcited, surrounded by their admiring and proud parents. They all flocked to Elsa and hugged her goodbye. And as she did so often, Elsa thought that teaching was so much better than any other job, particularly at Christmas. Imagine if you were in an office with interminable Christmas parties. How could anyone bear the false cheer, the fake bonhomie?

'Where are you going for Christmas, Miss Martin?' they asked her from the comfort and safety of their parents' arms.

Usually she said something vague and noncommittal, and that she would try not to eat too much Christmas pudding. But this year for some reason one of the children, little Marion Matthews, said confidently to the others, 'She's going to America. She told us she was.'

Had she? Elsa hadn't remembered saying anything of the sort.

'Remember? Miss Martin's going to make a wish for us from the Statue of Liberty,' cried Marion triumphantly.

Elsa remembered. There had been some story they read in class about people making a wish when they passed the Statue of Liberty in New York.

'Have you made a wish there, Miss Martin?' they had asked.

'No, not yet,' Elsa had said. 'But when I go I'll make a wish for you all.'

They had considered it with the seriousness of seven-year-olds. Would Miss Martin wish for the new hall for them? If they had a new hall, they could do all kinds of things, dancing classes, basketball, proper gymnastics. Elsa had said lightly that of course she would, but they must remember that all wishes didn't necessarily come true.

The Christmas vacation began. The children would have forgotten next term that Miss Martin was going to make a wish for them. Their minds would be too full of the adventures and gifts of a busy holiday. But Elsa didn't forget. She went to the drawer to look for her passport. Her face had looked different then, she thought, the eyes less weary, the mouth more relaxed. But perhaps this was fantasy.

At the back of the passport were ten folded notes each for twenty dollars. They had been there for five years, losing value. Why had she not changed them back into pounds? Perhaps it had all been too painful at the time, and then she had forgotten them. Still, it was a good omen. A whole two hundred extra dollars to spend on herself when she got there. She would give herself some little luxury. She would think not at all of what the money had been intended for. She didn't even know why it was there. Had she changed it herself? Was it a gift? Strange that she could remember so much about that time with frightening clarity and other things not at all.

It was surprisingly easy for a single woman to buy a ticket to New York and ask a travel agency to book her a hotel room. Nobody asked her why she was going there. Elsa was an adult, she presumably had plans of her own, her own *agenda*.

Other passengers read their books, watched the movie, or snoozed on the flight.

'Have a good Christmas, you hear?' the man at Immigration instructed her.

'Enjoy your stay,' ordered the man at Customs.

'Best city in the world,' volunteered the bus driver.

At the hotel the receptionist asked if she'd like a little Christmas tree in her room or not. 'Some folks do, some folks want to forget the holiday, so we always ask,' she said.

Elsa thought for a moment. 'I'd love a little Christmas tree,' she said. For five years she had not even placed a sprig of holly in her apartment at home.

She put on her comfortable shoes – she had already forgotten what time it was back in Britain – and went out to mix with the shoppers and the crowds coming home from work. She had heard that New York was a busy, frightening place where they pushed past you on the street, but the people seemed courteous to her, and smiled when they heard her accent.

She watched the skaters at Rockefeller Centre and marvelled at the fairy lights twinkling on every tree along the huge avenues of Manhattan. She stared, fascinated, into the windows of the great department stores, and the lavish displays of gifts. Exhausted, she returned to her own hotel and the individual tree trimmed in her honour by a little oriental chambermaid.

'Do your family celebrate Christmas?' Elsa asked. Back home she would never have asked a personal question about anyone's background or culture. Perhaps being in New York was changing her personality.

'Everybody love Christmas holidays, people are happy and good-tempered,' said the girl, as if it were the most obvious thing in the world.

At the reception desk they had a brochure advertising a Christmas Eve treat. It was a special tour: it began with children singing carols, then it took you around New York in a big bus pointing out the sights and the way various communities celebrated Christmas. There was a festive lunch and then a boat trip to blow away the cobwebs. They would go past the Statue of Liberty.

'Do people make a wish there or is that in my imagination?' Elsa asked.

'I don't know that they do, but then I was born and raised here so I wouldn't know. Perhaps all visitors or first-time people seeing the statue make a wish,' answered the receptionist.

Elsa studied the tour again. It was certainly full of interest, but it was expensive. Then she remembered her magic money, the ten twenty-dollar bills she had not known were hers. 'I'll book it,' she said.

There were twenty of them setting out. Couples and people on their own. They each wore a paper name badge as big as a dinner plate. 'Merry Christmas – I'm Elsa.' Some of them photographed each other.

'Shall I take one of you with your camera?' a man asked Elsa. She didn't like to tell him that there was nobody on the face of the earth to whom she would show such a picture, but he looked kind.

'I'd love that,' she said, not to disappoint him.

They got to know about each other, the people on the tour. There was a Japanese couple whose son had been killed in the war more than fifty years ago. They had corresponded over the years with an American couple whose son had been killed on the same day. This was their first visit. Elsa looked at the four old people in their seventies sitting together in such solidarity and mystification at what had happened to them all half a century ago. It made her own problems seem small.

There were a mother and daughter who fought good-naturedly and almost automatically as they had done for a generation and would do for another. There was a scattering of people on their own, all extroverts, all able to talk as if they were old friends. The only quiet person was the man with the kind face who had taken Elsa's photograph for her. He smiled as they passed places by. He looked as if he knew New York well, and might even be from the city, but that would be odd. Why would a native New Yorker take a guided tour of his own place?

Light snow began to fall as they approached the Statue of Liberty. Elsa looked at it with awe. You *must* be able to make a wish at a place like this, a symbol so important to so many people who had come to start a new life with hearts full of hope. She closed her eyes and wished that the children in her school would get a new hall.

'It's not a very important thing,' she said, struggling to be fair, mouthing the words without realising it. 'There must have been more important wishes made here, but I did promise the children I'd ask. And it would make a difference to music and concerts and everything as well as games. It's not just for showing off, and there aren't any funds left to build one, you see.'

She felt a camera flash; the man with the kind face had taken a picture of her.

'You were praying so hard I wanted to record it for you,' he said. He was easy to talk to. She told him about the hall and the schoolchildren back in London, and later when they were having eggnog in a tavern with the group she told him about Tim and how he had left her and about the dollars in the back of her passport.

And he told her about his friend Stefan, who had died six months ago. How every year on Christmas Eve, Stefan had come out to thank the Statue of Liberty for giving him a home in America, but that he had never been able to give Stefan a real home because his father was old and his mother frail, and they could not take on board their only son's having a friendship with a man. They still lived in hope that he would marry and that all their great wealth could be handed on to future generations.

He had never been able to spend Christmas Day with Stefan; for years he had sat, mute and miserable, trying to be cheerful for two elderly people who were disappointed in him, trying to put out of his mind the thought of Stefan sitting lonely and confused in an apartment drinking a bottle of vodka but assuring himself that he was loved even though it couldn't be acknowledged.

So every Christmas Eve they had been together and come out to salute the Statue of Liberty at the gate of New York's harbour. And sometimes Stefan played the violin to say thank you for being invited into America. People had smiled at him, some had thought it sentimental, some had thought it touching.

He had tears in his eyes as he spoke of Stefan and how he had promised him that one day he would build a great auditorium in his name so that everyone would know of him. He wouldn't be one more immigrant, he would be a violinist who loved this city. But he couldn't do it yet. Not yet while his parents were alive. He must allow them peace in their last years, months even. Stefan would understand.

'Did he play in concerts?' Elsa asked.

'No, he taught music in a school,' said the man with the kind face, and then suddenly they both knew how Stefan's monument could be built and where. A hall with his name on it could go up three thousand miles away. The children would be pleased but not astonished. Miss Martin had made a wish, that was all. And Stefan could be honoured in another great city until the time was right for him to be acknowledged in New York, his own home-town.

THE HARD CORE

Ellie liked them mainly. The old people who had come to live and die in Woodlands. There were very few trees in Woodlands, but that didn't matter, it was as good a name as most and better than some. The place down the road was called Rest Haven, and the one across the road, Santa Rosa della Marina. Woodlands had a bit more dignity somehow.

Ellie was popular with the guests, she didn't call them dear or dearie like some of the carers did. She didn't speak to them as if they were deaf or mad. She never asked how are *we* feeling today. She didn't lower her voice in respect of their huge age and imminent death. Ellie would admit to them when she had a hangover or had got involved yet again with a highly unsuitable man. She was twenty-seven, eager, untidy, and loud. She brought life and energy into their bedrooms with their early morning tea and into the Day Room with their midmorning coffee.

Kate Harris, the matron, watched Ellie with amused exasperation. She was certainly no advertisement for Woodlands with her stained white coat ... yet she had got those stains by helping the old people to move to more comfortable positions and maybe knocking over their coffee while doing so. Her hair escaped from its cap because she was always running to be somewhere that she was needed. She spent little time in the staff room preening herself at a mirror. Ellie had held the hands of dying men and women, she had prattled on to them about their families, she had a natural kindness that more than made up for a sloppy, careless, and overfamiliar style of going on. She remembered the names of the visitors, too, which was a bonus, and had a tendency to flirt with some of the sons or grandsons who came to visit the elderly.

Kate Harris felt that Ellie's judgment in men left a lot to be desired. The most recent one, a dark, brooding-looking man with an irritating tendency to hoot his car horn just at the time the residents were settling down to sleep, was no great addition to the scene. But then Kate Harris had not been a wise chooser of men: her ex-husband had left eventually with a woman half Kate's age and somehow without leaving Kate half the community property. It had never been sorted out, and it never would be.

Kate's mother had always said that it was an unwise marriage. It was doubly and trebly irritating that she had been proved right. There was nothing Mother had not been right about. She had even been right about the future.

'Don't come and live with me, Kate,' Mother had said. 'We would be enemies in a week. Get started in some kind of business. You had quite a brain before that man set about destroying it.'

She had decided to go into business herself and established Woodlands in a Melbourne suburb, an only moderately successful retirement home. Kate Harris sighed; she wasn't one to criticise young Ellie's poor choice in men. And at least she hadn't married any of them.

Ellie was going to spend her Christmas holiday in Sydney with the dark, brooding man called Dan. She had told them all about the apartment he had rented. Well, was going to rent. From people he knew, or friends of his knew. And they were going four days before Christmas or maybe three. There was no pressure, no fuss. It would be great. And somebody had asked Ellie yesterday did it have a sea view and she had bitten her lip and said yes, sure, probably.

Kate Harris got the impression that Dan and the apartment hadn't quite firmed up as expected. Still, let them work it out. It wasn't Kate's problem, she was not Ellie's mother, there was no need to advise or warn as her own mother had.

There were thirty-two people in Woodlands, twenty-eight of them were going out for Christmas. Four, the Hard Core, would remain.

Kate Harris would manage this herself, she had done so last year and the year before. These were the complainers, the moaners, the groaners. It was not hard to see why no one wanted them to spoil Christmas peace.

Twenty-eight old people would be collected and driven to their children and grandchildren, or to their nieces or the children of their cousins. They were people who would smile at a barbecue on Christmas Day, men and women who would choose presents from a gift catalogue, or arrange a case of a nice vintage to be delivered from a winery. They would come back with photographs of Christmas and New Year's festivities.

The Hard Core would sit, resentful and unyielding, refusing always to be interested in the activities of others. Kate sighed. It was not the most glorious and celebratory way to spend Christmas, listening to the collective complaints of the Hard Core. But she owed it to them. They paid to live here, it was their home, if they had nowhere else to go for Christmas, then she wasn't going to turf them out to other places like so many parcels. She couldn't say that Woodlands was closing so she could place them in Santa Rosa della Marina or Rest Haven and retrieve them later. Christmas was an unsettling time anyway and too full of memories. Besides, Kate was glad to be busy, it shut out the thoughts of her husband, the unhappy years before he left and the lonely years after he had gone.

She was unprepared for the phone call from Darwin. It came five days before Christmas as the guests and staff were beginning the long, slow business of winding down operations. Her mother had had a stroke, she was in hospital, miles away; a flight and a long drive.

The Hard Core would have to be resettled. Kate sighed a heavy sigh. At least it put the shock and flood of racing emotions about her mother onto one side. Would she call Rest Haven first? Perhaps they might take Donald. They might, but he was so choleric and bad-tempered and waved his stick so imperiously. Yet Rest Haven had pretensions about snobbery and class. Donald was the most top-drawer of the Hard Core. She wondered which was going to be harder, persuading Rest Haven or persuading Donald. Then there was Georgia. She would hate Santa Rosa della Marina, she would say that Italians and Spaniards made wonderful maids but one shouldn't have to talk to them socially. She had once gone to Rest Haven but then had been barred from there, so it was Santa Rosa or nowhere. And then there were Hazel and Heather, sisters who hated each other even more than they hated everyone around them, which was very deeply. Their days were spent plotting discomfiture and distress each for the other. Kate sat for a while, head in hands. Ellie came in and saw her.

'A few scoops too many last night?' She was quick to relate to what would have been her own reason for holding her head in her hands.

'No Ellie, this may come as a shock to you but I am not in the habit of getting drunk on duty.'

'Sorry, you look as if you're feeling crook.'

'My mother's had a stroke, I have to close Woodlands for Christmas, I have to relocate the Hard Core, wouldn't that make anyone crook?'

Ellie's face was full of concern and sympathy; she asked about Kate's mother, how much speech and movement had been lost, what was the prognosis. Not for the first time, Kate wished that Ellie had studied, qualified as a nurse, gone into paramedical management. She had so many of the right qualities. She was wasted on the loser Dan, the man with the dark, empty eyes and the unconfirmed plans for Christmas.

'But anyway, Ellie, these are the burdens of being a tycoon and running a place like this, a goldmine.' Kate's voice was bitter. Everyone knew that Woodlands only paid its way because she put in so many hours there.

'They'll throw Donald out on the side of the road,' Ellie said.

'Maybe *we* should have a long time ago.' Kate was reaching for her telephone book.

'And Georgia, she's actually barred from Rest Haven, you do know that?'

'I know, which is why I'm gritting my teeth and getting ready to face Santa Rosa.'

'Isn't it a pity there's nobody . . .' Ellie said.

'I know, but there *is* nobody . . . I just can't ask any one person to cancel her Christmas and stay here for the Hard Core. No money would pay them.'

'I know,' Ellie said.

Kate looked at her sharply. Could Dan have been darker and more brooding than usual and have forgotten Christmas? Kate couldn't ask. She reached for the telephone and dialed Santa Rosa.

'Stop for a minute,' Ellie said.

With great relief, Kate replaced the receiver.

'I'd need a lot of money,' Ellie said.

'It's yours,' Kate said.

'And double-time off afterwards.'

'That too.'

'You see, I thought I'd go to a health spa and have a makeover or whatever they call them. He likes smaller, younger, thinner girls, it turns out.'

'They all do, that's what it's about,' Kate said grimly.

'So after New Year's, I go for two weeks to one of these places and get a new me, and then I go off with Dan.'

'As you say,' Kate said, hardly daring to believe it.

'Well, pack your case and go see your mother,' Ellie said.

'You do remember how terrible the Hard Core is?'

'I do. Did we mention how much money?'

'We're talking about a week. Five times your weekly salary.'

'Six.'

'Oh come on, Ellie . . .'

'Think of Georgia in Santa Rosa, think of Donald in Rest Haven.'

'Six, but you have to cook properly and you are not to shout at them.'

'It's a deal.'

The Hard Core were not at all pleased when they were told that Ellie was in charge.

'A slattern, that's what we would have called her in the old days,' said Donald.

'She's not a nurse, she's a carer, a servant class,' said Georgia.

'I suppose her boyfriend has left her,' Heather said to Hazel.

'At least she had a boyfriend, which is more than you ever had,' Hazel said to Heather.

Kate Harris telephoned from the airport. 'I must have been mad,' she said to Ellie. 'My mind is unhinged, otherwise I wouldn't have left them to you.'

'Thanks for the vote of confidence,' Ellie said.

'Nothing personal. Listen, we could still get them in. Rest Haven owes me a favour or two, they'll take Donald and maybe the terrible twins.'

'Hazel is eleven months older, you *know* that,' Ellie said.

'Ellie, this is no time for inessentials.'

'If I am to look after the Hard Core until you get back, let me be the judge of what's essential and what's not. Kate, get on that plane, and be pleasant to your mother, for God's sake.'

'Don't alienate them, Ellie, please. Woodlands is all I've got; if they leave, we go under.'

'Safe journey, Kate,' said Ellie, and hung up.

She squared her shoulders and went in to face the grumblings of the Hard Core. It was going to be hard enough to tolerate them for a full week without the knowledge that the place was in worse financial condition than any of them had suspected.

'I suppose you're going to skimp on the food and pocket the profit for yourself,' said Donald, his face purple already with anger at the thought of it.

'If she ate less herself, she wouldn't have lost her boyfriend,' Heather said.

'Tell us how *you* would know what a boyfriend might or might not like,' Hazel countered.

'This is the last Christmas I spend here,' said Georgia. 'It was bad enough when Miss Harris tried to cope with us on her own, having let the staff go to save money, but to leave a carer. That's inexcusable.' Georgia sniffed so loudly, it was like a pistol shot.

'At least they have a cook in Santa Rosa,' said Hazel.

'And some company over what is meant to be the festive season,' said Heather.

'And people of one's own kind to talk to in Rest Haven ... they don't let the dross in,' said Donald, glaring at Georgia. It was generally known that Georgia was not allowed to darken the door of Rest Haven again.

Ellie's heart felt heavy. She had in her hands the future of four people, one-eighth of Kate Harris's clientele. They would all leave. Possibly during Christmas, with maximum publicity involving television coverage. Ellie could see Donald giving interviews and waving his stick as he crossed the road to Rest Haven. She could literally see the interview as if it had already happened, and could imagine Kate's face on the other side of Australia as she saw it too. And the place would close. Kate would lose her investment. Ellie would lose her job. Twenty-eight people would come back from their Christmas holidays and find that their home was under sentence. And these four difficult old horrors would have to be resettled somewhere. Not an easy task.

All this would happen simply because of the Hard Core and their selfish refusal to believe that Christmas could be hell on earth for lots of people, and their refusal to admit that their destiny was in their own hands. What a tragedy that she had promised Kate not to alienate them. It would be so good to tell the Hard Core what they were putting at risk.

'This place will close,' Ellie heard herself say. 'Between the four of you, you will manage to close it down. The rest of us will survive somehow. Kate will get something for the property if not the goodwill. The other guests are normal, they'll find other places to take them. I'll even get a job somewhere; as you're all so keen to point out I am a lowly person, there are still lots of lowly jobs about. But you four are the ones to worry about. I wonder where you will all be next Christmas. Wherever I am then, I will think of you, all four of you, and wonder.'

There was a silence.

Ellie couldn't believe that she had actually said it. Only five minutes after being pleaded with by Kate, who was on the way to her paralysed mother's bedside. How could she have been so selfish and thoughtless? But it had been said. And there were no words that could take back the insult and the hurt. She hardly dared to raise her head.

To her surprise, Donald wasn't pounding his stick on the floor, Georgia wasn't giving one of her unmerciful sniffs, neither Hazel nor Heather had said anything about Ellie's unlikely prospects of keeping any man if this was an example of her social behaviour.

The silence was more powerful than anything. It was not a feature of life with the Hard Core.

When she looked at them, she saw that their faces were stricken. They had all aged in front of her eyes. They looked what they were:

old, frail, and frightened. Ellie's eyes filled with tears. Tears for their future, for her own future when she was their age, for what she had said and done to them. And childish tears of frustration because she had no idea what to do now.

After what seemed the longest silence that Woodlands had ever known, Donald spoke. He spoke without moving his stick, and there was no sign of the sneer that Ellie had thought was built into his face.

'What should we do?' he asked.

Georgia also looked like a frightened child. 'I mean this is not the *worst* place in the world, and you, Ellie, even if you have no qualifications, you are . . . well, you are kind. They were not kind in Rest Haven. Even if they would have me again, which I gather they will not.'

Ellie looked at her open-mouthed. This was such forbidden territory, and here was Georgia admitting it.

Heather had begun to whimper, but Hazel reached out her hand. 'Now, now, none of that, Heather. I'm here, Hazel is here, didn't I always know what was best for my little sister?' she said.

Ellie blew her nose loudly, but somehow it only made her cry more. Dan was on his way to some job up on the Gold Coast. At the last minute there had been a job as a driver, driving lots of leggy girls to and from a resort . . . Surely Ellie would understand. It wasn't as if this Christmas was definite or anything. Was it . . .? Dan had looked at her with troubled eyes, and Ellie had been too hurt and tired and sad to tell him just how definite and important it had been. And Kate Harris, who had worked hard and been cheerful all her life, had been deserted by her rat of a husband, her business was about to collapse, her mother was going to be an invalid. But somehow saddest of all were these four self-destructive people who looked at her with frightened old eyes.

'I don't know what we can do.' Ellie found herself speaking to Donald as an equal for once. 'The place isn't quite making ends meet as it is, and if Kate's mother means she's going to have to be away a bit she won't have the money to pay a proper person to come in here.'

Georgia bit her lip. 'We don't need really proper people, we could sort of get by,' she said.

'But Kate's a qualified nurse, she mightn't be able to keep her license . . .'

'We don't need nursing,' said Hazel. 'We're as strong as horses, aren't we, Heather?'

'Horses,' Heather repeated dutifully.

'But there are no new people coming and it costs so much for Kate to advertise . . .'

'We could do word-of-mouth,' Donald said. 'You know, we could write and tell people it's a fine place.'

'But if they *do* come here, you'll just tell them that everyone is being poisoned,' Ellie said, with spirit.

'No, no, it would all be different.' Donald sounded as if he meant it.

'I could go and try and get some of the people in Rest Haven and lure them here,' Georgia said.

'Kate wouldn't allow that, no poaching on other people, that's always been her rule.'

'We could write to our old school, Heather,' Hazel suggested. 'Lots of past pupils of our age might like to know of a place to come.'

'Chaps who retired same time as I did,' Donald said. 'There's an office newsletter, I could write a first-person piece for it, I was always good with words, I could describe all the full days we have here . . .'

'But you *hate* it, Donald, you absolutely hate Woodlands, no point in luring them all here and then telling them the place is filled with dunderheads and lower-class people.' Ellie didn't want to raise Kate's hopes only to have them dashed again.

'I wouldn't if . . .' Donald didn't finish the sentence.

'You couldn't change overnight . . . people don't,' Ellie insisted. 'There's no one who wants this place to survive as much as I do, but come on . . . you're all old enough to know that it might only be a dream.'

She saw that they were looking at her with hope.

Suddenly Ellie realised that they never thought of her as someone with any real involvement in Woodlands. After all, she had only told them about her hangovers, the parties she went to, the fellows who came in and out of her life. Perhaps it was only now that they saw another side to her. The feeling that this place had been good to her and was in many ways her home.

'When I was in business,' Donald said, 'at the first sign of trouble we always called a meeting around a table to have a conference.'

'When I was a hostess, with anyone who was anyone in the state wanting to come to my dinner parties, I always began with a list,' said Georgia.

'When we ran the house for Father,' Hazel said, 'Heather and I would always work out with each other what was the very worst that could happen, and we sort of worked backwards from there.' Heather smiled proudly at her older sister.

'That's a good idea,' said Donald. 'Dealing with the negatives first.'

Ellie pulled up a table and they settled around it.

They would eat sparingly over the Christmas season, no need for festive banquets, they would save money for Kate there for a start.

'I'll forgo my bonus for looking after you,' Ellie offered.

How much was it, they wanted to know, and were horrified when they heard it was six times the weekly rate.

'But you *are* pretty terrible,' Ellie said, and they nodded. Almost proudly.

They listed the people they could contact about how much they loved Woodlands. Donald said they might contact a local television station to do a heartwarming interview for Christmas, about how four elderly people had refused all the offers to go to members of their family because they liked being together in their normal surroundings.

'Won't the members of our families who see it be surprised!' giggled Georgia.

'Wipe their bloody eyes for them,' said Donald.

Kate called when her plane got to the airport at her mother's town.

'Tell me it's all right, Ellie,' she said.

'Are you going to do this every day, are you going to waste the profits, meagre as they are, on interstate phone calls?'

'What about you taking six times your salary for one way of wasting the profits?' said Kate crossly.

'Oh well, yes, I sort of rethought that.'

'What are you trying to do now, bleed me dry?'

'No, double time will do.'

'Speak to me, Ellie, are any of them alive?' Kate begged.

'Have one quick word, say Happy Christmas to each of them and then hang up, this place isn't made of money,' Ellie ordered.

They all gave her a greeting.

'We decided not to be fulsome, in case she suspected something,' Donald said.

'Good senior management thinking,' Ellie said, and she got the first genuine smile Donald had managed since he arrived in Woodlands.

Late that night, they were still planning and structuring. They had cocoa and biscuits. A great car-hooting was heard outside.

'It's your young man,' said Heather.

'Let him come and knock at the door like a normal person then,' said Ellie.

Dan arrived. 'Didn't you hear me?' he said. 'I called to say that I asked them could you come to help. Told them you'd worked at a place, you know, a place. I didn't say it was like this.'

'No indeed,' said Ellie.

The Hard Core shook their old heads.

'So if you want to, you can come, company for the journey.'

'Happy Christmas, Dan,' Ellie said.

'Is that a yes or a no?' Dan asked.

'It's geriatric speak for goodbye,' Ellie said.

They sat in silence while his car roared off.

There was still postal time before Christmas, they must get letters into the mail tomorrow. There were phone calls too. Messages of goodwill to people estranged, cut off, or neglected because of real or imagined slights. Invitations to come and visit before the New Year.

'The place looks shabby,' said Georgia, 'they might not think it was smart enough. You know the way that some people judge by appearances.'

They agreed to ask local children to come in and whitewash the walls, help with the garden, build up the window boxes. Churches and community groups would co-operate.

On Christmas Day they were having a barbecue when the phone rang. Georgia answered.

'No, Kate, better not talk to Ellie, she's as drunk as a lord, Donald just insisted we get her some wine. She has been absolutely marvellous. How's your mother, by the way?'

Kate lost her power of speech, and sat down on a chair in the hospital corridor. Ellie was drunk. Georgia was cheerful. Donald had insisted that Ellie have some wine. They had remembered her mother was in hospital. The world was ending.

'I think I'll get back very soon,' Kate said in a strangled voice.

'Not until your mother is ready to travel,' Georgia said brightly.

'Travel?' Kate squeaked.

'Well, you will be bringing her home?' Georgia said. 'That's what the committee thought.'

'The committee?'

'Yes, we searched for a name but we decided to call ourselves the Hard Core,' Georgia said with the smile that had made her famous years ago, before she had fought with everybody and ended up with no friends.

Miles away, outside the ward where her mother was recovering but would always need permanent residential care, Kate held the phone and hardly dared to think about the spirit of Christmas.

'Kate, I think you should hang up now, Ellie said we must all be very careful of finances if Woodlands is to be the success we all want it to be.'

'Ellie said that?' Kate's voice was a whisper.

'When she's sober, which is most of the time, she is a fine person,' said Georgia in a tone that implied the only dissenting opinion had been Kate's.

'Give my love and thanks to the Hard Core,' said Kate.

Georgia was pleased. Pleased and surprised.

'You remembered the name,' she said approvingly. 'I think there's hope for this place yet.'

CHRISTMAS TIMING

꧁ ꧂

This would be their fifth Christmas together, or not together. But the principle was the same. Chris hated the smugness of married people who went on and on about anniversaries, as if a thing could only be celebrated when it was legit. She couldn't believe that her friends didn't know that she and Noel had got together in the winter of 1984. A magical winter when they kept finding out how much they had in common; they were both Christmas babies, one called Chris, one called Noel in deference to the season. They had both been bored rigid by the Olympic Games and never wanted to hear of a decathlon, a javelin, or a discus ever again. They had loved the film *Amadeus* and felt that at just touching thirty they were a little too old for Michael Jackson.

It had been the Christmas of Stevie Wonder and 'I just called to say I love you.' Chris would never forget that as long as she lived. And the way Noel *did* call to say he loved her, from every phone box, hotel foyer and railway station. And from the family home whenever his wife was out of earshot.

The children were so young in 1984. Noel's children. And of course, to be fair, his wife's children. They were very young, they were seven and eight. That was young. And oddly, as the years went by, they still seemed to be young. Chris couldn't understand it, everything else changed. But those children of Noel's were still clinging toddlers expecting him home, needing to be telephoned, wanting presents, demanding postcards daily on the few occasions when Noel and Chris *did* manage to get away together. They seemed to be getting younger in their photographs too. Or else dressing younger and assuming babyish positions. They were twelve and thirteen now. Why did they still get photographed cuddled up to Daddy, leaning on him, needing protection? Did a devilishly cunning wife always manage to snap them this way, knowing that these would be the pictures that got shown rather than complete family scenes?

They were very sensitive with each other, Chris and Noel. He never mentioned aspects of the family Christmas that might upset her, the parties for relatives and neighbours. She was the same with him, she never talked about how her parents always invited her father's junior partner, a man who had the huge advantage of being single. She never told him how her sisters talked to her darkly about the biological clock ticking away and how liberation was all very well but did one want to put off babies forever?

In fact Chris thought that they were much more courteous to each other and anxious not to offend than were most married couples she knew. She often did those quiz-type articles in magazines. 'Are you compatible?' In all of them, answering honestly, she thought they came out with top marks. They always listened, fascinated, to stories of the working day. They never slouched around the house in slovenly and unattractive gear. Neither of them would dream of turning on a television rather than having a conversation. They were tender and giving in their love-making rather than selfish. They didn't need to cheat. They were compatible.

Sometimes she did an 'Are you romantic?' test. And they were, they were!

He brought her a single flower; he remembered what she wore and praised it. She always served dinner on a table, no trays on the lap in Chris's flat.

And it was the same in the 'Is he a chauvinist pig?' tests. He wasn't, he wasn't. With her hand on her heart she could say that he admired her mind, thought her job was worthwhile, asked her advice about his own, treated her equally in all things. There was no way she could be considered his little bit of fluff.

There were no tests she shied away from. Not even the 'Will your love survive?' She went through it remorselessly and decided that it would. Triumphantly, when all others had fallen or cooled down.

They had all the right ingredients for survival. They were clear-sighted, they knew the limitations and yet could travel to the furthermost boundaries. Even the regular Christmas promise that next year they would be together. Properly. That wasn't a weak link in their love. It was a necessary pronouncing of commitment.

Noel loved doing these little psychological tests too. Sometimes he found more that Chris hadn't seen in management magazines. 'Is your love life suffering because of stress?' They would laugh confidently and agree that Noel's love life with Chris was doing nothing of the sort. He found a serious one called 'Are you a cheat?' They went through it very carefully and decided that he wasn't, because nobody was being let down. And that when the time was right everything would be out in the open.

So they had no fear of any Christmas Quiz dreamed up in a family newspaper to keep the readers happy and partially alert over Christmas. And though they were separated by many miles, they wouldn't be unhappy on Christmas Day. Noel had a picture of Chris sitting down in her family home surrounded by sisters and brothers-in-law, nephews and nieces, and good old family friends. He could imagine her sitting by the fire and picking up this marvellous questionnaire and filling it in quietly, smiling to herself in the knowledge that he, too, would be doing it by his fireside and that everything they answered to the questions would be almost word for word the same. Chris thought of Noel, after all the family fun with those two children who seemed to have reversed the ageing process, possibly getting rattles and soft toys in their stockings this year. He would ask for a little peace for Daddy to read the papers and it would be given to him. She could see him nodding and smiling over the kind of thing that might have other couples riddled with anxiety. Compatible, romantic, clear-sighted, non-chauvinist, non-cheating? They would win in every category. At around the same time on a crisp, cold afternoon on the day that was both Christmas and the day they had reached half of three score and ten, they sat down to do the Christmas Quiz.

This year it was in a different format. Not the usual boxes to tick for Yes and No and Possibly. Not the usual scoring scheme at the end: 'If you scored over 75 you are ridiculously happy' or 'If you scored under 20, are you *sure* this relationship is for you?'

This year it was a completely new layout. You had to write in words, sentences, not ticks and crosses. There was no scoring at the end, only the suggestion that you leave the newspaper around the house so that the loved one could read it. That's if you wanted the loved one to change. Deep in their armchairs miles from each other, Chris and Noel, the thirty-five-year-old Christmas babies, nestled in to do the questionnaire. It was called 'Those Little Irritations,' and under a whole lot of different headings you had to fill in the things about the loved one that caused you to wince. BE HONEST the headline screamed at you, and said there was no point in doing it unless you did it honestly.

In the house where Chris sat, children played with their new games by the tree, her sisters talked of new arrivals in the new decade, her parents slept contentedly in their chairs. Her father's junior partner, who had the merit of being single, mended the Christmas lights and put batteries into all the gadgets that had been gift-wrapped without them. He saw Chris take up the questionnaire.

'Only a couple who were seriously mad would attempt that,' he said genially.

Chris looked at him pityingly. He must not know about her happy love life in case he ever let it slip to her parents.

'Oh that's right, only us singles would dare to do it. Fantasy life and all that.'

He smiled at her; he looked kind of different this year, perhaps he, too, had a secret life. She drew the paper up to her closer so that she could begin without his seeing the pure contentment on her face.

In Noel's house the children had gone out with their friends; they said there was nothing to do at home and now that they had opened their presents, couldn't they please go up the hill and fly kites like everyone else. Noel's wife talked excitedly with her father and mother about the business she was going to start. Yes, of course it would mean a bit of travel, but the children were well grown up now and nothing made youngsters as independent as having to look after themselves a little in these formative years.

Noel opened the paper and smiled at 'Those Little Irritations.' He knew before he started that there would be no irritations, little or large, about his life with Chris.

Now, if it had been a questionnaire about him and his wife. Aha, *that* would be a different matter altogether! Look at the very first question.

'Does the loved one have any one phrase said over and over that drives you mad?' Chris hadn't. She was forever fresh and new in everything she said. But his wife, if she said 'Let's face it' once a day she must say it four hundred times. And her other phrase was 'To be strictly honest.' God, how he could scream when she said that. She always felt the need to say that she was being strictly honest when she told him the most trivial detail, like how long she had waited for a bus or what time somebody had telephoned. 'No, to be strictly honest it was at three o'clock she phoned not half-past two, but let's face it, she does phone every day.' No, there was nothing at all in that category that he could hang on Chris. His wife, however, had another phrase that he hated. It was 'Right?' Said as a question after the most banal statement. 'I saw the new next-door neighbours today. Right?' Why did she say 'Right?' With an effort Noel dragged himself away from this bubbling rage. The quiz was meant to be about him and Chris, for heaven's sake, and so far she had passed with flying colours. Now on to question two. 'Is there any item of clothing that the loved one wears which you would like to consign to the dustbin?' Well, yes of course, that hideous mink cravat, and the line of chat that went with it. 'I don't approve of killing animals for their fur, but mink are different, they're vermin, *and* they've never known freedom.' But wait, that wasn't Chris, that was his wife. Chris wouldn't wear any kind of fur, nor would she have a list of excuses ready if she did. She wore lovely soft colours, grey-blue like her eyes and lilac sometimes, then when he would least expect it she might appear in a scarlet dress, or a yellow sweater. No, nothing for the dustbin there. He sighed with pleasure as he thought of his luck in love. A girl who never said a word astray or wore a garment that he didn't love.

In another house Chris was being honest, as the headline had urged her to be. Any phrase, over and over? Well, only the way he *always* said 'I must go to the little boys' room' when they went out to dinner, or even when they had dinner in her flat. But that wasn't something you hated. Just a bit predictable. Oh, and of course he always said 'Ice and slice?' when he got her a gin and tonic, as if it were mint new. But that was sort of a joke, he had imaginary quotation marks around it. No, she wouldn't write it down, that would be nit-picking. Across from the fire she saw her father's partner. She thought he had been looking at her, but she must have imagined it, he was very busy installing new batteries. He had brought a seemingly endless supply of them, which was good thinking on the part of someone who didn't have any children of his own. Chris read on. Was there an item of clothing belonging to Noel that she would throw out, apart from the underpants with the words 'Hot Stuff' on them? Well, there was the red-and-white-striped nightcap that had been funny once, and the fur hat after the Gorbachev cult, and the socks with sandals in the summer, and the driving gloves that were perfectly reasonable gloves in themselves but looked self-important on a driving wheel somehow. But these weren't real irritations. Not in the sense of being able to find a list of them.

There were twenty questions in the list. Twenty times Noel found at least five flaws in his wife and not one in his girlfriend. When Chris answered the twenty questions, however, she found twenty flaws in Noel. Twenty times, with tears beginning to start at the back of her eyes. Yes, she had found three unpleasant eating habits, and yes, she had observed two signs of corporate dishonesty, as well as an alarming six signs of petty personal meanness. She wrote none of them down. She didn't need to. It wasn't a paper to be left around to improve his habits. It was an eye-opener. As the scales fell from her eyes so did the glory seem to fall from Noel. She knew he would call soon and sing the Stevie Wonder lines down the phone. She knew she would tell him now that she knew he would never leave his home for her and furthermore she didn't want him to. It would be a relief to him too. He wasn't a basically bad man, just a basically irritating one.

In another house, Noel had counted seven unpleasant eating habits in his wife, and such high levels of corporate dishonesty that he feared she would be in a major criminal league when she got her business going. Noel knew that this was the time he would tell his wife that he wanted to leave. He would tell her today, this very day. It would be fairer and she could go ahead with her plans without taking him into consideration. He hadn't realised just how far they had grown apart. Just how little his children needed him. What a revelation it had been.

He would tell her straight out and then phone Chris. And this time no need to go up to the bedroom saying he needed to go to the little boys' room to make the call. No need to go down the road to the phone box on the corner. He would be honest.

Noel could hardly wait to know what Chris would say. Perhaps she would leave home immediately and drive back to her flat in the city. What would there be for her to stay at home for? He would drive around to see her, take a bottle of tonic, possibly, and a lemon, she'd have gin, it would be silly to duplicate but he did know how she loved a gin and tonic with its ice and slice.

He wished he could see her now. But later, afterwards, he would ask her what it had been like in the hours before he had rung to tell her that he was free.

Chris sat and played a game of electronic ice hockey with the friend of the family, her father's partner, who happened to be single and who also happened to be very nice.

They were the only ones who heard the telephone ring, and he agreed with her that there was no point in answering it. Only very irritating people rang on Christmas Day.

THE CIVILISED CHRISTMAS

It had been a civilised divorce, people said. What did that mean? It meant that Jen never said a word against Tina, the first wife, the beautiful wife who had run away and run back half a dozen times. It was civilised because Jen wrapped Stevie up in his scarf every Saturday and took him by two buses to Tina's house without complaining. She smiled an insincere smile as Tina, often in a dressing gown, always lovely, came to the door. Tina used to ask her in at one time, but Jen had always said no, thank you, she had some shopping to do. Tina would repeat the word 'shopping' in wonder, as if it were a very unfamiliar and outlandish thing for someone to do on a Saturday. When Stevie's visit was over, Tina put him in a taxi and Jen took him out of it and paid the taxi driver. Tina had a house, a terraced house, she had a three-piece suite with beautiful flowers on it, she had a mirror with a big gilt frame in her hall, but she never had the taxi fare home for her son.

They said it was civilised because Tina hadn't contested the custody. Her job took her away from time to time – she was a casino croupier and was often called on to go to big functions in the country. Her hours were unsuitable, much better not to try and rear an eight-year-old boy, better for the child. And anyway, the boy's father wanted the child so much, let's be civilised about it, Tina had said. Martin was so delighted that there was no battle, he had started to think almost warmly about Tina. Stevie loved going to see his beautiful mother and her bright chatty friends. It was all much better than the days when Mum and Dad had been fighting and crying. They had told him it would be better this way and they were right. Mum had bought him a computer, so usually he spent the time at that when he went to Mum's house. All the people had wine and sandwiches and they would come in and watch him and say wasn't he marvellous. Mum had a big bottle of apple juice all for him, as well as the sandwiches, and she used to ruffle his hair and say he was very brilliant as well as handsome, and that he would look after her in her old age when all her looks and her friends had gone.

Mum's friends would pat him on the back approvingly and it was all very grown up and exciting. Mum even realised that he was old enough to take a taxi on his own. She would run lightly down the steps and whistle, a real ear-splitting whistle, and passers-by would smile as they always did at Mum.

At school people asked Stevie was it awful, his parents being divorced, and he said no, honestly, it was fine. He saw them both, you see, and they didn't fight, he was welcome in two places. And in the pub where Martin had his half pint on the way home from work, the kind motherly woman who polished glasses and listened to life stories asked him if it was all working out and if the boy was settling down with his new mother. 'Uh, Jen isn't his mother,' Martin would say happily. 'Nothing is ever going to replace his real mother, he knows that, we all know that.' The woman smiled as she shone up the gleaming brass on the pumps and said it would be a happy world if everyone was as civilised as Martin and his wife.

This would be their first Christmas together. Jen, Martin, and Stevie. Jen had planned every detail to make it perfect. She worked in a supermarket for five hours every Saturday morning, a tiring job particularly at this time of year. She worked the cash register and sat in a cold, windy part of the shop where the doors were always opening and the December wind came biting around her shoulders. They didn't like her wearing a jacket, so she wore three vests and a small jumper under her nylon coat. She looked much fatter than she did at school, where she was the secretary in a nice sensible wool dress. The school had central heating and nobody leaving doors open. Jen saved the supermarket money to make it a great Christmas for them all. She bought crackers and table decorations, she bought mincemeat for the pies, she got the kind of tin of biscuits they would never have dreamed of buying normally, she had a tin of chestnut purée and a box of crystallised fruits.

Jen wasn't a great cook, but she had planned their Christmas lunch so often that she felt she could now do it in her sleep. She even knew what time she should start the bread sauce. It would be the first *real* Christmas Day for Martin and Stevie, she reminded herself. The lovely Tina had never been very strong on home cooking, and she liked to spend the festive season drinking to people's health in wine bars or restaurants and clubs.

Jen felt a wave of unease, as she often did about Tina. She hoped there was no danger of Tina spoiling their first Christmas by arriving suddenly and being sweet. Tina being sweet was sickening. Martin seemed to forget how she had humiliated him so often and so publicly. How other men had been found sipping wine and eating dainty delicate sandwiches when Martin got home tired from work. In the days when Stevie was a toddler and well out of the way in his playpen and a wet nappy, Martin could barely remember the number of times when Tina had disappeared, overseas, sometimes for weeks on end, or how her working hours in the casino seemed to stretch to mid-morning and Martin had been unable to go to work until she returned.

Tina had been able to think of Stevie alone in the house; Martin had not.

But nowadays, when Tina was so charming and undemanding, it seemed that he could no longer remember the bad old days. Tina was so unfairly good-looking: long legs, long fair hair, and whatever she wore looked marvellous. She looked girlish and in many ways too young and irresponsible to be Stevie's mother. Jen, on the other hand, looked matronly, she told herself sadly, and as if she were the mother of many older children. Life was unfair, Jen was the same age as the leggy Tina, twenty-nine. Next year they would both be thirty, but one of them would never look it, not even when she turned forty in ten years time.

Jen pinned up the Christmas cards, attaching them to ribbons and trailing them across the wall.

'That's nice,' Stevie said approvingly. 'We never had that before.'

'What way did you put them then?'

'I don't think we put them at all. Well, last year Dad and I were in a hotel, remember, before you came along, and before that I don't think Mum had much time.'

He was neither wistful nor critical. He was just seeing things the way they were.

Jen seethed to herself. Mum had no time, indeed! Mum who had no real job, who just played about in that casino, had no time to put up Christmas decorations for her husband and little son. But plain old Jen had time, boring Jen who worked in a school from nine to four. Industrious Jen who dragged herself and Tina's son on two buses so that the boy could see his mother with minimum fuss. *And* took the money out of her own purse to pay for the taxi in order to keep the peace. But nobody ever said Jen hadn't got time to do anything. There was no mercy, no quarter given second time round.

Martin approved of the decorated house; he went round touching the sprays of holly and ivy over the pictures, the candle in the window, the tree that was waiting for them all to fill.

'This is lovely,' he said. 'It's like a house you see on telly not like a real house at all.'

It was meant as high praise. Jen felt a strange stinging in her eyes. It was a hell of a lot more real, she thought, when bloody Tina was here with her high-flying friends and her idiotic chat and no time to make a Christmas for anyone.

Well, at least this year, like last, Tina would be miles away on a cruise ship dealing the cards, calling the numbers, and looking divine for the passengers. That's what she had done last year, just before the divorce was final. Jen had gone home to her mother, who had warned her all through the five days of Christmas that it wouldn't be easy to marry a divorced man and raise his child. Martin said it had been a lonely Christmas in the hotel, though Stevie had enjoyed the organised games. They had both thought it was better not to spring too much on him at once, let him have a Christmas alone with his father to show him there was some stability in a changing world. He had only been seven, poor little fellow. Still he had adapted very well, all in all. He certainly didn't think of her as a wicked stepmother, and he didn't cry for his golden-haired mum. Jen just wished they wouldn't think of her as so ordinary and of Tina as something special and outside normal rules.

She had lit a fire for them and they sat, all three of them, around it talking. For once nobody asked what was on the television, Martin didn't say he had to go out to his workshop, Stevie didn't say he wanted to go to his room. Jen wondered why she had felt so uneasy about Tina and their Christmas. It was childish to have these forebodings. She laughed at the other school secretary who read her star signs carefully before taking any action each morning; people would laugh too at Jen with her premonitions and funny feelings that something was going to happen.

'Tina rang me at work today,' Martin said just then.

Martin hated being rung at work, he was on the counter in a busy bank, he hated being called away from his window. Only the greatest of emergencies would make Jen pick up the phone to call him. Surely it must have been the same with Tina, and this must have been an emergency.

'Her cruise has been cancelled apparently so she's not going abroad. Only told them at the last minute, and no money or anything. Very unfair of the company.' Martin shook his head at such sharp practice.

'So Mum will be at home at Christmas?' Stevie was pleased. 'Will I go over to see her in the morning or what?'

Jen found that her eyes were tingling for the second time that evening. Damn her. Damn Tina forever. Why couldn't she be ordinary? Why couldn't she have found a man and lived with him and married him like ordinary people did? Why did it have to be this flapper life of cruises and casinos and clubs? And Lord, if it had to be that, why did it have to be this shipping company of all of them that had to fail? There had to be a reason. Now they would have to disrupt their nice Christmas Day, just so that Tina could see her son for a couple of hours. A son she couldn't care about or why would she have given him away? It was so unfair. Martin was shaking his head doubtfully.

'That's the problem,' he said, looking from one to the other. 'You see, she had all her plans made to go abroad and she has nobody, nobody at all for Christmas. She doesn't think she could stay in her house all alone. She doesn't like the idea of being all alone for Christmas.'

'Lots of people are alone for Christmas,' Jen said suddenly before she had time to think.

'Yes, well sure they are. But this is Stevie's mum. And you know Tina, she likes to have a thousand people round her, but they all think she's going away.'

Jen stood up pretending to fix the curtains which didn't need to be touched at all. They didn't seem to notice her.

'So what will Mum do then if she doesn't want to be alone? Will she go away somewhere else?' Stevie wanted to know.

'I think she will, she said she was ringing round a bit,' Martin said. Of course she was ringing round a bit, but who better to ring first than the kind ex-husband. Just to make him miserable and guilty, just to make him offer her Christmas Day with her son, with a nice meal cooked for her. Yes, obviously Tina would ring Martin first, the old reliable, always there. No matter if she ran away, she knew he'd take her back. Until he met Jen and found that life could be lived on a normal level.

It had taken Jen to open Martin's eyes to Tina and her way of going on. But, Jen thought grimly, she mightn't have opened them enough. It was hovering in the air between them. *The invitation.* It had to come from Jen, but she was not going to issue it. No, she was most definitely not. She would pretend that she hadn't understood the tension.

'Then I won't be able to see her on Christmas Day?' Stevie said.

Jen was bright. 'If she had been on the cruise you wouldn't have seen her anyway, remember?' she said. 'And you've given her your Christmas present and hers to you is under the tree.'

'But if she has nowhere to go ...?' Stevie said.

'Oh Stevie, your mum has a thousand places to go, you heard your father say just a second ago she has a thousand friends around her.'

'I said, she likes a thousand friends – it's a different thing.'

Jen knew what she would like to do at that minute. She would like to have put her coat on and walked out in the rain and wind. She would like to have hailed the first taxi she saw and gone to Tina's house. Then she would have taken Tina by the neck and shaken her until there was only a flicker of life left in her body. Briskly she would get back into the taxi and come home to inquire if anyone would like drinking chocolate as a treat.

But Jen wouldn't do this because it was not a civilised thing to do. It would be considered the act of a mad-woman. In England, that is.

In the more hot-blooded Mediterranean countries it would be totally understood. But this was not a country of Latin lovers and passionate jealousy, this was a civilised place. So Jen fixed a slightly dim smile to her face, as if she were talking to a very senile man and a very young baby instead of her husband and stepson.

'Well, no point in us bothering about all that now, is there? Your mum is well able to sort out her own problems, Stevie. Would anyone like some drinking chocolate?'

Nobody felt like any, so Jen stood up deliberately and made some for herself. She knew if she had put three mugs on the tray they would all have had it, but why should she? Why should she play nanny to them both? While they stared into the changing pictures of the fire and worried about beautiful Tina and her troubled Christmas.

When Stevie had gone to bed, Jen talked about the supermarket. They wanted her to work Saturday, Sunday, and the two days before Christmas. Should she do it? It was a lot of money, in the middle of January they would be sorry if she hadn't done it. On the other hand, maybe it was just tiring herself out for the sake of a wage packet. Might they be happier if she were to stay at home a bit and relax? She wondered what Martin thought.

'Whichever you like best,' he said. His face still looked preoccupied to her. Suddenly it was all too much effort. Suddenly the mask of civilised behaviour fell right down to the ground.

'Whichever I *like*?' she said in disbelief. 'Are you actually mad, Martin? Whichever I *like*? Do you think anyone in the whole world would *like* to get out of a nice warm bed and leave a gorgeous man like you still in the bed, get dressed, flog over there and deal with bad-tempered customers, watch that people don't nick things at the till, see women with big rings on spending forty, fifty, sixty pounds a time on food? If you think anyone would choose to do that, you must be insane.' He looked at her, dumbfounded. Jen had never spoken to him like this before. Her eyes were blazing and her face was contorted with anger.

'But why did you . . . I mean, I thought you wanted to earn . . . you never said . . .' He was stammering, unable to cope with the woman in the other chair who had turned into a stranger.

'I wanted to have extra money to make this a nice home for you and Stevie and me, that's what I wanted. And I never allowed myself to think about the sum of money that goes from your salary every month towards Tina's mortgage. Not even on a Saturday afternoon when I look at her house, which is bigger and better than our house, do I question the fact that you pay towards its upkeep when we all know that sometimes Tina earns three times what you and I earn together. I know, I know her work is uncertain. Some weeks she might earn nothing. I know, but isn't she lucky, my, my, my, what a bit of luck that we never suggested that she should get a regular job like the rest of the world has to do?' Jen paused for breath and pulled away her hand which Martin was reaching for. 'No, let me finish, perhaps I should have said it before, perhaps I am the guilty one for pretending it doesn't matter, for putting on a brave little face, but that's what I thought you needed. You'd had enough tempers and tantrums with the last one, I thought you needed a bit of peace and calm around you now.'

'But I need *you, you're* what I want,' he said simply.

She went on, nodding her head in agreement. 'Well, that's what I tried to be, calm, and putting a good face on things, and I suppose that's what I'll go on doing. It was just when you asked me to suit myself or whatever you said – whichever I like – as if there was any question. Of course I'd like to be at home here, getting up late, pottering around a bit, maybe doing the plants and sort of just enjoying myself, like people do. Like some people do.'

'But I thought you found it a bit dull here, and that's why you like to run off and be with people, meet them, and have a bit of money as independence, you know.' His big honest face looked at her bewildered. No wonder Tina had walked over this kind, uncomplicated man.

Jen opened the kitchen cupboard and showed him the store of luxury foods, the crackers, the table decorations. She gestured to the bright, shining ornaments and the electric lights on the Christmas tree. She wordlessly touched the new standard lamp that stood up by his chair, the curtains on their smart new rail, the brass box that held the logs for the fire. 'This is hardly spending money just for me to fritter away. I got these things for our house. I don't hoard my salary for me any more than you do with yours. I spend it making a nice home for us all, and I'm sorry, Martin, I do *not* want to have Tina here to wreck our first Christmas, I really don't, and that's why I'm so upset. I just want you and me and Stevie and a bit of time. Time to talk. Is that so awful?'

'Tina? Come here for Christmas? There was never any question of that!'

'Oh yes, there was. I saw it in your eyes, you wanted brave Jen, nice calm Jen to say "Let's be civilised, let's ask Stevie's mother to share our groaning board". Well, I won't and that's that.'

'But you can't think I want Tina here, can you? After all the Christmases she ruined for me and Stevie, after all the heartbreak and the lies and the deceit. Why would I want her here again? I am divorced from her remember, I'm married to you. It's *you* I love.'

'Yes, but what about Tina's Christmas?'

'Oh, she'll find somewhere, don't worry.'

'I'm not worried. It was you who sounded worried when you were talking earlier. With Stevie, you definitely looked upset about her.'

'I was and I am a bit, you see I didn't finish while Stevie was there.'

'What was it?' Jen was anxious.

'Oh, just Tina upsetting people. As well as the Christmas fiasco, she has plans to go abroad in the New Year. More or less permanent job, she says. We had a talk about the house, her house. She won't need any more help towards it, she's going to let it apparently, and she said she's sending us something to recompense me.'

'I'll believe it when I see it.'

'Yes, well, so will I but the main thing is no more monthly cheque to her.'

'Are you upset because she's going?'

'Only for Stevie. I was thinking that he will miss her, but then tonight when I came home to this lovely place I think he'll only miss her for a little while, he's got such a good home here. You've made it for both of us a real home.'

But she wouldn't give in completely, she had come out in the open and she wasn't going to put on her gentle Jen mask again immediately.

'So what was the upset about if you're not going to miss Tina, and you think Stevie'll get over it. Why were you so depressed?'

'I was thinking that I might be a very dull sort of husband. Tina ran away from me, you ran off to work at weekends, I thought it was because I was dull.' He looked so sad, she knelt down in front of him.

'I thought I was dull too, I wanted to be tigerish like Tina, but I never thought you were dull for a moment, not for one second. I swear it.'

He kissed her in the firelight.

'Men are very silly really,' he said. 'We never think of saying the obvious. You are beautiful and fascinating and I've always been afraid since the first time we met that you might be too bright for me, and think I was a dreary sort of bank clerk encumbered with a son. I couldn't believe it when you wanted to take us both on. I never think of Tina except in relief that she gave me Stevie and that it turned out as it did. It never crossed my mind to compare you. Never.'

'I know.' She soothed him now, he seemed so worried. But he was struggling to find words. He was determined to pay her the compliment that was in his head and his heart but he had never been able to say.

'Years ago,' Martin said, 'they used to have mainly black-and-white films and when one was in colour, they used to say "In Glorious Technicolor ..." That's what you're like, Glorious Technicolor, to me.'

He stroked Jen's mouse-brown hair, and her pale cheek, he put his arms around her and hugged her to him in her grey cardigan and her grey and lilac skirt. He kissed her lips that had only a little lipstick left, and closed her eyelids that had no make-up, and kissed her on each of them.

'Glorious Technicolor,' he said again.

PULLING TOGETHER

Penny wrote an air letter to her friend Maggie in Australia every week. Every week she wrote about life in the staff room, how Miss Hall had become like a caricature of a schoolmarm, how the children were now *all* delinquents instead of just a steady thirty percent of them. She wrote about the parents, some of them filled with mad hopes and belief that their daughters were going to conquer the world. It was a hard thing to live in a land that seemed to have been ruled forever by a woman monarch and a woman prime minister, Penny wrote, it gave girls notions that they could get anywhere. That was nearly as bad as the old notions, the notions that they could get nowhere.

She wrote about the time passing so quickly that it was quite impossible to believe she was facing her fifth Christmas in this school. If anyone had told her that when she started. If anyone had said that at twenty-seven Penny would have had one job, and one job only, in a girls' school in a city miles from her home. In a small, shabby flat that she had never done up because she had never intended to stay in it. She wrote to Maggie about cold autumn evenings where she stood, hands deep in her pocket, cheering on the hockey team because it showed a bit of school spirit and pleased the games mistress, how she helped at the school play because it was solidarity and how, even now, without a note in her head she would help for the fifth time to organise the carol concert.

She didn't need to tell Maggie *why* she did all these things. Maggie knew. And Maggie was a good friend, she never mentioned it. Not once, not even in the middle of her own air letters about teaching in the bush, about having killed a kangaroo and thinking everyone would be furious but in fact they had congratulated her; about how the school seemed to empty at sheep-shearing time, about Pete the fellow she had a De Facto with. De Facto meant a real proper live-in relationship, it counted if you wanted to become an Australian citizen.

Maggie never inquired why Penny didn't leave if it was all so wearying. Maggie knew about Jack. And she knew enough about Jack not to ask any questions about him. In the first days of the romance Penny had written flowingly about him, about the way Jack had come into her life, suddenly and surely. Knowing that he loved her, knowing that he needed her. Jack had been so sure of everything, Penny felt foolish in her doubts. Doubts about his being married for one thing, about his not leaving home, about his wanting to keep it all quiet.

Jack loved everything about Penny that was funny, he said. Funny, lively, and free. She was so different from the predictable women who all came up with the same self-centred line over and over ... Penny felt that this line had something to do with wondering when, if ever, the man would be free. So that was a road which she had never gone down in the early days. She had sworn to him that she, too, wanted to be free, she couldn't bear the idea of being tied down, she couldn't change her horses in midstream now, she couldn't suddenly, when she passed her quarter-of-the-century mark, tell this man that she wanted a little security. She had picked up Germaine Greer's book *The Female Eunuch* and read again the chapter which said that there is no such thing as security. She willed herself to believe it, and refused to read any articles suggesting that Germaine Greer herself might have had a change of heart.

Because of Jack's position and the fact that he and his wife had to go out to a lot of functions, even though it was all meaningless, of course, and the smiles they had for the cameras were phony and empty ... Penny could tell nobody about their relationship, about how he came to the little flat whatever evenings he could steal and how she had to be there most of the time just in case, and not complain on the many evenings that he had *not* been able to steal time. She had hinted a little of that to Maggie at the start, but Maggie, secure in her De Facto, had been too kind to pursue it. Maggie had simply said that if you loved someone you did, and that was it. You took the package. You couldn't break down the kit and reassemble it, much as *she* would like to reassemble Pete without his insatiable thirst for ice-cold beer! It had been heartening, and Penny hugged the notion to herself when things were bleak, which was more and more of the time.

There had been three years of Christmas Days of loving Jack, and now a fourth was upcoming. They had been the saddest days of her life. Sitting watching gleeful television shows, telephoning her mother and stepfather miles and miles away, assuring them she was happy and thanking them for all the gifts. Fingering whatever scent bottle Jack had given her, and waiting all the time until he could steal the minutes. Last year he had only come for a quarter of an hour. He had pretended he needed to pick something up from his office, he said. The children had insisted on coming, he had left them in the park to play. He couldn't stay.

She had cried for two hours after he had gone. She had put on her dark raincoat and walked past his house later in the afternoon. It was full of lights and Christmas trees and cards on the wall, and mistletoe on the light. Who was that for? The children were too young. But don't ask him. Never let him know that she had seen it.

It had been so very lonely that this year she had decided to go away. To somewhere where there was sunshine, and preferably no Christmas. Morocco she had thought of, or Tunisia. Somewhere Muslim and warm. But Jack had been appalled. Hurt and even a little shocked.

'You must think very little of me, and how I have to go through this façade if you just run away,' he had said. 'We could all do that . . . run away from things. I thought you loved me and that you would be here. Have I ever failed to come and see you at Christmas? Answer me that.'

Penny realised it had indeed been selfish of her. But now that it was the season of fuss and school hysteria, now that the shops had been playing Christmas songs for weeks already and her eyes felt tired from looking at so many pictures of domestic bliss, Penny wished that she had been firmer, wished that she had told Jack in level tones without any catch in her voice that going away for eight days did not mean an end to the love that had consumed her for almost four years and would continue to be the centre of her being forever. She should have been strong enough, and found the words that didn't make it look like a gesture, a hurt little reaction . . . Something from the I-can-stand-on-my-own-feet brigade. But now it was too late. He was going to take her to supper on Christmas Eve, in a new place, very simple, no one he knew or his wife knew would go there. It sounded like a café from what he said, Penny thought glumly. She could imagine herself having sausage and beans and a nice cup of milky tea.

Still, it was better than . . . She stopped and racked her brains to think what it was better than. She looked over at Miss Hall, fifty-five possibly, same old jumper and skirt for years and years, same old shabby briefcase, sitting tucked away in a corner reading her newspapers, face grey, hair grey, outlook grey. Yes, it was much better than being Miss Hall, with her big house that must have been worth a fortune in the square and her lack of interest in anything except being left alone with her precious papers. Penny often wondered what, if anything, she ever read in them, she seemed to have no interest in current affairs, in politicians or in gossip columns. She had not been seen doing crosswords.

There was a knock on the staff room door, it was Lassie Clark. Lassie was one of the pupils that Penny liked least, a big sulky-looking girl with hair deliberately arranged so that it covered most of her face. She had a way of shrugging her disapproval and boredom without even seeming to move her shoulders. Without bothering to move the curtain of hair that hid her eyes and mouth, Lassie muttered that she had been told to report here at three-thirty.

'What was it for this time?' Penny asked. Lassie was one of the familiar faces reporting because of essays not done, excuses not given in by parents, homework unfinished.

'Don't know,' Lassie said. 'Something about an old school pageant, I think. Or else it was something else.'

Penny longed to give her a good hard smack. She must remember to tell Maggie in her next letter that teaching in an all-girls school, working in an all-female staff room, was definitely not natural. It made you mad, sooner rather than later. And in Penny's case, now.

She controlled her urge to attack the girl.

'How old are you, Lassie?' she inquired, her voice overpleasant.

Lassie looked out from the mane of hair suspiciously, as if this were a trick question.

'What do you mean?' she asked.

'Come on now, it's not one of the hard ones.'

'I'm fifteen,' Lassie admitted without any pleasure.

'Good, well by that age *I'm* sure you know what you were asked to report here about; was it the bloody pageant or was it some other goddamned thing? Say which it was and don't have us all here all night.'

Lassie looked up in genuine alarm. The teacher seemed to have lost control.

'It was the bloody pageant,' she said with spirit, knowing she could hardly be corrected about the word since the teacher had used it first.

'Well, what did you do? Not go to rehearsal?'

'Yeah.'

'What a fool you are! What a stupid, foolish girl who can't see further than her own foolish face. Why didn't you go to the rehearsal and get shot of it? Now you have to stay in and spend a half an hour in the classroom writing for no reason, and they'll be looking out for you tomorrow, and they'll probably insist you dress up as a shepherd or an angel or something. Why the hell couldn't you have just gone along with it and stood there like the rest of us have to year after bloody year just because it's easier?'

Penny had never seen Lassie's eyes before – they were quite alert, interested and frightened at the same time.

'I suppose so,' she said grudgingly.

'You can be sure of it. Right, come on, it's my day to take all the rebels, the burning young women protesting against the system.'

'What?' Lassie asked, confused.

'Forget it. I'm as bad as you are. I'll see you down in the hall.'

She went back into the staff room to collect her books and saw Miss Hall. The older woman was looking out of the window at the wet branches.

'Sorry for that outburst,' Penny said.

'I didn't hear you. What happened?'

'Oh, I shouted at Lassie Clark,' Penny explained.

'I wonder why her parents had a child if they wanted a dog,' Miss Hall said unexpectedly.

'Perhaps she made it up herself as a name.'

'No, she was always called that, for the last nine years anyway. I remember when she was in Juniors thinking how silly it was.'

Penny was surprised. Miss Hall wasn't noted for remembering anything about the children.

'Lord, but she's a troublesome child anyway, no matter what she's called,' Penny said. Her voice was down and unlike her normal cheer.

'It's just Christmas,' said Miss Hall. 'It brings everyone down. If I had my way I'd abolish it totally.'

Penny, who had been feeling precisely the same way, didn't think she could agree.

'Oh, come now, Miss Hall, it's lovely for the children,' she said.

'It's not lovely for people like Lassie,' Miss Hall said.

'Nothing would please *her*, spring, summer, autumn, or winter.'

'I think Christmas is particularly hard, we have such high expectations, and it never lives up to them.'

'You sound like Scrooge,' Penny said with a smile to take the criticism out of her voice.

'No, it's true, whoever felt as happy on Boxing Day as on Christmas Eve? Child or adult.'

'That's too gloomy.'

'What about you, you're a cheerful little soul. Since you came here you have always been able to see the bright side, even when there *is* no bright side. But isn't it true what I say? You will have a happier day before Christmas looking forward, than after it looking back.'

Penny had never had a conversation like this with the crabbed Miss Hall before. Definitely Christmas brought out if not the best in people, at least something different.

'Funnily enough, in my case Boxing Day will be better, because then Christmas will be over and I won't have to sit on my own worrying and waiting for it to be over. But I do take your point for other people.'

Miss Hall's eyes rested on her, and she thought she saw tears in them.

Penny had been so brave for years that she bristled at the thought of pity or even a hint of sympathy. 'No, no, I don't want you to feel sorry for me,' she said hastily.

'I don't have time to feel sorry for you, Penny, I feel so sorry for myself there isn't room for anyone else in my sympathy.'

The older woman looked so wretched that Penny, with her hand on the door and about to leave to supervise those girls who had been kept in after school, paused.

'Is there anything I could do . . .?' She was hesitant. Miss Hall was always so sharp and caustic. Even now, having admitted she felt miserable, she would surely somehow turn against any warmth that might be offered to her.

But Miss Hall looked not her usual confident self, she looked as if she were teetering on the brink of saying something, of giving a confidence.

'No . . . thank you . . . you are very kind to ask. But it's not something anything can be done about really.'

'Something can be done about everything,' Penny said with false cheer, as if she were talking to a child.

'Then why can't you do something about *your* Christmas and make it a day to be happy about instead of sitting wishing it was over?' The old teacher spoke with concern, not with malice. There was no way the question sounded offensive.

'I suppose because, in my case, there are things I don't *want* to change. And I have to take what goes with my having made this choice.'

'Yes, that's reasonable, if you know it's something you can cure by choice, then I agree you're right in saying that something can be done about everything.' Miss Hall nodded, as if pleased to have teased out the logic of the thing.

'And in your case?' Penny felt very bold, as if treading on dangerous ground.

'It's not a matter of simple choice, there's something I should have done years ago, or rather not done years ago. But let's leave me for a moment. That poor sulky child, Lassie, I don't suppose she has much choice.'

'She could make herself a bit more pleasant,' Penny complained.

'Yes, but it's not going to affect her Christmas. Pleasant or unpleasant it will still be the same.'

'How do you know?' Miss Hall had never been heard to speak a word about the children, as if they had no lives outside the school wall.

'Oh, the usual way, through the gossip. Her parents are divorcing, her mother is already pregnant by the new chap, her father has already moved into a flat with his girlfriend. The last thing any of them want for the festive season is the big gloomy face of the child they called Lassie lurking around them.'

'So what's she going to do?'

'What can she do? Demand as much attention in each place as she can, make them all feel miserable and guilty. That looks like the form. No amount of being charming is going to bring about what she really wants, which is her old home back again as it was. Solid and safe.'

There was such sympathy in Miss Hall's voice, such understanding. Penny dared to speak again of personal things . . .

'I am on my own at Christmas, as I told you. If there's any way I could come and see you or meet you . . . or . . .' She couldn't ask the woman to her flat in case she would be there when Jack found his stolen half hour. He would be speechless with rage to find an old schoolmarm on the premises. But at least she could offer to go to the old woman's huge terraced house later in the evening, when Jack had gone back to what she considered the bosom of his family and what he described as an empty charade which he had to stay in for the sake of the children until they were old enough to understand.

'No, no, you are very kind.'

'You *said* that already. Why not? *Why* can't I come?' Penny sounded bad-tempered now.

'Because I won't be there. My house is no longer mine. It has had to be sold.'

'I don't believe you. Where are you living now?'

'In a hostel.'

'Miss Hall – is this a joke?'

'It would be a very unfunny one if it were.'

'But why? That was your home for ages I heard, your father and grandfather lived there. Why was it sold?'

'To pay my debts. I'm a gambler, a compulsive gambler. I would like to say I *was* a gambler, but like alcoholism, we must always use the present tense.'

'You can't live in a hostel . . . forever.'

'I may not have to. When the sale of the house is completed I shall probably have enough to get myself something small.'

'But how terrible for you. I had no idea.'

'No, nobody has any idea, nobody except my group . . . you know, the support group, and of course the people I owe money to, they know only too well. It would be disastrous if at this stage the school were to know. I don't think the Head would extend a great deal of seasonal charity and understanding, I'd much prefer if she weren't to find out.'

'No, no, of course,' Penny gasped.

'There can always be some cover story about my selling the house and the pictures, and all the lovely furniture because it was too big for me, too much to manage.'

'Was it horses or cards, Miss Hall?'

Miss Hall smiled. 'Why do you ask?'

'I suppose it's all so unlikely, and I wanted to keep the conversation sort of down to earth rather than getting upset on your behalf.'

Miss Hall approved of this. She gave a wry sort of smile.

'Well, to make it even more unlikely still, let me tell you it was *chemin de fer*.'

'In a club?'

'Yes in a plush club an hour's journey from here by train. Where nobody knows my name. Now you've heard everything.'

Penny realised that she must leave. This minute. There were no parting shots. No sympathetic reassurances. Just close the door behind her.

In the hall, sitting sulkily at her desk, was Lassie. Alone.

'Leave it and go home,' Penny said.

'I can't, I *have* to do it. You said yourself it was silly not to have gone to the thing, I'd better not be done twice.'

'True. I just thought you might like to get home.'

'No point really, no one there,' Lassie said.

'Like me,' Penny said with a grin.

'Yeah, but you chose it, and you're old.'

'No, I didn't choose it, and I'm not old.'

'Sorry.' Lassie managed a half smile.

'Get on with it then, I'll just think something out.'

Penny sat in the big classroom they used as a detention hall. In front of her Lassie Clark struggled with a page and a half of essay, 'Changes in the Neighbourhood,' which nobody would read once it was written. Its only function was to be a punishment.

Penny thought about her mother and stepfather and how it was too late now to go home to them for Christmas even if she wanted to, which she didn't. It would startle them, it would bring back too many memories of the house when Daddy was alive, when she had been a little girl, when there were no problems ahead.

It was too late to go on the trip to a country where there would be no Christmas, only swimming pools and palm trees and buffets in the sun.

But it would not be too late to rescue Christmas if she *chose* to. If she *chose* to open up some of the windows in her heart that Jack had made her close. That she had closed out of blind love for him that was not real love, it was infatuation and fear of losing him.

She thought it all through, slowly, clearly, and without emotion. It would suit them all, but there would be problems, of course, foolish not to face the problems.

There must be no aura of pity about it. No hint of the Last Chance Saloon. If Penny were going to do it, she would spend not one minute of her time trying to keep the peace between the gruff and distant Miss Hall and the sulky, resentful Lassie. She took a deep breath and looked at the child sitting at the desk in front of her. Was it her imagination or had she actually pushed her hair behind her ears? Her face looked if not alert, at least responsive.

'Lassie,' she said.

'Have you thought it all out?' Lassie asked.

'Yes, and I'm going to offer you something. A lot depends on what you say, so listen to me until I've finished.'

'All right,' Lassie said agreeably.

She listened and there was a silence.

'Do you have a nice big flat?' she asked.

'No, it's *not* very nice, I never did much with it, I never thought I'd stay there long, you see. But there is room. A spare room with a sofa bed for Miss Hall, you could bring a sleeping bag and have the sitting room and the telly if you turn it down low. I have my own room.'

'There's ten days before Christmas,' Lassie said impassively.

'Yes. So what?' Penny didn't know whether to be pleased or annoyed that the child was taking it all so matter-of-factly. To be invited to stay with two teachers for Christmas was surely not something that came your way every day.

'I meant we could get it looking nice, paint it up a bit maybe, put up a tree, practice cooking. I don't suppose any of us are much use at that.'

'No.' Penny couldn't hide a smile.

'Will she have any money?' Lassie cocked her head towards the staff room.

'No, I don't imagine so, but I have enough. Nothing luxurious.'

'They'll probably give me some money, I can bring that, I mean they'll be so glad to get rid of me.'

'You can't live with me *forever*, you know, Lassie, just Christmas.'

'That's all right, that's all we'll need each other for,' Lassie said.

'I'll go and tell Miss Hall. I'm sure she'll agree.'

'She'll be mad if she doesn't,' Lassie said sagely.

Miss Hall listened impassively. Penny began to wonder was the world filled with people who took everything very lightly.

'Yes,' she said eventually, 'that would be very nice. I'm glad you told her about my predicament, after all, I told you about hers. So *we're* all right. *You're* the only problem.'

'What do you mean I am the problem?' Penny was so indignant, she could hardly speak. Here she was offering these two misfits a home for Christmas and now suddenly *she* was defined as the one with the problem.

'Well, it must be a man, a married man,' said Miss Hall without any condemnation in her tone. 'And since you haven't had time to discuss this new arrangement for Christmas with him, is there not a possibility that you may regret your invitation to us, or that he'll resent it, or that it will seem somehow the wrong thing to have done?' Miss Hall asked as mildly as she might have asked were there more biscuits with morning coffee.

'No. No, there is no possibility of that. None whatsoever,' Penny said.

'And you mustn't take this kind of thing on every year, dear.' Miss Hall was solicitous. 'You are such a good warm girl, it would be easy to find yourself taking on lame ducks instead of taking on someone undamaged to love them and to be loved back.'

It was said softly and with great warmth, and yet Penny knew she must respond in practical brisk tones.

'You *are* good to say that.' She smiled. 'And of course you're right, it's just one-off, just this Christmas, after that we'll all be cured and ready to get on with whatever there is to get on with.'

She would have plenty to write to Maggie about, and little to say to Jack. Because Jack would know it was no empty gesture, no seeking his attention. Just a sign that she was indeed cured and well on the way to recovery.

A HUNDRED MILLIGRAMS

If you stayed with Helen's mother until Easter, she'd still complain that you were leaving too early after Christmas. So this year they decided to be firm. They would arrive on the Sunday night and they would leave on Thursday. Four nights under her mother's roof and almost four full days. This year, their tenth Christmas together in Mother's house, they would avoid all the pit-falls of other years. They would list them in advance.

There was the cold. Mother's house was freezing. So they would give her a gas heater, one you could buy cylinders for, then she couldn't complain that it was eating electricity or running away with fuel bills since they would provide the cylinders. They would wear warm clothes and take two hot-water bottles each. They would never shiver in public nor would they spend any time at all trying to persuade her to get central heating.

Then there was the matter of drink. They would just provide their own bar up in the bedroom, cunningly disguised as part of their luggage. They would need many more drinks than Mother's sideboard would offer, and they would have to take them in private. Mother was a great one for spotting broken veins, shaking hands, signs of liver damage where none existed. Then there was Mother's advice. They would listen to it with blank, polite faces. This year they would not rise to the bait, this year they would not be drawn into an argument they couldn't win. They would say to themselves and each other as soon as they woke, the tips of their noses freezing in that igloo of a bedroom ... they would say, 'Mother is not technically very old. But Mother has always had the mind of an old woman. She will not change so we must change and not allow ourselves to be hurt by her.' They would chant that at each other. Then surely it couldn't be too bad.

And indeed it wasn't too bad. This tenth Christmas was a lot better than the ones that had gone before. The house was warmer for one thing, and they had invited neighbours in for sherry and mince pies at intervals. That cut down on the amount of time left for Helen's mother to shake her head sadly and say she didn't know what the world was coming to, and that values had all changed and not for the better.

It was Thursday morning. Today they were going to leave. They had planned to take Mother out to lunch. The boot of the car would be packed already. They would drop her home after the meal in the hotel and they would fly off home, guilty but free, and this year congratulating themselves on having kept the peace.

Helen leaned over and gave Nick a kiss. He reached for her but she leapt smartly out of bed. That was another thing that you couldn't do in Mother's house. It felt wrong, you had the notion she could come in the door at any time. Anyway there was plenty of time for all that back home.

'I'll make us a cup of tea instead,' she said.

'All right,' Nick grumbled.

Her mother was in the kitchen. 'Wouldn't you think he'd get up and get you a cup of tea.' There was a hard, thin line of discontent. Helen reminded herself to watch it, she must not allow herself to become defensive, she must let no note of anything mutinous into her voice.

'Oh, we take it in turns,' she said lightly.

'A lot else he has to do. Any man in his position should be glad to make you tea and take it up to you – honoured to be allowed to make you tea.'

'Look, while I'm here why don't you go back to bed too and I'll bring you a cup.'

'No, I'm up now. I might as well stay up. It's back to normal for me now that you have to go. I thought you were going to stay till the

New Year at least, and Miss O'Connor was saying that she was surprised ...'

'Yes, she has a great capacity for being surprised, I've noticed that,' said Helen, banging out the cups and saucers. Then she remembered. Only five more hours. Be nice, be calm. Nobody except us gets hurt in the end.

'Did she have a nice Christmas herself, Miss O'Connor I mean?' she asked in staccato tones.

'I've no idea. She goes to a sister. It's all she has.'

The kettle was taking an age to boil.

'Does he lie in bed all day at home now? Does he get dressed at all?'

Calm, Helen. Slow. Fix on the smile. 'Oh, we usually get up about the same time, you know. One day I make the breakfast, the next day he does. Then we take Hitchcock for a walk and I get the bus; Nick gets a paper and goes home.' Her voice was bright and sunny, as if she were telling a tale of an ideal lifestyle.

'And has he turned his hand to cooking even?'

'Oh yes indeed. Well, you saw over Christmas how much he likes to be involved with everything.'

'He only carried plates in and out, from what I could see.'

The kettle must have two holes in the bottom of it, no container ever took three hours to boil. Helen smiled on and fussed with a tray.

'Trays, is it? There used to be a time when two mugs of tea did fine in the morning.'

'You have such nice things here, it's a pity not to use them.'

'I suppose he can't wait to get his hands on them altogether. I saw the way he was admiring that cabinet. Fetch a good price, he said.'

'I think Nick was trying to reassure you, Mother. You said that you had no possessions, no antiques. Nick was pointing out to you that you do have nice pieces of furniture.'

'He's in a poor position to point anything out, a man who did what he did. I wouldn't thank him for pointing things out to me.'

'That would be a pity, Mother.' There was steel in her voice. Helen knew she was on the thinnest ice yet. Usually it had been hint and innuendo. Now it was being said straight out.

'No I mean it, Helen, to humiliate you and me. To make us the object of pity here. Don't think that everyone doesn't know.

Everyone knows. It's only because I have always been on my own, always had to bear the burden, that I'm able to do it again.'

'I don't think it's a humiliation for me or for you that Nick has been made redundant. All over the country people are being laid off work. The one it's worst for is Nick, and we're lucky that we have something coming in. And that we don't have five children like some of his colleagues have.'

'Well, that's another thing. Ten years married and no children, just a dog with a ridiculous name, Hitchcock. Who would call a dog a name like that?'

'We thought it was a nice name, and we love him. And we don't inflict him on you, now do we? He's in a kennel, looking out, waiting for us.'

Wrong. Wrong. She shouldn't have said that. It showed an eagerness to be away. Too late to try to retrieve it. Was that actually a sound out of the kettle, did it intend to boil after all?

'I don't know how you put up with it, Helen, you who had everything. I really don't know how you take it all, instead of having some spirit.'

'If I could get Nick a good job in the morning there's no one who'd be more delighted than myself.' She had the smile of a simpleton on her face now, willing her mother to drop the conversation, to go no farther down the path where she was leading.

'I don't mean just about the job. I mean about the other thing,' her mother said. And now it was said, it had to be acknowledged.

'Yes?' Polite, interested, but giving nothing away.

'Don't yes me, Helen, you know what I mean. The woman. Nick's woman.'

'Oh yes, well, that's all over now.' Still light, no evidence of the heavy lump of putty gathering in her chest.

'What do you mean it's over? It's not like Christmas that it's here and then it's gone. It's not simple like that.'

'It is really, Mother, that's exactly what it is.'

'But how can you let him away with it? How can you bear him with you after ... after all that?'

'Nick and I are very happy, we love each other, that was just something that happened. It was a pity that people got to know about it but they did.'

The kettle had boiled. She scaled the teapot.

'And you go on as if nothing has happened, after all that.'

'What is the alternative, Mother? Just tell me. What else would you like me to have done? What would you have liked, Mother, if I had asked you?'

'I'd like for it never to have happened.'

'So would I, so would I, and I think so would Nick and so would Virginia. But it did happen.'

'Is that her name, Virginia?'

'Yes, that's her name.'

'Well, well. Virginia.'

'But tell me, Mother. I'm interested now, what would you like me to have done? Left him? Got a barring order? Tried to get an annulment? What?'

'Don't raise your voice at me. I'm only your mother who wants the best for you.'

'If you want the best for me, then stop torturing me.' Helen's eyes filled with tears. She went upstairs with the tray of tea. 'I've blown it,' she sobbed to Nick, 'on the last bloody morning I've blown it.'

He laid her head on his shoulder and patted her until the sobs ceased.

'Let's put some brandy in our tea,' he said, 'and get back under the covers before you become a relic of the Ice Age.'

It would have been nice if nobody had known about Virginia, Helen knew. She had known from the start, but she had said nothing. She thought that it would not last. Virginia was young and pretty and silly and worked in Nick's office. That kind of thing happened all the time, very very rarely did it break up people's marriages. If the wife was sensible and kept her head. Only confrontations were dangerous, and why make a perfectly decent, honourable man like Nick be forced to choose between his practical wife, Helen, and the pretty little Virginia? Why not take no notice and hope that Virginia found some other man? That is precisely what would have happened and was about to happen, and it would all be past history if it hadn't been for the accident.

It was two Christmases ago and there was Nick's office party. Helen had begged him not to take the car. The place would be full of taxis. Why have the responsibility? They had argued good-naturedly about it at breakfast. They worked out milligrams, how many would make you drunk. They agreed that they could both drive a car perfectly after four times the permitted amount, but that some people couldn't so that was why the rules had to be so strict and the limit made so absurdly low. He had promised that if they all got really bad, he would leave the car there and sneak in for it the next morning. Helen knew that his romance with Virginia was coming to an end, she had been happier then than for a long time before.

She realised that Nick wasn't staying out so late, there were fewer furtive phone calls. She congratulated herself on having weathered the storm.

At seven o'clock Virginia had telephoned her very drunk and tearful. Virginia had asked her to be especially nice to Nick over Christmas because Nick was a wonderful person, a really wonderful person, and would need a lot of consolation. Helen agreed, grimly thinking that the only thing worse than being sober and receiving a telephone call from a drunk was to be the wife receiving a telephone call from the mistress. The combination of the two was heady stuff.

A little later Nick had phoned saying he hoped that some of the girls hadn't phoned her saying anything silly. Helen said it was all incomprehensible but please don't drive home. Nick said he had to take this silly girl home, she was making a fool of herself. He hung up before Helen could beseech him to get a taxi.

Nick had told her later that the drive was something he would remember for the rest of his life. The drive rather than the accident.

The streets seemed to be full of tension and danger, the lights of every car were hostile, there were drivers peering through windscreens in the rain, there were unseasonal hootings, and abuse was hurled in a most unfestive manner.

Beside him Virginia, who had been sick, was sobbing and clutching at his arm. She hadn't meant to telephone Helen, but it came over her that Helen should be informed. Earlier that day she had told Nick she was going away for Christmas with someone else. Now she seemed full of regrets and second thoughts, she wanted reassurance that she had done the right thing at every turn. Nick was concentrating hard on the road and didn't answer, she pulled his arm and the car swerved into the left lane right into the path of a big truck.

Virginia lost two teeth, broke her shoulder, and cracked two ribs.

Nick lost his driving license for three years, the firm lost the car, but since it also lost Nick and most of his colleagues some months later that wasn't very important. The case went on and on, and insurance companies provided more and more explanations on each side, and Virginia gave an interview to a paper about how her chances of matrimony might well be lessened by her facial injuries and referred to having a fling with a married man in her office, a married man who had managed to destroy her life completely. Somewhere in the world there is always someone who sees things in papers and brings them to the attention of other people, and somewhere there was somebody who managed to send it to Mother's friend Miss O'Connor, with the name of the firm and the coincidence of the accident and everything they thought Helen's mother should know.

For two years she had managed not to speak aloud about it, only making allusions. But this morning it had come out. And Helen hadn't been ready. 'I'm sorry,' she snuffled into her brandy-flavoured tea. 'You've been so marvellous, and now I've thrown it all away. She'll sulk during lunch, and it's all been wasted.'

Nick warmed his ice-cold hands on the nice cup of tea and brandy and stared ahead of him. Downstairs they could hear Helen's mother banging the furniture about a bit. It was a message as clear as any drumbeat in a jungle, a message that she was annoyed and upset and that things would not be easy when they got up.

'If only we didn't have to come here. Just one Christmas, the two of us on our own with Hitchcock,' Helen said wistfully.

Nick's eyes seemed misty, she thought, or was the early morning's brandy making her feel a bit dizzy.

'I wonder how many milligrams there are in this tea?' she asked. More to cheer him up than anything else. He turned and looked at her. She had been right, there were tears in his eyes.

'Remember that plate you broke here years and years ago?' he said.

She was surprised. 'Yes, the one that Mother made such a fuss about.'

'Well, we mended it, remember, you held bits of the plate with an eyebrow tweezers and I painted on the glue.'

'And you couldn't see the cracks in the end.' She wondered why he was thinking of this, it had happened years ago, just another occasion when her mother had behaved badly and Nick had smoothed it out.

'But when it was done she wanted to use it at once and we had to say no and put it high, high up so that it would have time to harden. It looked all right but it wasn't really. You couldn't use it. Touch it and it would all fall apart.'

'Yes, we put it in one of those little plate stands?' There was a question in her voice. What was he talking about?

'If anyone came into the room and looked at that plate, they'd have said to themselves that it was a perfectly sound plate, they'd have no reason to think otherwise. But it wouldn't have been. Not until the glue hardened. It was fine in the end, of course, but for a long time it was only pretending to be a real plate.'

'Well, yes.'

'It's a bit the same here, isn't it? We've been pretending to be real plates in front of your mother. We won't let her see any of the cracks or the glue or anything. We've been putting on such a brave face for her. We've not stopped to ask ourselves is it real or is it not?' He had rarely sounded so serious.

'Yes, I suppose it was a way to go. We could have endless discussions and analyses, and what happened and why, and where did we go wrong, but I don't know. Would it have made things much better?'

'It might have been more honest. You might have wanted to throw me out but couldn't, not with us having to put on an act all the time for your mother, pretend that this was the successful lovey-dovey marriage of the century.'

'Well, it's been a pretty good marriage most of the time, hasn't it?' Helen said.

'Is that you talking or is it you talking for your mother's ears?'

'It's me talking, do you not think the same?'

'I do, but I'm the villain, the cheat, the partner without a job, the drunk driver, I'm in no position to make definitions.'

'Oh Nick, don't be so ridiculous, what's over is over. I said that ages ago.'

'No, you've got too used to pretending, you're being too tolerant . . .'

'Listen to me.' Her face flashed with anger. 'When my mother attacks you I feel a sense of loyalty to you so strong it almost sweeps me away, when she says one word against you I become so fiercely protective you would never believe it. Perhaps she has done some good for us in that way, because her every attempt to drive us apart only glues us together.'

'Is it real glue, is it good firm glue, do you think, or are we only pretending to get along fine?'

'I don't know how you test these things. We could go downstairs and fling the plate on the floor, for example, and if it broke we could say, "Boo hoo the plate wasn't properly stuck together."'

He looked very pleased. 'In a way your bad-tempered old mother has a lot to be thanked for. She stopped us making any decision before the glue had hardened. It has hardened, hasn't it, Helen?'

There was an almighty banging downstairs. The noise had increased in case it wasn't being heard. Nick and Helen got up and tore the linen off the bed they wouldn't have to sleep in that night. They heaved the furniture round the room for pure devilment and realised that for them there would be nothing gained by examining the cracks and pulling them to see if they would come apart. Other people might want to talk it to death, but they knew the face they had shown the difficult woman downstairs was a real face, and they only had four more hours of putting slightly phony smiles on it. The kinds of smiles a million other people were putting on their faces like children's masks over Christmas.

THE CHRISTMAS
BARAMUNDI

She had met him first at the fish market on Christmas Eve. It was very early in the morning, but already crowded. Their hands touched as they each pointed to the same ocean perch.

'That one,' they said at the same time.

They all laughed, Janet the schoolteacher, Liam the banker, and Hano the younger son of the fish merchant.

'You have it,' Liam said gallantly.

'No, no, you were the first,' Janet countered.

Hano said, 'He has many brothers and sisters, you can have one each.'

'I don't like to think of his brothers and sisters,' Janet said.

'I know, but we're very hypocritical, aren't we?' Liam had a crinkly smile that lit up his face.

'Who was it said they could never eat anything that had a face?' Janet looked thoughtfully at the slabs of fish, each one with a very definite face, some of them indeed with expressions that you could almost define.

'Hey, you'll have us eating bread and cheese for Christmas,' he said.

Janet sighed. 'No, that's the problem, point out all the disadvantages about something and then go ahead and do it all the same.'

'Mine's different, I favour the ostrich technique; pretend things don't have faces, or brothers and sisters. Just grill them and eat them.'

'Poach them surely, or cook them in foil. This is much too big to grill.' Janet took things literally.

'Have coffee with me,' Liam said suddenly.

Hano wrapped their fish for them. Janet paid in cash, Liam used a gold credit card. He took her by the elbow and they went to where people drank small cups of coffee and ate delicious Italian bread. Hano waved them goodbye. He would love to have gone with them, to have talked and laughed as they did so easily. Instead he would have his father's eye on him and his uncles' and the eyes of his two older brothers. This was one of the busiest days of the year. He should be working, reaching out towards customers, not dreaming.

More and more people bought fish for Christmas Day. Going to the market in Pyremont was now almost a tradition. The customers enjoyed the experience as much as the fish they bought. Look at that couple, for example: the man was rich, he had a jacket that Hano would have to work for five years to earn. His watch was gold. He didn't even look at the docket he signed. He surely didn't *need* to come here and buy fish; someone could have got it for him. Perhaps he was lonely; maybe he had a fight with his wife. Possibly he was a bachelor or a divorced man. He must be about thirty-five or forty.

Janet was asking herself all these questions, too, as they went together for coffee.

But by the time they were sipping their espresso and eating the warm foccacia she didn't care if he was married or single, if he had twenty people waiting at home for him or nobody. He was just so easy to talk to. They sat on high stools and talked about Christmas Eve in other lands. Liam had been in New York some years, always a wet cold day. He remembered coming out of his office and trying to join the throngs getting last-minute gifts in stores where a million others had the same idea. They took such short vacations in New York City. Not like here in Sydney, where the world closed down for weeks.

'Well, it is our summer holidays,' Janet said, a trifle defensively. She was always apologising for the long school vacations that teachers enjoyed. Her other friends said her life was a holiday. But their lives weren't filled with shrill young voices, clamouring young personalities, and the need to be on stage from the moment the first bell rang to the last. Of course, she had never wanted to be anything else but a teacher, she told Liam, and she told him about a Christmas she had spent in France that was meant to improve her French but actually had only improved her interest in wine.

And then they talked about wines they both liked, and around them people wandered around the fish counters and water gushed through the drains and lumps of ice that hadn't yet melted fell to the ground. They talked, Liam and Janet, with the excitement of people getting to know each other and afraid to ask the question that might nip it all before it got started. Each was buying a fish large enough to feed a family. Neither wore a ring, but that meant nothing. They each noticed that the other was in no hurry to go home, but again that might have no significance. When their third set of empty coffee cups was taken away they could pretend no longer.

'I suppose I'll have the shakes if I drink any more,' Liam said.

'Me too.' Janet looked glum suddenly.

'What's wrong?' he asked.

'I wish sometimes that I could get out of that school-girl habit of saying *me too*, and *me first*. It's the only downside of working with children; you start talking like them.'

'Do you have children?' His question was sudden and direct.

'About two hundred and eleven at last count,' she said, and then as if trying to make up for being flippant, added, 'but I say goodbye to them each day at four o'clock.'

'I see.' He seemed pleased.

'And you?' She hoped her voice sounded light.

'About ninety at last count, but that's only in the bank,' he said. And she knew that he left them behind when he left the bank too.

'I see.' She was very pleased. She might have to fight a woman for him, but no adorable little toddlers who needed their Daddy.

They had been there for a long time.

'Would you like to meet again?' he asked simply.

'Yes please,' she said. It was a jokey thing to say. It hid her eagerness, her great relief. Would he ask her phone number? Would he give her his? When would he suggest? Janet felt the breath almost choke her.

'So what do you suggest?' he asked. He was leaving the decision to her.

'I think saying *same place, same time, next year* is a bit on the long finger.' She looked at him with her head on one side, waiting. Janet hated women who behaved like this, but she felt she had to. It was the only alternative to letting him see the eager longing in her face to see him again, to get to know him better.

'Oh, I hope to know you very well by this time next year,' he said softly. 'Very well indeed.'

Janet felt herself shiver. It was the kind of shiver that her mother said meant someone was walking over your grave.

'Well then,' he said. 'Well then.' He suggested a restaurant, he suggested lunchtime three days later.

'Will they be open?' Janet asked. She didn't want to risk their missing each other.

'Oh yes, they'll be open.'

They looked at each other as if there was still something more to be said. He picked up a brochure advertising all the different kinds of fish that were on sale and tore a piece off. It had a picture of a baramundi. He quickly wrote some figures.

'In case you change your mind,' he said.

She tore another baramundi off and wrote her number.

'In case you change yours,' she said.

'No, it's the highlight,' he said, with a mock bow of his head.

'I look forward to it,' Janet said, and skipping the puddles of water made from the hosing of the fish stands, she made her way to her car. She turned around to look back once, and he was still standing there. She wondered why they hadn't wished each other Happy Christmas. Everyone else was saying that to people that they had only just met. Perhaps it was because they each believed the other had something to do at Christmas, something to unpick or sort out.

Janet shared a house with three other teachers. They each had a large sunny room that acted as their own bed-sitting-room. They had a huge shared kitchen and two bathrooms. They had a small garden with four sun beds placed around it. Everyone said they were mad to rent this expensive property. They could each have found a deposit and a mortgage for a house of their own, but at this point none of them wanted that. And they got on very well together for women in their twenties and thirties. They didn't live each other's lives. They paid a woman to come in once a week to clean, nobody kept their television up too high, and if lovers were invited into people's rooms, it was not discussed, nor was anything untoward ever audible. They always laughed about their living arrangement, calling it Menopause Manor. But they could do that because it was far from the truth.

This year none of them had gone away for Christmas. They would eat together in their garden. There were various reasons. Janet had a new stepmother; she wanted to give the woman a breathing space before descending on her for holiday festivities. Maggie had a married lover who was not available for Christmas Day. Kate was writing her thesis and had decided to give it three solid weeks of six hours a day in Menopause Manor. Sheila was from Ireland; sometimes she flew the whole way back there, but this year she had not saved the money and couldn't find the enthusiasm for rain and sleet, so she too was staying in Sydney. It would be a happy, undemanding day for the four of them. They would be unsentimental, probably a little tipsy. They would not mention Maggie's man, and the futility of it all; they would not make Sheila sad about the Emerald Isle by singing 'Danny Boy'; they would be supportive about Kate's MA thesis; and they wouldn't know that Janet had just met the most marvellous man in the whole world, so they could have no attitudes about it.

On Christmas Eve, Janet sat out in the garden; the night was warm and smelled of flowers. She could hear the sea in the distance. She wondered where he was at this moment, the man called Liam with the crinkly smile, who said he was in banking. He had not said he worked in a bank; that was a subtle difference. It was ten o'clock. The telephone rang. Although she felt sure it must be from Ireland for Sheila, Janet went to answer the call.

'Janet?'

'Liam?' she said immediately.

'Just thought I'd wish you Happy Christmas. We forgot to do that today.'

'So we did. Happy Christmas,' and although she hated waiting, she managed not to say any more.

'Have you still got the baramundi?' he asked.

'Yes, yes indeed.' Another pause.

'Have a happy day,' he said.

'You too.'

They hung up. Janet went back to the garden and hugged her knee as she looked up at the starlit sky. She knew exactly why she had been so unforthcoming. She wanted to be allowed to dream over this Christmas. She wanted to think of Liam and his smile, and the fact that he had been thinking of her at ten o'clock on Christmas Eve night. She did *not* want to hear about his wife and children if they existed, or his longtime live-in lover who understood him, or his messy divorce. She wanted to think of him as a man who was looking forward to seeing her in three days time. A man who could talk about anything and who understood everything. A man who said that this time next year they would surely know each other very well.

She sat and hugged her secret to herself. She had not been in love for six years. Not since she was twenty-two. Since then there had been people, but nothing that counted as real love. She had forgotten how utterly wonderful it felt; how silly and feathery and quite unconnected with the real world. She heard bells ring and she knew there must be church services. She heard merry-makers calling good night down the street. It was Christmas Day.

There was no breeze, but still she shivered. That was the second time today. For no reason Janet remembered her mother helping to zip her into her first formal dress on her eighteenth birthday.

'I'm so happy,' Janet had said, looking delightedly at her reflection in the mirror.

'You'll never be as happy as you are now this minute,' her mother had said. Janet had been furious. Her mother had taken all the gold and glitter away from the moment. And she had never forgotten it, even though her mother had been wrong.

Janet had been happier than on her eighteenth birthday. When she was twenty-one she had fallen in love with Mark and been happy for fourteen months, every day and every night. Why did she have to remember her mother's words now, the words of a woman who was never truly happy, who always saw the bleak side? Too much laughter meant tears before bedtime, too much good weather meant headaches later on, people being nice and warm and welcoming meant that sooner or later they would prove to have feet of clay.

Janet's mother had been dead for four years. Her father had married again; a different kind of woman, small and round and giggling. Janet couldn't understand what they saw in each other, but that was not remotely important. Maybe they found what she and

Liam had found, however unlikely it seemed. After all, her father had met Lilian at a television studio where they were both members of a studio audience, and now they were married. Janet had met Liam at the fish market this morning, and he had told her that this time next year they would know each other very well indeed. He had just telephoned to wish her Happy Christmas. The good times were only starting.

On Christmas Day the others said that Janet must have had some attitude-changing substance. She had a funny, happy smile all day. Janet made the salads, set the table in the garden, baked the potatoes, and chilled the wine. Not the most domesticated of the four in the household, she insisted on doing it all this time. She cooked the ocean perch lovingly. This was a fish that Liam had touched with his own hand. This was a fish they had laughed over, a fish that brought them together.

The day seemed curiously long; happy but long. Janet thought that it must be seven o'clock when it was still only five o'clock. Somehow the time passed. And then it was the morning. The morning of the lunch. Janet realised that she had shadows under her eyes because she had slept so poorly. She was placing far too much hope on this, too much importance, reading more into it than there was. Very probably, but it still didn't make her sleep. There was no hairdresser open so she shampooed her hair and spent hours trying to get into the kind of shape she wanted. She had planned to wear her peach-coloured shirt and a grey denim skirt, but she thought it made her look as if she had stepped from the chorus of *Oklahoma!* It was too hot for a jacket, too smart a place for a beach dress. Janet had been wearing jeans when she met him at the fish market. She wanted him to know she had other clothes.

By the time she had settled on a tartan skirt and plain white T-shirt, it was time to call the taxi. The taxi was late. Janet was red-faced and anxious when she arrived at the restaurant.

'I ordered us oysters,' he said, his eyes anxious to know if he had done the right thing.

Normally Janet hated the pushy male thing of ordering for the little woman. But he was trying to be generous, to make a gesture. She smiled such a smile, her face nearly broke in half.

'What could be better?' she asked.

The lunch was like their coffee break at the fish market only better. They talked about the world of banking and how hard it was for Liam to meet real people anymore. Instead he met corporate people and committees and read reports and acted on them. And Janet told him eagerly about school and how there was no time to get to know the children and find out what they really wanted to do, and what they were like and what they hoped for. Instead you had to follow a curriculum, and get them to pass exams, and achieve a good result for the school.

They couldn't finish the prawns, the sauce was too rich. As they pushed them around their plate he said unexpectedly.

'Will you spend the afternoon with me?'

'Yes, of course, where?' she asked.

'I have a place.'

Her smile was broad again. He couldn't be married or tied up or have a whole complicated lifestyle that he was cheating on. Not if he said he had a place.

'Oh, really?' Janet said, face full of hope and eagerness.

'Well yes, I booked, just in case, just in case you'd say yes,' he said.

It was a motel. A place you book. He had been so sure of her, he had thought it worthwhile to make a reservation. Her heart felt heavy, and her face must have shown it.

'Something's wrong,' Liam said.

'No, not at all.' Her smile was brave and his came back. He was so simple, really, and straightforward. He had liked her, liked her enough to invite her to lunch, to call her on Christmas Eve, to order oysters, to book a place for the afternoon, to be with her. Perhaps *she* was the selfish one, she was the one demanding commitment, assurances that he was available, and a catch, and maybe even a meal ticket. She was a liberated woman. Janet knew you could meet and enjoy each other as equals if you wanted to. The days of demanding that a man be a protector or a provider were long gone.

'So shall we stop pretending to eat these prawns?' he asked with a laugh.

'I've given up the struggle,' she agreed.

They drove to the motel. A place Janet had often passed and wondered idly how it made a living. Now she knew; they rented by the hour. It was clean and functional. He had a bottle of wine in a cool bag that he had brought with him, another sign that he had known she would agree to the motel, and he poured her a glass. It was a good wine from a vineyard they had talked about, but today it tasted like vinegar. He was a gentle and courteous lover, and he lay afterwards with his arm around her shoulder, protectively, as if they had often lain like this before and would for many more years. Her heart lifted for a while. Perhaps this is the way people were nowadays. Behaviour had changed. You didn't have to play games, pretend to be hard to get, exchange sexual favours for continued attention, trade sex for commitment.

'I got you a little gift, a silly thing,' he said, and he reached out for a wrapped parcel that he had on the bedside table. She couldn't have loved him more. She was glad that she hadn't played at being outraged when he suggested an afternoon in a motel.

'What is it?'

No present she had got this Christmas could compare. It was a little tin fish, the kind of thing you might hang on a Christmas tree or, if it had a magnet, it could be stuck to the refrigerator door.

'It's a baramundi,' he said, pleased with what he saw as her pleasure. 'To remind you of when we met pointing at that fish and fighting over it, and then becoming friends.' His arm was around her again, squeezing tightly.

'Great, great friends,' he said, appreciatively. She turned over the little fish in her hand.

'It's great,' she said. She knew her voice was flat, her pleasure was not real.

'Well, it's a jokey gift,' he said, embarrassed.

'No, it's great.' She wanted to be a million miles from here. Why had she not taken her car? She tried to remember. It had something to do with being available for him. Well, she had been that all right. In spades. Now she would have to ask him to drive her to somewhere near her home or to a taxi rank. It would be squalid. But she would not let it be that way. If only she could guard herself, not say anything foolish.

'Where does your wife think you are?' Janet heard herself ask.

He looked as if she had hit him, but he rallied.

'She didn't ask. I didn't say.'

'And your children?'

Why was she asking these things, ruining what was good between them.

'They're in the pool. They don't know where I am. I work such long hours they don't expect me to be around.'

He had answered her truthfully. He had asked her nothing in return.

They left the bed where they had been so happy, so close, and she noticed he took a very long time having a shower. As if he had been to a sports club or a gym. He passed her a clean towel when she went into the shower, and she held it for a long time to her face to force away the tears that she thought might come.

In the car he was still boyish and happy. But he was so intelligent, surely he must know that whatever they had was over? He asked where she lived and she suggested that he leave her in Balmain.

'No, no, door-to-door service,' he laughed, then looking at her face, realised it might be crass. He patted her on the knee.

'I didn't mean to be flip. It was lovely,' he said.

'Yes indeed.' She tried, but she couldn't put any life into her words.

He drove her to the gate. Out in the back garden Maggie might have been half sleeping in the sun, dreaming of her married man who could not leave his family at this festive time. Kate would be in her room studying. Sheila might have gone to play tennis and beat back the guilt about not having gone home to Ireland for Christmas Day. None of them would know that Janet's heart had cracked in two.

Liam was looking at her.

'Will we meet again?' he asked; his face was enthusiastic. He liked talking to her, laughing with her, holding her, making love with her. He couldn't see any reason why it could not go on, as sunnily and easily as it had begun.

Struggling to be fair, Janet couldn't see any reason either, except that she knew it was over.

'No, but thank you, thank you all the same,' she said.

He looked at her sadly.

'Was it the fish? Was it the little Christmas baramundi?' he asked anxiously.

'Why do you say that?' Janet asked.

His face was troubled.

'I thought you'd like it. I thought it was silly and sentimental and not commercial. I could have got you a pin, a brooch or something for five hundred dollars, but I thought it looked wrong somehow.'

'The fish is great,' Janet said.

'And we did meet over a baramundi,' he said.

'Or something,' Janet said.

There was a silence. Liam looked at the house.

'It's a nice place to live,' he said, as if trying to bequeath her a good life.

'Oh yes, it is.' She realised he didn't know. He had never asked if she lived with a man, a husband, or children. He just assumed she was a free spirit who could live life in compartments as he could.

'Has it a garden at the back?' They talked like strangers now, like people at a cocktail party.

'Yes, a small garden. Do you know, Liam, I was happier there on Christmas Eve than I ever was in my life, and than I ever will be again.' She knew her voice was very intense and that he was looking at her uneasily. But somehow it was a great relief to have something defined. They said that women became more like their mothers as they grew older.

Janet shivered. She felt that she was becoming very like her mother. Soon her face would tighten in a hard smile. What a pity there was nobody she could talk to about it. The man who was saying goodbye at her gate was someone who might have understood, had things been different.

THIS YEAR IT WILL BE
DIFFERENT

❧ ❦

Ethel wondered had it anything to do with her name. Apart from Ethel Merman there didn't seem to be many racy Ethels; she didn't know any Ethels who took charge of their own lives.

At school there had been two other Ethels. One was a nun in the Third World, which was a choice, of course, but not a racy choice. The other was a grey sort of person, she had been grey as a teenager and she was even greyer in her forties. She worked as a minder to a selfish personality. She described the work as Girl Friday; it was, in fact, Dogsbody, which scanned perfectly, and after all, words mean what you want them to mean.

These were no role models, Ethel told herself. But anyway, even if it weren't a question of having a meek name, a woman couldn't change overnight. Only in movies did a happily married mother of three suddenly call a family conference and say that this year she was tired of the whole thing, weary of coming home after work and cleaning the house and buying the Christmas decorations and putting them up, buying the Christmas cards, writing them and posting them so that they would keep the few friends they had.

Only in a film would Ethel say that she had had it up to here with Christmas countdowns, and timing the brandy butter, and the chestnut stuffing, and the bacon rolls, and bracing herself for the cry 'No sausages?' when a groaning platter of turkey and trimmings was hauled in from the kitchen.

She who had once loved cooking, who had delighted in her

family's looking up at her hopefully waiting to be fed, now loathed the thought of what the rest of the world seemed to regard as the whole meaning of Christmas.

But there would be no big scene. What was the point of ruining everyone else's Christmas by a lecture on how selfish they all were? Ethel had a very strong sense of justice. If her husband never did a hand's turn in the kitchen, then some of the blame was surely Ethel's. From the very beginning she should have expected that he would share the meal preparation with her, assumed it, stood smiling, waiting for him to help. But twenty-five years ago women didn't do that. Young women whooshed their young husbands back to the fire and the evening newspaper. They were all mini-Superwomen then. It wasn't fair to move the goalposts in middle age.

Any more than it was fair to stage a protest against her two sons and daughter. From the start those children had been told that the first priority was their studies. Their mother had always cleared away the meal after supper to leave them space and time to do their homework, or their university essays, or their computer practice. When other women had got a dishwasher, Ethel had said the family should have a word processor. Why should she complain now?

And everyone envied her having two strong, handsome sons around the house, living with her from choice. Other people's twenty-three- and twenty-two-year-olds were mad keen to leave home. Other women with a nineteen-year-old daughter said they were demented with pleas about living in a bed-sitter, a commune, a squat. Ethel was considered lucky, and she agreed with this. She was the first to say she had got more than her fair share of good fortune.

Until this year. This year she felt she was put upon. If she saw one more picture of a forty-seven-year-old woman smiling at her out of a magazine with the body of an eighteen-year-old, gleaming skin, fifty-six white, even teeth, and shiny hair, Ethel was going to go after her with a carving knife.

This year, for the first time, she did not look forward to Christmas. This year she had made the calculation: the thought, the work, the worry, the bone-aching tiredness on one side of the scales; the pleasure of the family on the other. They didn't even begin to balance. With a heavy heart she realised that it wasn't worth it.

She didn't do anything dramatic. She didn't do anything at all. She bought no tree, she mended no fairy lights, she sent six cards to people who really needed cards. There was no excited talking about weights of turkey and length of time cooking the ham as in other years. There were no lists, no excursions for late-night shopping. She came home after work, made the supper, cleared it away, washed up and sat down and looked at the television.

Eventually they noticed.

'When are you getting the tree, Ethel?' her husband asked her good-naturedly.

'The tree?' She looked at him blankly, as if it were a strange Scandinavian custom that hadn't hit Ireland.

He frowned. 'Sean will get the tree this year,' he said, looking thunderously at his elder son.

'Are the mince pies done yet?' Brian asked her.

She smiled at him dreamily.

'Done?' she asked.

'Made, like, cooked. You know in tins, like always.' He was confused.

'I'm sure the shops are full of them, all right,' she said.

Ethel's husband shook his head warningly at Brian, the younger son.

The subject was dropped.

Next day Theresa said to the others that there was no turkey in the freezer, nor had one been ordered. And Ethel turned up the television so that she wouldn't hear the family conference that she knew was going on in the kitchen.

They came to her very formally. They reminded her of a trade union delegation walking up the steps to arbitration. Or like people delivering a letter of protest at an embassy.

'This year it's going to be different, Ethel.' Her husband's voice was gruff at the awkward unfamiliar words. 'We realise that we haven't been doing our fair share. No, don't deny it, we have all discussed it and this year you'll find that it will be different.'

'We'll do all the washing-up after Christmas dinner,' Sean said. 'And clear away all the wrapping paper,' added Brian. 'And I'll ice the cake when you've made it. I mean after the almond icing,' Theresa said.

She looked at them all, one by one, with a pleasant smile, as she always had.

'That would be very nice,' she said. She spoke somehow remotely. She knew they wanted more. They wanted her to leap up there and then and put on a pinny, crying that now she knew they would each do one chore then she would work like a demon to catch up. Buzz, buzz, fuss, fuss. But she didn't have the energy, she wished they would stop talking about it.

Her husband patted her hand.

'Not just words, you know, Ethel. We have very concrete plans and it will begin before Christmas. Actually it will begin tomorrow. So don't come into the kitchen for a bit, we want to finalise our discussions.'

They all trooped back to the kitchen again. She lay back in her chair. She hadn't wanted to punish them, to withhold affection, to sulk her way into getting a bit more help. It was no carefully planned victory, no cunning ploy.

She could hear them murmuring and planning; she could hear their voices getting excited and then shushing each other. They were trying so hard to make up for the years of not noticing. Yes, that is all it was. Simply not noticing how hard she worked.

It just hadn't dawned on them how unequal was the situation where five adults left this house in the morning to go out to work and one adult kept the house running as well.

Of course, she could always give up her job and be a full-time wife and mother. But that seemed a foolish thing to do now, at this stage, when the next stage would be the empty nest that people talked about. They were all saving for deposits, so they didn't really give her much, and they were her own children. You couldn't ask them for real board and lodging, could you?

No, no, it was her own fault that they hadn't seen how hard she worked and how tired she was. Or hadn't seen until now. She listened happily to the conversation in the kitchen. Well, now they knew, God bless them. Perhaps it hadn't been a bad thing at all to be a bit listless, even though it hadn't come from within, it wasn't an act she had put on.

Next morning they asked her what time she'd be home from work.

'Well, like every day, around half-past six,' she said.

'Could you make it half-past seven?' they asked.

She could indeed, she could have a nice drink with her friend Maire from work. Maire, who said that she was like a mat for that family to walk on. It would be deeply satisfying to tell Maire that she couldn't go home since the family were doing all the pre-Christmas preparations for her.

'You could always go to the supermarket.' Theresa said.

'Am I to do any shopping?' Ethel was flustered. She had thought they were seeing to all that.

She saw the boys frown at Theresa.

'Or do whatever you like, I mean,' Theresa said.

'You won't forget foil, will you?' Ethel said anxiously. If they were going to do all this baking, it would be awful if they ran out of things.

'Foil?' They looked at her blankly.

'Maybe I'll come back early and give you a bit of a hand ...'

There was a chorus of disagreement.

Nobody wanted that. No, no she was to stay out. It was four days before Christmas, this would be a Christmas like no other, wait and see, but she couldn't be at home.

They all went off to work or college.

She noticed that the new regime hadn't involved clearing away their breakfast things, but Ethel told herself it would be curmudgeonly to complain about clearing away five cups and saucers and plates and cornflake bowls and washing them and drying them. She wanted to leave the kitchen perfect for them and all they were going to do.

She wondered that they hadn't taken out the cookery books. She would leave them in a conspicuous place, together with all those cookery articles she had cut from the paper and clipped together with a big clothes-peg. But she must stop fussing, she'd be late for work.

Maire was delighted with the invitation to a drink after work. 'What happened? Did they all fly off to the Bahamas without you or something?' she asked.

Ethel laughed; that was just Maire's way, making little of the married state.

She hugged her secret to herself. Her family who were going to do everything. Things were exciting at the office, they were all going to get new office furniture in the new year, the old stuff was being sold off at ridiculous prices. Ethel wondered would Sean like the computer table, or would Brian like the small desk. Nothing would be too good for them this year. But then, did secondhand goods look shabby, as if you didn't care?

With the unaccustomed buzz of two hot whiskeys to light her home, Ethel came up the path and let herself in the door.

'I'm back,' she called. 'May I come into the kitchen?'

They were standing there, sheepish and eager. Her heart was full for them. While she had been out drinking whiskey with lemon and cloves in it, stretching her legs and talking about the new office layout with Maire, they had been slaving. Poor Maire had to go back to her empty flat, while lucky Ethel had this family who had promised her that things would be different this year. She felt a prickling around her nose and eyes and hoped that she wasn't going to cry.

She never remembered them giving her a treat or a surprise. This is what made this one all the better. For her birthday it had been a couple of notes folded over, from her husband a request to buy herself something nice. Cards from the children. Not every year. And for Christmas they clubbed together to get her something that the house needed. Last year it had been an electric can opener. The year before it had been lagging for the cylinder.

How could she have known that they would change?

They looked at her, all of them waiting for her reaction. They wanted her to love it, whatever they had done.

She hoped they had found the candied peel – it was in one of those cartons without much identification on it, but even if they hadn't she'd say nothing.

She looked around the kitchen. There was no sign of anything baked or blended or stirred or mixed or prepared.

And still they looked at her, eager and full of anticipation.

She followed their eyes. A large and awkward-looking television set took up the only shelf of work space that had any length or breadth in it.

An indoor aerial rose from it perilously, meaning that the shelves behind it couldn't be got at.

They stood back so that she could view the full splendour of it.

Sean turned it on with a flourish, like a ringmaster at a circus. 'Da-daaaaa!' he cried.

It was black-and-white.

'Terribly sharp image,' Sean said.

'More restful, really, on older eyes, they say,' Theresa soothed her.

'And you wouldn't need more than RTE 1 anyway, even if you could get it. I mean, too much choice is worse than too little,' said Brian.

'I *told* you this Christmas was going to be different to the others.' Her husband beamed at her.

From now on she could look at television as well as the rest of them; she'd be as informed and catch up on things and not be left out, just because she had to be in the kitchen.

All around her they stood, a circle of goodwill waiting to share in her delight. From very far away she heard their voices. Sean had known a fellow who did up televisions, Dad had given the money, Brian had gone to collect it in someone's van. Theresa had bought the plug and put it on herself.

Years of hiding her disappointment stood to Ethel at this moment. The muscles of her face sprang into action. The mouth into an ooooh of delight, the eyes into surprise and excitement; the hands even clasped themselves automatically.

With the practiced steps of a dancer she made the movements that they expected. Her hand went out like an automaton to stroke the hideous, misshapen television that took up most of her kitchen.

As they went back to wait for her to make the supper, happy that they had bought her the gift that would change everything, Ethel got to work in the kitchen.

She had taken off her coat and put on her pinny. She edged around the large television set and mentally rearranged every shelf and bit of storage that she had.

She felt curiously apart from everything, and in her head she kept hearing their voices saying that this Christmas was going to be different.

They were right, it felt different; but surely it couldn't be on account of this crass gift, a sign that they wanted her forever chained to the kitchen cooking for them and cleaning up after them.

As she pricked the sausages and peeled the potatoes it became clear to her. They had done something for her for the very first time – not something she wanted, but something; and why? Because she had sulked. Ethel hadn't intended to sulk, but that's exactly what it had been. What other women had been doing for years. Women who had pouted and complained, and demanded to be appreciated. By refusing to begin the preparations for Christmas, she had drawn a response from them.

Now, what more could be done?

She turned on the crackling, snowy television and looked at it with interest. It was the beginning. She would have to go slowly, of course. A lifetime of being a drudge could not be turned around instantly. If, as a worm, she was seen to turn too much, it might be thought to be her nerves, her time of life, a case for a nice chat with some kind, white-coated person prescribing tranquillisers. No instant withdrawal of services. It would be done very slowly.

She looked at them all settled inside around the colour television, satisfied that the Right Thing had been done, and that supper would be ready soon. They had no idea just how different things were indeed going to be from now on.

SEASON OF FUSS

Mrs Doyle used to begin fussing around October. There was so much to do. The Christmas cakes, the puddings, getting everything out. It drove her children up the wall and down again, particularly since they weren't children anymore. They were grown-ups.

It would start when she realised that she had lost Theodora's recipe for the cake, and everything would be turned out on the table. This would reveal new horrors – letters not replied to, knitting patterns that had been promised to friends. All was in disorder, all was confusion, and the very mess that was created served as further proof of how much there was to be done.

'I bought her an album for her recipes,' wailed Brenda. 'I even started clipping them out and putting them in for her, but she actually takes them out again and loses them. It's too bad.'

Brenda's own flat was something that a business efficiency expert would envy. She was always able to retrieve Theodora's recipe for the cake or the latest posting dates to America. She would photocopy them for her mother, but it only seemed to add to the fuss. Mrs Doyle would speculate about where she could possibly have put the originals.

Her other daughter, Cathy, used to have to lie down with cold compresses on her eyes after any hour of Mrs Doyle's fussing about the Christmas dinner. To Cathy it was the simplest meal in the whole year. You put a bird into the oven and when it was cooked, you took it out and carved it and ate it. There were potatoes, sprouts, bread sauce, and stuffing to consider, but honestly, unless you were about to throw in the towel, you shouldn't be frightened of that lot. Mrs Doyle would go through her schedule over and over, planning all she should do the night before, and what time she should get up. It was as if she were in charge of mission control in Cape Canaveral instead of lunch for her two daughters and son and two extra spouses. It was a meal for six, not a space shuttle.

Michael Doyle said that he sometimes wanted to lie down on the floor and not get up until Christmas was over when his mother began to talk about the cost of everything. In vain would he urge her not to worry about the price of things. She only had to pay for a turkey and some vegetables. She would have made the pudding and the cake well in advance. Brenda, Cathy, and Michael provided all the wine and the liqueur chocolates, the little extras like a tin of biscuits, or packets of crisps, or a spare set of lights for the Christmas tree to cope with the annual failure of the bulbs to glow.

They all went away drained, back to their houses weary and tense, the spirit of Christmas snuffed out by the buzzing and bustling of the woman who was unable to relax and enjoy the family that gathered around her for Christmas Day.

It was Brenda who decided that this year should be different. Brenda was single and successful at her work and allowed to be a little more bossy than the others. In fact, it was a role she was almost meant to play, and this year she played it for all it was worth.

Cathy had a small baby to think of, a gorgeous five-month-old boy who would be no trouble to anyone, who would sleep peacefully through the hurricane of fuss downstairs, if only Mrs Doyle would allow him to. Cathy was tired this year, unused to the wakeful nights. She should not have to go through all this business with their mother. And Michael's wife, Rose, was pregnant, so she too must not be stressed out by this restless, unsettling atmosphere. She should be allowed tranquillity and a chance to talk about birth and babies to her sister-in-law, Cathy.

In September, Brenda decided on her plan of action. They told Mrs Doyle that as a treat *they* would cook the Christmas meal. Cathy would make the cake, Rose would make the puddings, and on the day Brenda could cook the main course. Mrs Doyle was to put her feet up. They would find a Christmas tree for her and decorate it. They would even buy her Christmas cards well in advance and get the stamps so that she did not have to queue for hours at the post office. Mrs Doyle protested. No, they all said, you've been doing it long enough for us; just this once for a change let us do it instead.

Coming up to Christmas they wondered why this had never occurred to them before. Mrs Doyle was calmer than any of them remembered her having been in her whole life. Sometimes she would begin sentences of urgency, but then she would remember that she had no great onerous duties this year so she would fall silent again. They all lived near enough for her to have a visit from one of them almost every day, and Brenda, Cathy, and Michael congratulated themselves and each other on having reduced the level of fuss by eighty percent. She still worried about icy roads, and whether she had put enough stamps on the calendar she had sent to her cousin, but that kind of thing was just literally incurable. They had cured all that was available for cure. On Christmas Eve the house looked festive. They had put up a tree, bigger and much better decorated than before. Michael and Brenda had enjoyed doing that, they laughed and poured themselves small vodka-and-oranges. It was like being children again. Cathy had come and decorated the room with holly.

Brian had tacked it up high so that it didn't fall down and scrape people's foreheads, as often happened when Mrs Doyle had tried to shove small spiky bits behind pictures. They had bought cheerful red paper napkins and colourful crackers. Michael had seen to it that there were plenty of briquettes to keep the fire going and an extra box of firelighters. They had set the table for lunch before they left. They kissed Mrs Doyle and looked forward to the happiest Christmas yet.

She walked around the warm, neat house. Brenda had taken the opportunity of doing a little tidying, as well as just getting things ready for the next day's meal. The saucepans that held the potatoes and sprouts were shinier, the turkey with its chestnut stuffing, and sausage-meat stuffing as well, was covered with foil. She was to put it in the oven at eleven a.m. That was all she had to do. Perhaps she might look through that kitchen drawer and sort out some of those old recipes. It would please Brenda to see them in that album. But fancy that! Brenda had already stuck them in for her. The drawers were suspiciously tidy, and though she couldn't actually pinpoint anything that was missing, she felt that a lot of things must have been thrown out.

She would tidy up the food cupboard so that it would impress them when they helped with the washing-up. It was very tidy, actually, and nice clean paper lining the shelves. That was new, surely. Yes, that must have been what Cathy and Rose were doing as they laughed about babies and backache and insisted that Mrs Doyle sit in at the fire out of their way. And her tea towels had all been washed and were stretched over chairs, so that they would be crisp and dry for tomorrow, and a tray had been set for her own breakfast, the boiled egg she would have when she came back from Mass and waited for them to come. Waited doing nothing after she had made the big journey to the oven to put in the turkey at eleven a.m. The day would be so peaceful, compared to other years. They were very good to her, her children. Very good indeed.

She sat down by the fire and thought about James. She even took down his photograph from the mantelpiece and looked at it hard. This was her twelfth Christmas without him. He would only be sixty-two if he were alive, the same age as she was. It wasn't old. A lot of their friends had been older than they were and both husband and wife were still alive. It was far too young to have been twelve years a widow at sixty-two. James shouldn't have died like that. They had hardly had time to say anything to each other and he was gone. Her eyes filled with tears as she heard carol singers going by. Christmas was very hard on widows and people who lived alone.

She was determined not to let her eyes get puffy for tomorrow. Her daughters would peer at her suspiciously and interrogate her.

No. She would remember the good bits of when James was alive; how excited he had been when the children were born; how he had bought drinks for total strangers when his first daughter arrived, and ran around to the neighbours knocking on their windows at the birth of his first son. How he had told everyone of their successes, the number of honours in their exams, the unfairness of Michael's not getting that job because of somebody else's pull. She would think of him coming back from work laughing. She wouldn't think of those last months with the pain and the bewilderment in his eyes, and the constant question, and the constant lying reply. 'Of course you're not going to die, James, don't be ridiculous.'

Somehow this Christmas it was harder to put things out of her mind. She couldn't think why. But it was.

They arrived, arms full of presents, up and down the street people saw that Mrs Doyle was loved and cared for by her children. They saw she had a bright Christmas tree in her window, and they may even have noticed that her brasses were nice and shiny. Brenda had given them a surreptitious rub when her mother wasn't looking.

The lunch was effortless. Their mother sat in her chair, the baby upstairs slept happily through it all, and Michael and Rose talked happily of next Christmas when their own baby would come to the feast. Brenda was the life and soul of the party and said that she had serious designs on a widower who had recently come to the office, and if she played her cards right she might bring him home for Christmas next year.

They all agreed that it had been the happiest Christmas they had spent.

'Since your father died,' Mrs Doyle said.

'Of course,' Michael said hastily.

'Naturally we meant that,' Cathy said.

'Obviously, since Daddy died, that's what we meant,' Brenda said.

They were surprised. Normally she never mentioned Daddy at Christmas, but she didn't seem upset. It was as if she was saying it for the record.

This time they didn't all rush home. The washing-up was done in relays, with others staying by the big roaring fire talking to Mrs Doyle. There was some television viewing, a walk for everyone except Cathy and Rose, who minded one baby and talked about the next.

There was tea and cake, and much later a small plate of cold turkey with some of Brenda's excellent homemade bread. They all said he would be a lucky widower if Brenda trapped him.

They were gone and the house was warm and tidy still. The wrapping paper had been folded up and stored in the bottom of the dresser. Mrs Doyle could never decide other years whether they should keep it or not; this year the decision had been made for her. Her presents were all on the sideboard. Perfume, talcum, a pen and pencil set, a subscription to a magazine, a hand-embroidered cover for the *RTE Guide*, a bottle of oranges in Grand Marnier, gifts to a woman who was always remembered at Christmas. Why did they make her feel a little uneasy? Perhaps it was the list beside them. Brenda had written out who had given her what. So that there would be no confusion, Brenda had said, when writing to thank. Well, yes. It was useful, of course, but she was sixty-two not ninety-two. They didn't have to put a bib around her neck and feed her. They didn't talk baby language to her. Why write down who gave her what? She had little enough to hold in her mind today. She might have enjoyed thinking over who gave which gift.

Normally Mrs Doyle went to bed exhausted on Christmas night. This year she sat on long at the fireplace and took down the picture of Jim again and wondered why if God was so good, as the priest had said this morning, he had let Jim suffer for all those months and be so frightened and then let him die. She found no answer to the problem, only guilt at thinking badly of God. She went to bed and lay with her eyes open in the dark for what felt like a long time.

They all dropped in over Christmas week. This had always been the way, they would pop in and out as they felt like it. Usually she would fuss and say she had been about to make scones, but this year it was organised like some military campaign. When Rose and Michael came in the morning, they took her a plate of ham sandwiches just in case anyone dropped in. Then when Cathy and Brian came in the afternoon, hey presto, there was their tea! And Cathy brought a bottle of something that was lemon and cloves and whiskey, you just added hot water. So, lo and behold, when Brenda came by there was a nice unusual little snack for her to try.

But they all thought that something was wrong somewhere. Their mother was too quiet. It wasn't natural for her to be so quiet. She didn't speak until somebody spoke to her. She didn't have any views or complaints or in fact anything at all much to say.

They conferred with each other. It didn't look like flu. She assured them she had no pains and aches. They began to notice it on Stephen's Day and on Thursday it was still there. By Saturday she was positively taciturn.

Brenda worked it out. She had nothing to fuss about, but she also had nothing to do. The central core of their mother's life had become fuss, like the epicentre of a hurricane. Take that away and she was left with nothing. The others wondered was Brenda being too extreme. After all, it had been a wonderful Christmas.

'For us,' Brenda said darkly. 'For us it was.'

On Saturday afternoon she called to see her mother. She had given her no warning and there was nothing prepared. She waited patiently until her mother revved up the fussing batteries and got into the mood where she would sigh and groan and complain about shops being open and not being open and how you never knew which they would be. Brenda nodded in sympathy. She did not produce food from her own well-stocked freezer and larder, as she had been about to do. She allowed the fuss to blow up into a good-sized storm.

Then she played her trump card.

'Are you going to the sales?' she asked. 'They're always so crowded, so hard to decide what to get.'

Mrs Doyle showed a flicker of enthusiasm.

'I don't know why we do it,' Brenda said. 'They're real torture, but on the other hand there are great bargains. Now would you think that it's best to go in first thing on the very first morning with the queues, or do you think that it's better to wait till the rush has died down a bit?'

She was rewarded. Life, a sort of life, had come back to Mrs Doyle's face again. She entered eagerly into the confusion of it all, the exhaustion, the value and the lack of value, the problem of knowing what was rubbish just brought in for the sale and what was a genuine bargain, and as she went to rummage and find the pieces of paper she had cut out during the year about things that would be good value if they were reduced by a third, Brenda sighed and realised that the Season of Fuss had returned and all was well again despite the setback of the perfect Christmas.

'A TYPICAL IRISH
CHRISTMAS . . .'

Everyone in the office wanted to ask Ben for Christmas. He was exhausted trying to tell them that honestly he was fine.

He didn't look fine, he didn't sound fine. He was a big sad man who had lost the love of his life last springtime. How could he be fine? Everything reminded him of Ellen. People running to meet others in restaurants, people carrying flowers, people spending a night at home, a night away.

Christmas would be terrible for Ben.

So they all found an excuse to invite him.

For Thanksgiving he had gone to Harry and Jeannie and their children. They would never know how long the hours had seemed, how dry the turkey, how flavourless the pumpkin pie, compared to the way it had been with Ellen.

He had smiled and thanked them and tried to take part, but his heart had been like lead. He had promised Ellen that he would try to be sociable after she was gone, that he would not become a recluse working all the hours of the day and many of the night.

He had not kept his promise.

But Ellen had not known it would be so hard. She would not have known the knives of loss he felt all over him as he sat at a Thanksgiving table with Harry and Jeannie and remembered that last year his Ellen had been alive and well with no shadow of the illness that had taken her away.

Ben really and truly could not go to anyone for Christmas. That had always been their special time, the time they trimmed the tree, for hours and hours, laughing and hugging each other all the while. Ellen would tell him stories about the great trees in the forests of her native Sweden, he told her stories about trees they bought in stores in Brooklyn, late on Christmas Eve when all the likely customers had gone and the trees were half price.

They had no children, but people said this is what made them love each other all the more. There was nobody to share their love but nobody to distract them either. Ellen worked as hard as he did, but she seemed to have time to make cakes and puddings and to soak the smoked fish in a special marinade.

'I want to make sure you never leave me for another woman . . .' she had said. 'Who else could give you so many different dishes at Christmas?'

He would never have left her and he could not believe that she had left him that bright spring day.

Christmas with anyone else in New York would be unbearable. But they were all so kind, he couldn't tell them how much he would hate their hospitality. He would have to pretend that he was going elsewhere. But where?

Each morning on his way to work he passed a travel agency that had pictures of Ireland. He didn't know why he picked on that as a place to go. Probably because it was somewhere he had never been with Ellen.

She had always said she wanted the sun, the poor cold Nordic people were starved of sunshine, she needed to go to Mexico or the islands in winter. And that's where they had gone, as Ellen's pale skin turned golden and they walked together, so wrapped up in each other that they never noticed those who travelled on their own.

They must have smiled at them, Ben thought. Ellen was always so generous and warm to people, she would surely have talked to those without company. But he didn't remember it.

'I'm going to Ireland over Christmas,' Ben told people firmly. 'A little work and lot of rest.' He spoke authoritatively, as if he knew exactly what he was going to do.

He could see in their faces that his colleagues and friends were pleased that something had been planned. He marvelled at the easy way they accepted this simplistic explanation. Some months back if a collegue had said he was doing business and having a rest in Ireland, Ben would have nodded too, pleased that it had all worked out so well.

People basically didn't think deeply about other people.

He went into the travel agency to book a holiday.

The girl at the counter was small and dark, she had freckles on her nose, the kind of freckles that Ellen used to get in summer. It was odd to see them in New York on a cold, cold day.

She had her name pinned to her jacket – Fionnula.

'That sure is an unusual name,' Ben said.

'Oh you'll meet dozens of them when you go to Ireland, if you go,' she said. 'Are you on the run or anything?'

Ben was startled, it wasn't what he had expected.

He had handed her his business card with a request that she should send him brochures and details of Irish Christmas holidays.

'Why do you ask that?' he wanted to know.

'Well, it says on your card that you're a vice-president, normally they have people who do their bookings for them. This seems like something secret.'

She had an Irish accent and he felt he was there already, in her country where people asked unusual questions and would be interested in the reply.

'I want to escape, that's right, but not from the law, just from my friends and colleagues – they keep trying to involve me in their holiday plans and I don't want it.'

'And why don't you have any of your own?' Fionnula asked.

'Because my wife died in April.' He said it baldly, as he had never done before.

Fionnula took it in.

'Well, I don't imagine you'd want too much razzmatazz then,' she said.

'No, just a typical Irish Christmas,' he said.

'There's no such thing, any more than there's a typical United States Christmas. If you go to one of the cities I can book you a hotel where there will be a Christmas programme, and maybe visits to the races and dances, and pub tours . . . or in the country you could go to somewhere with a lot of sports and hunting – or even maybe rent a cottage where you'd meet nobody at all, but that might be a bit lonely for you.'

'So what would you suggest?' Ben asked.

'I don't know you, I wouldn't know what you'd like, you'll have to tell me more about yourself.' She was simple and direct.

'If you say that to every client you can't be very cost effective; it would take you three weeks to make a booking.'

Fionnula looked at him with spirit. 'I don't say that to every client, I only say it to you, you've lost your wife, it's different for you, it's important we send you to the right place.'

It was true, Ben thought, he had lost his wife. His eyes filled with tears.

'So you wouldn't want a family scene then?' Fionnula asked, pretending she didn't see that he was about to cry.

'Not unless I could find someone as remote and distant as myself, then they wouldn't want to have anyone to stay.'

'Isn't it very hard on you?' she said, full of sympathy.

'The rest of the world manages. This city must be full of people who lost other people.' Ben was going back into his shell.

'You could stay with my dad,' she said.

'What?'

'You'd be doing me a huge favour if you did go and stay with him, he is much more remote and distant than you are, and he'll be on his own for Christmas.'

'Ah, yes, but . . .'

'And he lives in a big stone farmhouse with two big collie dogs that need to be walked for miles every day along the beach. And there's a grand pub a half a mile down the road, but he won't have a Christmas tree because there'll be no one to look at it but himself.'

'And why aren't you there with him?' Ben spoke equally directly to the girl Fionnula, whom he had never met before.

'Because I followed a man from my hometown all the way to New York City, I thought he'd love me and it would be all right.'

Ben did not need to ask if it had been all right, it obviously had been nothing of the sort.

Fionnula spoke. 'My father said hard things and I said hard things, so I'm here and he's there.'

Ben looked at her. 'But you could call him, he could call you.'

'It's not that easy, we'd each be afraid the other would put the phone down. When you don't call that could never happen.'

'So I'm to be the peacemaker.' Ben worked it out.

'You have a lovely kind face and you have nothing else to do,' she said.

The collie dogs were called Sunset and Seaweed. Niall O'Connor apologised and said they were the most stupid names imaginable chosen by his daughter years back, but you have to keep faith with a dog.

'Or a daughter,' Ben the peacemaker had said.

'True, I suppose,' Fionnula's father said.

They shopped in the town and bought the kind of food they would like for Christmas, steak and onions, runny cheese, and up-market ice cream with lumps of chocolate in it.

They went to midnight Mass on Christmas Eve.

Niall O'Connor told Ben his wife had been called Ellen too; they had a good cry together. Next day as they cooked their steaks they never mentioned the tears.

They walked the hills and explored the lakes, and they called on the neighbours and they learned the gossip of the neighbourhood.

There had been no date fixed for Ben's return.

'I have to call Fionnula,' he said.

'She's your travel agent,' Niall O'Connor said.

'And your daughter,' said Ben the peacemaker.

Fionnula said New York was cold but back in business, unlike Ireland which had presumably closed down for two weeks.

'It went great, the typical Irish Christmas,' Ben said. 'I was about to stay on and have a typical Irish New Year as well . . . so about the ticket . . .?'

'Ben, your ticket is an open ticket, you can travel any day you like . . . why are you really calling me?'

'We were hoping that you could come over here and have a quick New Year with us,' he said.

'Who was hoping . . .?'

'Well, Sunset and Seaweed and Niall and myself to name but four,' he said. 'I'd put them all on to you but the dogs are asleep. Niall's here though.'

He handed the phone to Fionnula's father. And as they spoke to each other he moved out to the door and looked at the Atlantic Ocean from the other side.

The night sky was full of stars.

Somewhere out there two Ellens would be pleased. He took a deep breath that was more deep and free than any he had taken since the springtime.

TRAVELLING HOPEFULLY

~·≈ ≈·~

They were full of envy at the office when Meg told them she was going to Australia for a month on December 11.

'The weather,' they said, 'the weather.'

She would miss the cold, wet weeks in London when the streets were so crowded the traffic was at a standstill, when people were fussed and it was also so commercialised.

'Lucky Meg,' they said, and even the younger ones, the girls in their twenties, seemed genuinely jealous of her. This made Meg smile to herself.

Even though she was fifty-three, which didn't feel terribly old, she knew that most of the people she worked with thought she was well over the hill. They knew she had a grown-up son in Australia, but because they knew he was married they weren't interested in him. That, and because he didn't come back home to visit his mum. Married or single they would have been interested had they only seen her handsome Robert. Robert who had been captain of his school, who got so many A levels. Robert, aged twenty-five and married to a girl called Rosa, a Greek girl that Meg had never met.

Robert wrote and said the wedding would be quiet, but it didn't look very quiet, Meg thought, when she got the photographs. There seemed to be dozens and dozens of Greek relatives and friends. Only the groom's family was missing. She tried hard to keep her voice light when she asked him about this on the telephone. He had been impatient, as she had known he would be.

'Don't fuss, Mum,' he had said – as he had said since he was five years old and appeared with blood-soaked bandages around his knee.

'Rosa's people were all here, you and Dad would have had to come thousands of miles. It's not important. You'll come someday when we all have more time to talk.'

And, of course, he had been right. A wedding where most of the cast spoke Greek, where she would have to meet Gerald, her ex-husband, and probably his pert little wife, and make conversation with them ... it would have been intolerable. Robert had been right.

And now she was off to see them, to meet Rosa, the small dark girl in the photographs. She was going to spend a month in the sunshine, see places that she had only seen in magazine articles or on television. They would have a big party to welcome her once she had got over the jet lag. They must think she was very frail, Meg decided; they were giving her four days to recover.

Robert had written excitedly: they would take Meg to the Outback, show her the real Australia. She would not be just a tourist seeing a few sights, she would get to know the place. Secretly she wished he would have said that she could sit all day in the little garden and use the neighbours' swimming pool. Meg had never known a holiday like that. For so many years there had been no holiday at all, as she saved and saved to get Robert the clothes, the bikes, and the extras that she hoped would make up for the fact that he was missing a father. Gerald had done nothing for the boy except to unsettle him about three times a year with false promises and dreams, and then gave him a battered guitar which had meant more to the boy than anything his mother had worked so hard to provide. It was while playing his guitar during his year in Australia that he had met Rosa and discovered a love and a lifestyle that were going to be forever, he told his mother.

In Meg's office they clubbed together and bought her a suitcase. It was a lovely light case, far too classy for her, she thought. Not at all the case for someone who never made a foreign journey. She could hardly believe it was hers when she checked it in at the airport. The plane was crowded, they told her, this time of year all the rellies were heading down under.

'Rellies?' Meg was confused.

'People's grannies, you know,' said the young man at the desk.

Meg had wondered whether Rosa might be pregnant. But then they would never be heading for the Outback, wherever it was. She must not ask. She steeled herself over and over not to ask questions that she knew would irritate.

They settled into the plane and a big square man beside her put out his hand to introduce himself.

'Since we're going to be sleeping together in a manner of speaking, I think we should know each other's names,' he said in a broad Irish accent. 'I'm Tom O'Neill from Wicklow.'

'I'm Meg Matthews from London.' She shook his hand, and hoped he wouldn't want to talk for the next twenty-four hours. She wanted to prepare her mind and practice not saying things that would make Robert say 'Don't fuss, Mum.' In fact, Tom O'Neill from Wicklow was an ideal neighbour. He had a small chess set and a book of chess problems. He perched his spectacles on his nose and went methodically through the moves. Meg's magazine and novel remained unopened on her lap. She did a mental checklist. She would *not* ask Robert what he earned a year, whether he had any intention of returning to the academic studies he had abandoned after two years of university, when he went to find himself in Australia and found singing in cafes and Rosa instead. Meg told herself over and over that she would say nothing about how infrequently he telephoned. She wasn't aware that her lips moved as she promised that she would allow no words of loneliness or criticism to escape.

'It's only a bit of air turbulence,' said Tom O'Neill to her reassuringly.

'I beg your pardon?'

'I thought you were saying the Rosary. I wanted to tell you there was no need. Save it till things get really bad.'

He had a nice smile.

'No, I don't say the Rosary actually. How does it work?'

'Irregularly, I would say, like maybe one time out of fifty, but people are so pleased when it does, they think it works all the time and they forget the times it doesn't.'

'And do you say it?' she asked.

'Not nowadays, I did when I was a young fellow. Once it worked spectacularly. I won at the horses, the dogs, and poker. All in one week.' He looked very happy at the memory.

'I don't think you were meant to pray about those kinds of things. I didn't think it worked for gambling.'

'It didn't in the long run,' he said ruefully, and went back to his chess.

Meg noticed that Tom O'Neill drank nothing and ate little; he had glass after glass of water. Eventually she commented on it. The meals were one of the few pleasures of long-haul flying, and the drink would help sleep.

'I have to be in good shape when we arrive,' he said. 'I've read that the secret is buckets and buckets of water.'

'You're very extreme the way you take things,' Meg said to him, half admiring, half critical.

'I know,' Tom O'Neill said, 'that has been the curse and the blessing of my life.'

There were still fifteen hours to go. Meg didn't encourage any stories of his life. Not so early in the trip. When they had only four hours left she began to ask him about his life. It was a story of a daughter who had been wild. Once the girl's mother had died, Tom hadn't been able to control her. The girl had done what she liked when she liked. Now she was living in Australia. Not just staying there, mind, but living there. With a man. Not a husband, but what they called a De Facto. Very liberal, very modern, his daughter living with a man openly and telling the Australian government this too, proud as punch. He shook his head, angry and upset by it all.

'I suppose you will have to accept it. I mean coming all this way, it would be a bit pointless if you were to attack her about it,' Meg said. It was so easy to be wise about other people's business.

She told him in turn about Robert, and how she hadn't been invited to the wedding. Tom O'Neill said wasn't it a blessing? She'd have had to make conversation with her ex and a lot of people who hadn't a word of any language between them. Much better to go now. What was a wedding day? It was only a day – not that he seemed likely to be having the opportunity of seeing one in his circumstances.

His daughter was called Deirdre, a good Irish name, but now she signed herself Dee, and her man friend was called Fox. What kind of name was that for a human being?

The blinds were raised. They had orange juice and hot towels to wake them up. Meg and Tom felt like old friends by this stage. They were almost loath to part. As they waited for their luggage they gave each other advice.

'Try not to mention their wedding day,' Tom warned.

'Don't say anything about the living-in-sin bit. They don't think that way here,' she begged.

'I wrote out my address,' he said.

'Thank you, thank you.' Meg felt guilty that she hadn't thought to write her son's address. Perhaps it was because she did not want Robert to think she was pathetic, picking up a strange Irishman on the plane and giving him her phone number.

'I'll leave it to you then ... to get in touch or whatever,' he said, and she could sense the disappointment in his voice.

'Yes, yes, what a good idea,' Meg said.

'It's just a month is a long time,' he said.

Earlier they had both told each other that it was a very short time. Now they were on Australian soil and both of them slightly nervous of meeting their children ... it seemed too long.

'It's in Randwick,' Meg began.

'No, no, you ring me if you'd like a cup of coffee someday. Maybe we could have a bit of a walk and a chat.'

He looked frightened. The endless glasses of water had left him in no state to deal with a man called Fox on equal terms. He didn't look like a man who was going to remember that his daughter called herself Dee and that she thought she *was* married, a De Facto being more or less the same. Meg felt protective of him.

'Certainly I'll call you. In fact, I think we will both possibly need to escape a little from the culture shock,' she said.

She knew she looked anxious. She could feel the frown developing on her forehead, the squeezing of her eyebrows together which made people at work say that Meg was getting into a tizz, and made her son beg her to stop fussing. She wished she could go on talking to this easy man. Why couldn't they sit down on chairs and talk for an hour or so, get themselves ready for a very different kind of Christmas than they had ever had before, and for a different lifestyle.

She realised suddenly that this was what they were both doing. They were coming to give their blessing to new lifestyles. Tom was here to tell Dee that he was glad she had found Fox and he didn't mind about their not being married properly. She was here to tell

Robert that she couldn't wait to meet her new daughter-in-law and all her family, and not to hint that she ever gave her absence from their actual wedding day a thought. It would be good to meet Tom again and to know how it was all going. If they had been old friends, then obviously they would have done, but being single and middle-aged and having just met on the plane it would call for many more explanations. Possibly Robert would pity her. Or else Rosa would think that it was wonderful, perhaps, that Mother had actually found herself a bloke on a plane trip. In either case it would have been embarrassing.

'I thought I might tell Deirdre, *Dee*, her name is Dee. Lord God, I must remember her name is Dee,' Tom began.

'Yes?'

'I thought I might tell her that you and I were friends from way back. You know?'

'I know,' she said, with a very warm smile.

They could have said more, a great deal more. In fact, they needed to find out a bit more about each other if they were meant to be friends. But it was too late. They were wheeling their trolleys through the passage to where a crowd of sun-tanned, healthy-looking young Australians waited for the crumpled rellies to stagger from the long journey. And people were calling and crying out and raising children up in the air to wave. And it seemed to be the middle of summer.

And there was Robert in shorts with long, suntanned legs and his arm around the neck of a tiny little girl with huge eyes and black curly hair biting her lip anxiously as they raked the crowd to find Meg; and when they saw her, Robert shouted, 'There she is!' as if nobody else had travelled all those hours on the plane, and they were hugging her and Rosa was crying.

'You are so young, too young to be a grandmother,' she said, and patted her little tummy with such pride that Meg started to cry too. And Robert held her and didn't ask her not to fuss. Over her son's shoulder Meg could see Tom O'Neill's beautiful daughter, the girl who had been wild all her life but didn't look wild anymore. Dee was shyly introducing a round-faced, redheaded, bespectacled boy who was loosening the unaccustomed collar and tie he had put on specially to meet the father-in-law from Ireland. Tom was indicating the boy's hair, making some joke maybe about how he knew now why he was called Fox. Whatever he said, they were all laughing.

And now Robert and Rosa were laughing too as they wiped their tears and led her toward the car. Meg looked back in case she could catch the eye of her friend Tom O'Neill, the old friend she had met by chance on the plane. But he, too, was being bundled off. It didn't matter. They would meet here in Australia, maybe two or three times so that they would not always be in the young people's way. But not too often, because a month was a very short time for a visit. And Christmas was for families. And anyway they could always meet back on the other side of the world in a time and a place where there wouldn't be so much to do.

WHAT IS HAPPINESS?

They had called him Parnell to show how Irish he was. At school they called him Parny, so that was it. Anyway Katy and Shane Quinn could always explain it to anyone who mattered that his real name was Parnell, like the great leader. It was just as well nobody asked them too much about the great leader. They were somewhat hazy about what he was leading and when and why. They liked the Parnell Monument when they came to Dublin, but they didn't like at all the news that the great leader had been a Protestant, and a womaniser. They hoped that this was just a local story.

Parny liked Dublin, it was small and kind of folksy. People seemed poor compared to at home and it was hard to find the downtown area, but it was much better than being at home for Christmas. Much much better.

At home there would have been Dad's receptionist, Esther. Esther had worked for Dad for nine years, since Parny was a baby. Esther was a wonderful receptionist but a sad, lonely person according to Dad. Esther was a nutter who was in love with Parny's father according to Mum. Last Christmas, Esther had come to the house and sat down on the doorstep and cried until they had to let her in for fear of the neighbours complaining. She had shouted at them and gone round and banged on windows. Esther had said that she would not be cast aside. They had all asked Parny to go to bed.

'But I've only just got up. It's Christmas Day!' he had cried, not unreasonably. They begged him to go back to bed with his toys. He agreed grudgingly because his mum had whispered that mad Esther would go sooner. He had listened on the stairs, of course, it had been very bewildering indeed.

He gathered that Dad must have had a romance with Esther at one stage. It sounded impossible what with Dad being so old, desperately old now, and with Esther looking like she did, terrible. And it seemed hard to know why Mum was so upset, she must be well finished with Dad now. But that was definitely what it was about.

There were enough kids at school who had mums and dads split up for him to know about this, and Esther kept shouting that Dad had promised to divorce Mum as soon as the brat was old enough. Parny was very annoyed to be called a brat and bristled on the stairs, but both Mum and Dad seemed very annoyed too and had rushed to his defence, so Esther had lost out on that one, and at least his parents seemed to be on his side. Parny gave it up after a while and had gone back to his room to play with his presents as they had advised.

'I want some happiness. I want to be happy too,' he heard Esther shouting downstairs. 'What's happiness, Esther?' he had heard his father asking wearily.

They had been right, it was the best thing for him to go upstairs. Later when she was gone, they came to get him. They were full of apologies. Parny was more interested in it all than frightened.

'Did you plan to divorce Mum and go off with her, Dad?' he inquired, for the record, as it were. There was a lot of bluster.

Eventually Dad said, 'No, I told her I would, but I didn't mean it. I told her a lie, Son, and I'm paying for it dearly.'

Parny nodded. 'I thought that was it,' he said sagely. Mum was pleased with this explanation of Dad's. She patted Dad's hand.

'Your father is a mighty brave man to admit that, Parny,' she said. 'Not all men are so severely punished for straying from the home.'

Parny said that having Esther screaming on the doorstep was a terrible punishment all right. Did she scream and rave in the surgery too, he wondered?

No, apparently not, she was nice and calm and official when wearing her white coat. It was only in leisure times and particularly high holidays that she became upset and carried on. Labour Day, and Thanksgiving she had called, but she had not been so disturbed. During the year Esther had come to the house again; she came on

New Year's Eve, and on Dad's birthday and in the middle of the St Patrick's Day party they held, and they saw her turning up for the Fourth of July picnic just as they were unpacking the barbecue, and Dad and Mum had leapt back into the car and they had driven for miles looking over their shoulder in case she was behind.

So this year, to escape her, they had come to Ireland. They had always wanted to visit the home of their ancestors, they had said, but now with Parny being old enough to appreciate everything, and the dollar being such a good little spender in terms of Irish money, well, why not? And actually things were getting very urgent now. At this year's Thanksgiving Esther had arrived wearing a spaceman suit and they thought she was a singing telegram and opened the door. Then she was in like a flash.

So that's why they were in the land of his ancestors at last. Parny was glad, he missed his friends at Christmas but he was becoming as edgy as Mum and Dad about any celebration in case he saw the red mad face of Esther appearing.

He had half hoped she would turn up at his own birthday. It would have been something for the school to talk about for months. But she didn't. It was only official celebrations and Dad's birthday. She must be nearly mad enough to be put away, Parny thought. Seriously he wondered why nobody had. 'She had nobody to put her away,' Mum had explained.

Parny thought this might be Esther's bit of good luck. If you had had as much bad luck as she had, then maybe it was only fair that fate should deal you the good card of having nobody around to get you locked up. She could roam free for a bit longer.

He asked why Dad couldn't fire her. Dad said there were laws about this sort of thing, and if Esther was a very good worker, which she was, and not at all mad in the office, if he fired Esther there would be a huge protest and he might be sued.

Dad and Mum seemed nice and relaxed now that there was no Esther. Parny saw that they held hands sometimes, which was very embarrassing to watch, but at least there was nobody here that would know them so it was okay.

The hall porter became a great friend of Parny's: he told the boy all about the days when there were dozens and dozens of American tourists staying in the hotel, when they came and hired his brother out to drive them all over Ireland and then back to the hotel again. The porter's name was Mick Quinn, and he said it was an undeniable fact that he and Parny must be some kind of relations, otherwise why would they be called the same name? Mick Quinn had all the time in the world to spare for Parny since the hotel was almost empty, and Parny's Mum and Dad were given to looking into each other's eyes and having long conversations about life.

This was all to the good. Parny used to go with Mick to collect the newspapers in the morning and helped with the luggage; he even got a tip once.

He was most useful to Mick by holding the cigarettes. Mick wasn't supposed to smoke on duty, so it just looked as if Parny was a forward American brat allowed to do what he liked, including smoking at the age of ten.

Parny was great at sidling up when the coast was clear to give Mick a drag. Mick was married to a woman called Berna. Parny asked a lot about Berna. 'She's not the worst,' Mick would say. 'Who *is* the worst?' Parny always wanted to know. If Berna wasn't, someone must be the worst, but Mick said it was only a manner of speaking. Mick and Berna had grown-up children now, they were away, all of them. Three in England, one in Australia, and one at the other side of Dublin – which was the same as being in Australia.

What did Berna do all day when Mick was in the hotel, Parny wondered? His mum worked in a flower shop, which was very smart and a perfectly fine place for a dentist's wife to work. But Berna worked nowhere.

She spent the day in a state of discontent, Mick revealed one time. She didn't know the meaning of happiness. But he seemed ashamed he had told Parny this and never wanted to bring the subject up again.

'What is happiness exactly, Mick?' Parny asked.

'Well, if you don't know, a fine young fellow like you who has everything he wants, then it would be hard for the rest of us to know.'

'I suppose I do have a lot of things,' Parny said. 'But then so has Esther, and not only is she not happy but she's crazy as a box of birds.'

'I don't think there is anything crazy about a box of birds,' Mick said unexpectedly.

'No, neither do I,' said Parny. 'It's like you said about Berna not being the worst. It's only a manner of speaking.'

'I'm very fond of birds in fact,' Mick Quinn said, having a quick drag out of Parny Quinn's cigarette. 'I'd have liked pigeons, but Berna said they were dirty.' He shook his head sadly and Parny felt that Berna must be very nearly the worst.

'Who is this Esther anyway?' Mick said, anxious to drag his thoughts and conversation away from the unsatisfactory Berna.

'It's all too long and complicated to explain, unless we had time,' Parny said. You couldn't do justice to the madness of Esther in the fairly uneasy atmosphere of the hall, waiting for a manager to appear suddenly or a guest to need some assistance and advice.

In fact something made Parny wonder if his new friend Mick would ever understand about Esther. 'Maybe you might like to come on a tour with me this afternoon, you could tell me then?' Mick said.

'Yes, and you could tell me about the birds you might have,' Parny said.

'I'll show you some birds, that would be better still.'

Parny's mum said they had been neglecting him. She and Dad had been feeling very guilty, but they had many important things to talk about. This very afternoon they would take him to a movie house. He could choose which one and if they could bear his first choice, they would all go to that, but if they really couldn't bear his first choice, they might ask him to make a second choice. Parny said that he and Mick were going to visit some birds.

'That means girls in this part of the world,' Parny's dad said.

'No.' Parny was very clear on this, it didn't. Not with Mick. Mick had his fill of women, he had Berna who was always in a state of discontent, he wanted no more truck with women, he had told Parny that personally.

Parny's mum thought Mick had made a right choice. She looked meaningfully at Parny's dad and said sooner or later most men come to that conclusion.

Mick looked different in his ordinary clothes, not as splendid as in the porter's uniform, but he said he felt free as a seagull that soared when he put on his old jacket and trousers. He led Parny to a bus. 'Is it an aviary?' Parny asked, interested.

'No. It's more a house of a fellow. I have a part interest in some pigeons. Hardly anyone knows that except you and me,' Mick said, looking round in case anyone on the bus might have heard it and confronted them with the information. 'They don't know at the hotel,' he whispered.

'Would they mind?' Parny whispered back. He didn't see the harm in having a part interest in pigeons. But it was obviously fraught with danger.

'I just don't want them to know my business. They'd be asking how are the pigeons. I couldn't be doing with that.'

Parny understood immediately. To have people who knew nothing about it asking, would diminish the pigeons. 'I'm afraid I'm not what you'd call an expert myself,' he said, in order to make sure there were no grey areas.

'I know that, son, but you have an open mind. A young open mind.'

'Esther said that to me once. She said I had a young mind that wasn't closed up like the older generation.' He was lost in wonderment that here at the other side of the earth someone should say exactly the same thing to him. He hoped this didn't mean that Mick was crazy, too, like Esther. 'Have you anyone to put you away if you go mad?' he asked solicitously.

Mick was delighted with him. 'You're a living entertainment, Parny Quinn. Who's Esther, is she your sister?' Parny noticed that they asked each other questions and never replied one to the other. It didn't matter somehow, the questions weren't that important. They got off the bus and went into a house that seemed rather poor to Parny. He hoped it wasn't Mick's house, he'd like Mick to have had more comfort. 'Is this where you live?'

'Indeed not.' Mick sounded wistful, looking at the shabby cupboards and the piles of newspapers on the floor, the dishes on the draining board, and the empty milk bottle on the table. 'No, I live at a place where you have to take off your shoes almost. No indeed, in my house there'd be a commotion that you'd hear at the other end of the country if I brought you in without an act of Parliament being passed first. This is Ger's house.' He said it with pure envy.

Ger was out in the back. He seemed pleased to see Parny, asked him was he a betting man, and Parny said he was sure he would be when he was old enough to know what to bet on and to have some money to bet with. Ger accepted this as a reasonable answer and didn't apologise for having assumed that Parny was rarely out of a bookie's office. Ger was an all right guy, Parny thought to himself.

They showed him the loft, they explained the rules. Man to man, the three of them discussed the singularly poor record of Ger and Mick's pigeons compared to other pigeons they knew and envied. They were homing pigeons certainly, the back yard was full of them, but would they go back into the box? Would they hell! Race after race could have been won if these birds could only have followed the rules. But no. Instead they came and sat and cooed in the yard, delighted to be back to Ger and Mick. Some of them were definitely not the full shilling, Parny was told though it was a view that would not be expressed beyond these four walls. Parny had to admit that he didn't know whether there was any pigeon fancying in the States, but he would inquire when he got back; he would write and tell Ger and Mick all about it.

'A young fellow like you won't think of writing,' Ger said philosophically as the pigeons swooped down on Parny and perched on his shoulders, glad to have a new playmate in this friendly place, a playmate that didn't seem obsessed with their timings.

'I'm very good at writing letters,' Parny protested. 'I've written to everyone I said I would . . .' He paused. 'Well, except Esther.'

'I think you'd better tell us about Esther,' Mick Quinn said.

In the small back yard with the big soft birds landing and taking off, with the comforting warbling sound of their cooing as Muzak in the background, Parny Quinn told Ger and Mick about Esther. He could never have asked for a better audience, it was like telling a film, they said to each other as they demanded details of her appearance at each festivity. Would you credit that? The family had to cross the Atlantic to escape her.

'And why would she want you to write to her?' Mick asked eventually.

'The day before we left, she said she knew we were going somewhere, and would I write her just one letter, to let her know if we had found happiness wherever it was we had gone. But I couldn't write. I couldn't tell Esther that Mum and Dad look sort of happy with all this awful holding hands. She'd flip completely if she knew that.'

He stood there as the pigeons came and went, he stroked their feathers and they didn't seem frightened, he held one in his hand and felt its heart beat under its plump chest. He closed his eyes as they swirled around. There wasn't much to beat this, the company of birds and men. Undemanding, satisfying. He had a feeling that he might never be as happy as this again.

'You could send the poor woman a card,' Mick said.

'Not committing yourself to anything,' said Ger, who had always travelled alone in life and thought it was the best way to be.

'It's too late now. We're going back on Friday, it won't get there.'

'We could ring her from the hotel,' Mick said.

'Call Esther? Mum would turn blue and die,' Parny said.

'Without telling your ma.'

'I wouldn't be able to afford it, calling the States is very expensive.' Ger and Mick nodded at each other. It could be done, they said. If he had anything to say to the poor tortured woman, then at Christmas time, the season of goodwill, he should say it.

Parny wondered had he explained how crazy Esther was, and how she wanted to run away with his father. But still Mick and Ger were so kind, it would be very bad-mannered to go against them.

The afternoon passed in a welter of feathers and timings and soft sounds. Then it was back on the bus to the hotel. It was six o'clock, so it would be Esther's lunchtime. From the phone box in the hall Parny talked to the international operator, they found directory inquiries and they found Esther. Parny also inquired how much it would cost and had to hold on to the door of the box for support. He told Mick it was out of the question. Mick was back in his uniform again, he worked a split shift some days, he had only the afternoon free. He looked up and down the hall.

'Get back in the box,' he said, and like lightning he dialed from the desk the number written on a piece of paper. Parny heard the phone ringing, he swallowed. Esther's voice was surprisingly thin, not like the excited roar he had come to know and fear.

'It's Parny Quinn,' he said.

Esther began to cry, softly, it was definitely crying.

'Did your father ask you to call me?' she sniffled.

'He doesn't know I'm calling you. Listen, Esther, the mail is very bad here, and you asked me to let you know about happiness and everything . . .'

'What's happiness?' Esther said.

Parny was impatient. Why do people always say that, he was calling her long distance to answer her damn fool questions, now she just asks them back.

'Yeah sure, it's hard to know but you did ask me to let you know if I'd found it, so I thought I'd call you and say it has a lot to do with birds.'

'Birds?'

'Yes, birds, pigeons, you could go to the library and get a book on them. I think you'd enjoy that, honestly, Esther.'

'Has your father taken up the bird business too?'

'No, Esther, just me, you wanted to know what I thought and if I had found happiness, I did, so I thought I'd call you.'

He was annoyed that she was ungrateful. 'Who cares what you think, kid?' Esther said. 'Put me on to your father.'

'He's not here,' Parny said, tears of rage stinging the back of his eyes. After all his kindness and Mick risking his job connecting him on the hotel phone. 'Dad and Mum are in Dublin Casino, they're not back yet.'

'You're in Dublin,' Esther screamed triumphantly. 'What hotel, speak to me, Parnell, you dumb child. Speak. What hotel?'

Parny hung up. Mick was waiting outside. 'You did your best, lad, you kept faith with her. And there's always the pigeons as consolation, remember that.'

Esther got a list of hotels in Dublin and she had found Katy and Shane Quinn by seven p.m.

'I guess she must have traced us through the airlines or travel agent,' Parny's pop said.

'They really will have to put her away this time,' said Parny's mum with a grim little smile.

'Fancy saying that Parny called her.'

'She seemed very definite about that.' Parny's dad sighed. 'Said he'd called her up to tell her that he had taken up ornithology. It's sad, really sad.'

'I wonder why she fixed on Parny this time. She's always steered clear of talking about him, she knows how upset it makes us.'

Parny sat there thinking about the events of the day. It could have been worse. Esther couldn't get a flight what with it being Christmas, she was just going to haunt them by telephone. Dad had to ask the switchboard to say they had left the hotel. Parny had said nothing about his part in it all. He had thought it through very carefully. If they thought she was making it all up about his having called her, that would be further proof of her madness. It might speed up the day they put her away. And anyway he hadn't been going to say anything about Ger and Mick's part share in the pigeons. He remembered that Mick never spoke of the pigeons in the hotel, they were too precious. Parny felt like that too.

Anyway Esther had called him a dumb kid and said nobody cared what he thought about anything. Why should he bail her out? Why should he? He would keep his interest in pigeons a secret, just like Mick did, and one day when Esther was safely locked up he would pretend to have read a book about them, and he'd have his own loft. And he would have no truck with women. Ever. You could see that Ger in his free-and-easy house was like a king compared to people like his father and Mick who were heart-scalded.

Parny sighed happily and read the movie listings. He liked the sound of *The Company of Wolves*, but you had to be eighteen to get in. He wondered could he tell the people at the cinema that he was from the States and more mature than other kids of his age.

THE BEST INN IN TOWN

꧁꧂

They should have liked each other, the two mothers. They were birds of the same showy kind of feather, after all. Full of notions, full of what they each liked to think of as style. But they hated each other the very moment they met eighteen long years ago – in 1970, when their respective son and daughter got engaged to each other. Noel's mother, who became Granny Dunne a year later, had a lip that curled all on its own without being given any instructions; and Avril's mother, who had become Granny Byrne, had a line in tinkling laughs that would freeze the blood. They had both had husbands back at the wedding, mild men who managed to put the children's happiness before their own territorial struggles, but not even the shared experience of widowhood had brought the two women together. They met one day a year, and that was Christmas Day. They met to terrorise and destroy what might have been a fairly reasonable family Christmas.

Noel was called Noel because he was a Christmas baby. Granny Dunne never tired of telling that. How the pains had come during Christmas lunch. How there had been mistletoe and holly and paper streamers all around the maternity ward. Oh, they knew how to celebrate Christmas in those days, she would say accusingly to Avril, as if a labour ward in 1950 was somehow like the Versailles Ball in comparison with the kind of entertainment she was being offered these times.

Granny Byrne never failed to explain that Avril had been given her name because she was born in April. A lovely month, full of sunshine and fresh flowers, and little lambs and everything full of hope. In those days. There would be a sad, chilling tinkle of a laugh and a glower at Noel. The implication was easy to read. Life had lost its spring freshness since her daughter had married at the age of nineteen and thrown away all that hope forever.

Noel and Avril had triumphed over their mothers' great mutual dislike. In fact it had cemented them further together over the years. They were lucky, they said, in that the scales were fairly evenly balanced. For every one of Granny Dunne's clangers there was a reciprocal salvo from Granny Byrne. And they were careful to treat each mother equally so that no comparisons could be made. On the first Sunday of each month they visited one or the other parent alternately. The three children liked Granny Dunne's house because she had an aquarium, and Granny Byrne's house because she had a Manx cat and a book about Manx cats which they would read six times a year with total fascination.

No, it was no trouble for the children going to either granny's house. For Noel and Avril it was always a trial. Granny Dunne had a very strong line about cats spreading diseases and that if you had to have a cat, wasn't it perverse getting a poor dumb animal that was bred deformed and had its nether regions on display. Granny Byrne always managed to bring up what she thought of people who had warm tanks of stale water and poor crazed orange fish in them swimming despairingly around for the sole purpose of being soothing for neurotic humans.

Granny Byrne usually said it was wonderful that Avril managed so well without all the newest modern appliances which most husbands bought for their wives. Avril just gritted her teeth and squeezed Noel's hand to show him that her mother was not mouthing her own discontents. Then Granny Dunne would say, with a lip curl that might have remained permanent if the wind changed, that she really admired young women like her daughter-in-law who didn't bother with make-up and dressing properly just to please their man and do him credit. Noel's turn for hand-squeezing would come then. They agreed that they were forced into a great deal of reassurance and positive stating that they loved each other, just to counteract the effects of both mothers. And that this might be no bad thing.

They had called their children Ann, Mary, and John as a reaction against their own fancy tricksy names. Both mothers thought these names sadly unimaginative and each blamed the child of the other for the lack of vision and style.

Ann was seventeen and had been put in charge of the entertainment programme for Christmas Day. Ann was good at computer studies at school, which was a help because it was becoming more and more difficult to organise the grannies' entertainment. The problem was the increase in television channels and the availability of videos. This Christmas there was far too much choice. Ann explained seriously to her parents that it had been much simpler in the days when it was only *The Sound of Music* and then the usual row about the Pope and the Queen. Avril's mother, Granny Byrne, thought that anyone with a bit of class watched the Queen's message; it was nothing to do with being pro-English or West Brit or anything, it was just what one did. Noel's mother said it had never been part of their culture to watch the Royal Family. But then she did remember that a long time ago the maids in the house had indeed been very interested in reading little tidbits about royalty, so perhaps some people did find it all very fascinating. For her own part, even though she didn't go along with every single thing about Pope John Paul, she did think it would be a poor sort of Catholic who couldn't find it in her heart to kneel for a papal blessing just one day out of three hundred and sixty-five.

Noel and Avril had stayed sane by incorporating both dignitaries into their Christmas Day. There were other ingredients too, like a good healthy walk after the Pope and before the mince pies and presents. They had agreed it would be straitjackets for supper if they had to remain cooped up all day. Even in the rain or the snow they got the show on the road and down to the strand. They used to walk past other families, and Noel and Avril often wondered if they were really happy or whether each family group was like their own, a powder keg, a volcano, a collection of disasters waiting to happen.

And then, after the heavy cocktails which went with the Queen there was the Christmas lunch, and Serious Viewing combined with snoozing, until the Good-Lord-is-that-the-time? What about a nice cup of tea and Christmas cake before we drive you both home?

Since they had got the video, life had been easier. It wasn't a question of zapping from channel to channel, nor of trying to decide on the spot. For the past couple of years the family had studied the advance Christmas schedules with the intensity that had been given to the Normandy landings. Pop shows were out because of the torrent of abuse they would unleash. Comedy shows were doubtful. They wouldn't be worth all the side looks and wondering if Granny Byrne had got the point or if Granny Dunne was about to say that for the life of her she couldn't understand people who took offence over nothing. It was always impossible to programme the grannies. One year one would have a high moral tone and the other have become bawdy, but you never knew which would be which. It was like the Christmas presents, a feast or a famine. Indulge them while they're young, or give them a sense of proportion.

Ann felt very important to be allowed to choose the entertainment, but she admitted that there were a lot of problems. If they recorded *Back to the Future* on one channel during lunch, then it would be ready to watch at five o'clock, but could the grannies take a time machine on board?

The children would like to see *The Empire Strikes Back*, Ann reported. They had been hoping that she would be able to fit it into the recording plan. But it went on from four till six and probably they'd need to be watching something then, and most likely something already on a video, so that meant they wouldn't be able to record at the same time.

Ann wondered if they might record *Storm Boy* earlier; it sounded more suitable family viewing than *Falling in Love*. They didn't know what *Falling in Love* was going to be about, but if it had Meryl Streep and Robert De Niro there could be a lot of groping involved, and nobody knew how the grannies might respond to screen fondling.

Noel and Avril watched their daughter's serious face as she juggled the schedules. The *Jo Maxi Show* that Mary and John loved had to be out; the grannies couldn't take anything like that. Something called *Play the Game* was described as a Christmas frolic, and it was always unwise to think that a frolic might please either Mrs Dunne or Mrs Byrne. *Glenroe*, obviously, at eight o'clock, but not necessarily the *Non-Stop Christmas Show* – it was too varied for the grannies. They might love the Dublin Boy Singers, but would it be worth it for the tirades that might erupt at Johnny Logan or the Dingbats?

Ann said she'd consult again with the younger ones: there had to be a way. All families must have the same problems at this time of year, she said sagely, it was just that the youngsters kept bleating about *Top of the Pops* and other things that were out of the question. It wasn't as if Christmas was meant to be for children.

Avril and Noel's hearts were filled with sadness. Their daughter was not being even remotely ironic. All her life she had thought that Christmas Day had to do with the grannies and keeping them as contented as either would allow herself to be.

Avril bit her lip at the memory at what seemed like a thousand Christmas days when Granny Dunne had looked her up and down and asked her when she was going to change, and then with a lip curl apologised and said of course, of course, she had changed, and how sensible she was not to get dressed up in anything smart.

She remembered another thousand festive seasons when Granny Byrne had examined the label on the supermarket wine bottle and asked Noel who his wine merchant was and had they chosen something special this year. A thousand times Noel had patted her hand under the table. It didn't matter, he had told her. We have all our lives.

True, but their children were not having the Christmas Days they should have been having.

If there were no grannies, think what it would be like. Think.

Avril indulged herself. They could get up later, they could have breakfast in their dressing gowns. Cup after cup of tea watching the video of *Fawlty Towers*. The episode of Manuel's rat. They all loved that. There would be no sneaking glances at the two good armchairs to see how it was being received.

They could all have a short walk and wear old clothes and maybe go somewhere with a bit of mud and point things out to each other and laugh. Like they did on ordinary days. Not walking at Granny speed and fielding a battery of Granny interrogation and point-scoring.

They need watch neither Pope nor Queen. Their Christmas messages would be in their own family.

The turkey would taste better when it didn't have to be analysed and explained and apologised for. They could have Greek yogurt with the Christmas pudding, which they all loved instead of making a brandy butter for show. The children could laugh out loud at the jokes in the crackers instead of nodding sagely with the grannies that it was a sin crying out to heaven for vengeance buying crackers that were such poor value.

Noel too felt a surge of resentment toward his two brothers and his sister who never thought of having Mother for Christmas. Not even once. It's tradition that she goes to Noel and Avril, they all said with huge guilty relief, and gave her bottles of sherry and fleece-lined hot-water bottles plus tiny boxes of liqueur chocolates, which she was instructed to keep for herself and which she did.

And couldn't Avril's sister in Limerick take Mrs Byrne? Just once, just one year? Why did it have to be a tradition? The old bats would even *like* a change, a bit of variety, Noel thought despairingly.

But it was too late this year to think about it. The plans would have to be made long in advance, and it must never be allowed to look like ... well, to look like what it was.

Avril and Noel looked at each other and for once they didn't reach out to pat, to reassure, to remind each other of a lifetime shared and to underline that one day wasn't much to give up. For the first time, it did seem too much. The day that everyone was meant to enjoy; and their family seriously believed that it wasn't meant to be a day for children.

The feeling lasted through the days that led up to Christmas. The children knew there was something wrong. Their mother and father, normally so full of requests and pleas and urgings, seemed to have lost the Christmas spirit somehow.

They didn't even have those embarrassing middle-aged hugs and hand-pattings that used to go on. When Ann or Mary or John asked about plans for the grannies, they got scant answers.

'Will we bring down the screen in case Granny Byrne gets a draught?' Ann asked.

'Let her get a draught,' her mother said unexpectedly.

'Where's the magnifying glass for the *RTE Guide*?' John asked on Christmas Eve. 'Granny Dunne likes to have it handy to see the small print.'

'Then let her put on her bloody glasses like the rest of us,' said his father.

They were very worried about them.

Ann thought her father might be having the male menopause: Mary wondered whether their mother might be having a midlife crisis. She didn't know what it was, but there had been a programme about it on television with lots of white-faced women of their mother's age saying they were going through it. John thought they were just in bad tempers like teachers at school got into bad tempers that seemed to last half a term. He hoped his parents would get over it. It was very glum with them like this, biting the head off everyone.

The night before Christmas the family sat beside the fire. They all wanted to see the same film; in a few minutes they would turn on James Stewart. There would be no sense of peevishness about who sat where, about the position of honour nearer the fire or nearer the set. Nobody was hunting for a magnifying glass or a draught excluder.

Noel and Avril sighed.

'I'm sorry about the grannies!' Avril said suddenly.

'It would be nice if you could have normal Christmas Days like other children do,' said Noel.

Their three children looked at them in disbelief. This was the first time that an apology had ever been made. Usually they had been told how lucky they were to have two grannies and even luckier that these grannies came for Christmas Day.

They had never believed it, of course, but it was like crusts being good for you and fast food bad for you – they heard it and accepted it as something people said. It had been said for so long now, it was part of the scenery. Much easier to listen to and ignore than this new unease between their parents and this sudden revelation that grannies were not a Good Thing after all.

Ann and Mary and John didn't like it. It changed the natural order of things. They didn't want things changed. And certainly not at Christmas.

'It's your day too, you know,' Avril said.

'More yours than theirs, in fact.' Noel's face was eager to explain.

In the firelight his three children looked up at him. They were going to hear no explanation. No accusations about aunts and uncles who didn't do their fair share. No words like 'burden' and 'nuisance.' Not at Christmas time.

They had to speak quickly to prevent things that shouldn't be said being spoken.

'We thought that we could record *Star Trek Three*, and sort of give them an update on who they all are, you know – Kirk and Spock and Scotty,' said John.

'And Granny Byrne might be one of her remembering-Dracula-and-Frankenstein moods,' Mary said hopefully.

Ann, who had grown up this Christmas and understood almost everything, suddenly said in a gentle voice:

'And there really couldn't be much room for them in any other inn or they would have gone there, so they're lucky this is the best inn in town.'

dig

1495